THE LAST HOPE

The Last Hope

A Maggie Hope Mystery

SUSAN ELIA MacNEAL

BANTAM

NEW YORK

Copyright © 2024 by Susan Elia

Published in the United States by Bantam Books, an imprint of Random House, a division of Penguin Random House LLC, New York.

BANTAM BOOKS is a registered trademark and the B colophon is a trademark of Penguin Random House LLC.

LIBRARY OF CONGRESS CATALOGING-IN-PUBLICATION DATA
Names: MacNeal, Susan Elia, author.
Title: The last hope: a novel / Susan Elia MacNeal.
Description: First edition. | New York: Bantam Books, 2024. |
Series: Maggie Hope | Includes bibliographical references.
Identifiers: LCCN 2023054046 (print) | LCCN 2023054047 (ebook) |
ISBN 9780593156988 (hardcover; acid-free paper) |
ISBN 9780593156995 (ebook)
Subjects: LCSH: Women spies—Fiction. | Targeted killing—Fiction. |
World War, 1939-1945—Secret service—Great Britain—Fiction. |
World War, 1939-1945—Secret service—Spain—Fiction. | World War,
1939-1945—Spain—Madrid—Fiction. | Chanel, Coco, 1883-1971—
Fiction. | Heisenberg, Werner, 1901-1976—Fiction. |
LCGFT: Historical fiction. |
Spy fiction. | Novels.
Classification: LCC PS3613.A2774 L37 2024 (print) |
LCC PS3613.A2774 (ebook) | DDC 813/.6—dc23/eng/20231127
LC record available at https://lccn.loc.gov/2023054046
LC ebook record available at https://lccn.loc.gov/2023054047

Printed in the United States of America on acid-free paper

randomhousebooks.com

2 4 6 8 9 7 5 3 1

First Edition

Title-page art by WINDCOLORS/Adobe Stock

In memory of OSS spies

Aline, Countess of Romanones,

and Moe Berg

Underneath the glamour of Chanel beats the throbbing pulse of history—the history of fashion and the history of the world.

—Marie-Pierre Lannelongue, French journalist

It is possible that the Germans will have, by the end of this year, enough material accumulated to make a large number of gadgets [atomic bombs] which they will release at the same time on England, Russia, and this country.

—Letter from Hans Albrecht Bethe and Edward Teller to
Robert Oppenheimer, about their worries that
the American effort wasn't moving fast enough,
from Craig Nelson's *The Age of Radiance*

Oh, lay that pistol down, babe,
Lay that pistol down,
Pistol packin' mama,
Lay that thing down before it goes off, and hurts somebody!

—Al Dexter's "Pistol Packin' Mama," sung by
Bing Crosby and the Andrews Sisters

THE LAST HOPE

Prologue

July 1943

General Walter Friedrich Schellenberg, cigarette dangling from the corner of his mouth, raced his black Mercedes coupe through the dense pine forest and then up the cobblestone drive to the gates of the looming castle. Only that morning, he'd been at his desk in Berlin when he'd received word Reichsführer Heinrich Himmler wanted to see him. No reason had been given and none was needed. When the Reichsführer asked for something—anything—it was done immediately.

Schellenberg knew Wewelsburg well; Himmler had taken over the Renaissance castle early in the Nazis' rise to power. It was to be his own vision of Wagner's *Parsifal,* the place where he would raise up a new order of Teutonic knights, a brotherhood of the "racially pure."

Over the years, Himmler had fashioned it as his personal lair and a shrine to the SS elite. There was an enormous dining hall inspired by stories of King Arthur and the Knights of the Round Table, complete with inscribed silver plates and special chairs with hand-carved names. Schellenberg had always questioned Himmler's obsession with a British king who fought Saxon invaders, but he was too politic to ever bring it up. Nor did he ever comment on what he thought of as Himmler's interest in the occult, astrology, and ancient Aryan history.

Because Schellenberg had grown up in the Saarland, a German region on the French border, he spoke both German and French fluently. His mastery of French, and his astonishing facility with other tongues—not to mention his ambition and acumen—helped his entry into the Nazi party. Reinhard Heydrich himself had recruited Schellenberg from the University of Bonn, where he'd been a member of a far-right fraternity and studied law. And under Heydrich's mentorship, he rose quickly to the top of the Sicherheitsdienst, the SS intelligence agency known as the SD. It was different from, and often in competition with, Wilhelm Canaris's more conventional military intelligence service, Abwehr.

Before leaving Berlin, Schellenberg had carefully donned his black dress SS uniform, including the Iron Cross First Class medal pinned at his throat. A slim man in his early thirties, with thick hair brushed back from a broad forehead and large, wide-set eyes, he was aware of the power of the uniform. He used it alongside his devastatingly charming smile—despite the long white dueling scar on his cheek. But while he looked the part of a conquering Nazi hero, on his left pinkie was a large gold signet ring containing a cyanide capsule. Just in case.

The war, now spread across the globe, was unraveling for Germany. Hitler's glory days of the late thirties and early forties were a memory. The Soviets had stopped the German advance at Stalingrad and forced the Sixth Army to surrender. Hamburg had burned to the ground in a devastating air raid. The Germans had been defeated brutally in both North Africa and Italy. At the end of the Casablanca Conference in Morocco, the Allies had announced their decision to accept nothing less than the unconditional surrender of the Axis. Most of the Nazi leaders had realized winning the war was no longer a possibility.

While a few still dreamed of a devastating new weapon—a fission bomb or long-range ballistic missile—most had given up hope. They knew it was just a matter of time before the Allies invaded France. And with the Soviets pushing relentlessly toward Germany, the situation would soon become dire.

As Schellenberg approached, he noted the long red swastika flags, which had once snapped so proudly in the western breeze, were now still. The castle, with its striking thick stone walls, narrow slit windows, and turrets, looked more like a prison.

At the sentry box before the castle's moat, two SS officers waved for Schellenberg to stop. He hit the brakes, rolling his eyes at the ornate lightning-strike SS runes carved into the gate's stonework. A sergeant approached the driver's side, clicked his heels together, and saluted smartly. "Heil Hitler!" Schellenberg rolled down the window and returned a salute with less enthusiasm.

The guard peered into the car. Beside him was a large-jawed, muscular Alsatian, teeth bared, that was pulling on a black leather leash.

"General Schellenberg, Reichsführer Himmler is expecting you." The sergeant was also in dress uniform, his empty jacket sleeve pinned to hide his missing left arm. "He's asked me to escort you to the west wing. The corporal will attend to your vehicle. Follow me, sir."

Schellenberg exited the car, cracking his neck and stretching his arms after the long ride from Berlin. The air was charged; a cold front was moving in. He gazed up at the high stone walls of the castle, its three phallic towers covered in long red banners, glowing like coals in the late afternoon gloom. "Subtle," he said under his breath, spitting his cigarette to the gravel, grinding it under the heel of his well-polished boot. "So very subtle."

"General?" the sergeant called back over his shoulder. "Did you say something?"

Schellenberg shook his head and followed.

Inside, the castle was silent as a monastery, and the cool, damp air smelled of moldering tapestries. Schellenberg was left in an oversize sitting room in the first tower, lit from above by an iron wheel chandelier. The dark oak furniture was heavy; a large sword collection covered the thick walls.

He looked up at the Führer's portrait, hung in the place of honor over the fireplace's mantel. *The Standard Bearer* portrayed a young and suspiciously handsome Hitler in profile as a medieval knight, on horseback and wearing shining armor, carrying the SS flag. On the stone floor in front of an empty stone hearth, a skinned lion grinned up at Schellenberg with yellowed teeth, glass eyes glinting. The general crossed his arms and faced the lion, meeting its eyes, taking its measure.

Through the mullioned windows, he could hear the rumbling engines of fighter planes flying low—American, by the sound of them, probably on their way to Berlin. Everything shook, and the overhead lights flickered. He took a swastika-engraved platinum case from his breast pocket, selected a cigarette, and lit it, blowing out a succession of rings that rose and dissolved over the painted Führer's head like vanishing halos.

"No cigarettes!" Heinrich Luitpold Himmler snapped. His reedy voice, with its light Bavarian twang, echoed in the tower room. The Reichsführer was short, and now almost frail, his hooded eyes magnified by round glasses. He had a receding chin and small, delicate hands. Unlike Schellenberg, he was in mufti, wearing a dark gray chalk-striped wool suit and heavy gold watch, his hair parted severely and brilliantined in place. For someone who revered warriors and knights in shining armor, Himmler appeared the opposite, looking more like the chicken farmer he'd once been than Hitler's right-hand man.

"I beg your pardon, Reichsführer," Schellenberg said smoothly, bowing and clicking his heels. His smoking had been no mistake, though. While Schellenberg and Heydrich had been on a first-name basis, Himmler treated Schellenberg formally. Himmler had never once, even after so much time, uttered his colleague's Christian name. To retaliate, Schellenberg liked to infuriate the Reichsführer with his smoking. He crushed out the cigarette in a large silver cup, evocative of King Arthur's Holy Grail. "How may I be of service?"

Himmler gave a smile that never quite reached his eyes. "Walk with me," he ordered the younger man. "We've much to discuss."

Schellenberg followed. He was used to humoring the Reichsführer on various subjects, from poultry rearing to the Ahnenerbe organization to Vril theory. This would be no different, he assumed.

Himmler led the way down damp halls to the North Tower, where the grand SS Generals' Hall stood empty. Their footsteps echoed on the stone floor as they walked to the still-unfinished space. The consecration hall was dimly lit, a single bulb hanging from a wrought-iron fitting. Somewhere, water dripped steadily into a bucket.

The Reichsführer stopped at the room's center, in front of the place where an eternal flame was planned. Spears of light slanted down through narrow slits onto the twelve seats set into the walls, one for each elite SS member. Overhead, a swastika extended its crooked arms. Embedded in the floor was a black sun wheel, circled in gold plate that glinted in the dim light. Schellenberg and Himmler stood on opposite sides, the toes of shining boots facing alligator shoes three feet apart. Schellenberg waited.

The Reichsführer closed his eyes as if in prayer, then took a deep breath. "Tell me your thoughts on the current situation."

Schellenberg inhaled. "Most in Berlin think unconditional surrender to the Allies would be a disaster. Especially to the

Soviets. However—" The general chose his words carefully as the water continued to drip. "Fighting a second front, in France, at this stage, would be . . . challenging."

"And so"—Himmler clasped his hands—" 'total final victory' is no longer an option. We fight to the death in 'total war.' Or . . ." The Reichsführer seemed to force the words out with a certain reluctance. Or was it fear?

"Germany's only chance of survival now is to negotiate a separate peace. We've known this for months, but the window of time before the invasion's growing smaller. If we don't act soon . . ."

A separate peace with the Allies—minus the Soviet Union— was something Schellenberg himself had contemplated for some time. He'd proposed numerous ways to make overtures, had countless unofficial "exploratory" conversations. He'd secretly tested how Swiss and Swedish representatives might be used to negotiate. He'd even collaborated with Felix Kersten, Himmler's private medical adviser and masseur.

But his attempts, without support, never stood a chance of success. Himmler had been unwilling to oppose Hitler, sabotaging Schellenberg's efforts at diplomacy with Swiss intelligence at the last minute. But now?

Schellenberg was canny. "A separate peace, sir? With the British?" He paused and pretended to consider. "Yes, fear of Communism and of Soviet control of Europe after the war is one thing we have in common with the British and the Americans." He nodded. "It could work."

Himmler stepped across the circle, clapping Schellenberg on the shoulder. "We must, to save Germany. After all, Hitler's weakening. He's showing more symptoms—tremors in his hands, impaired balance, issues with his jaw."

Schellenberg had heard the rumors of various ailments, as well as those of advancing venereal disease, and wondered how long it would be until the higher-ups of the Third Reich turned on Hitler. "I agree, sir. If we still have the power to fight, we retain the power to bargain. It's important we act now."

"I've always maintained this war between Britain and Germany is like a war between brothers," Himmler mused, rubbing his chin. "It never should have happened. I've always admired the English government and political system." He straightened his bony shoulders. "It would be good to mend fences. For all involved."

"True . . ."

"The Americans are already talking about a declaration of 'total surrender,' of course," Himmler continued, his thin voice echoing in the vast hall. "And as for the Soviets . . ." He shrugged. "Well, you know what we did there. . . . But the British will *always* see us as a lesser evil than the Communists."

Schellenberg had seen the grim statistics coming from the Soviet Union and knew of Nazi atrocities. He knew, better than Himmler, how the rest of the world would react. It was only a matter of time until the facts of the Germans' actions came to light. The cold, damp air was heavy; the monotonous drip continued. "But what about Hitler?"

Himmler cleared his throat—a sign of nerves, Schellenberg thought. "You know he would never agree to surrender. And the Allies would never accept an offer with his name attached."

"Then . . ."

Unspoken words between the two men hung in the heavy air of the crypt. During the Stockholm negotiations, the Brits had made it clear they'd only agree to peace in the West with the removal of Hitler from power, preferably dead. And yet, there was a very real threat that even speaking of the assassination of Hitler could land them in the Gestapo cellars at Prinz-Albrecht-Strasse—or worse.

Himmler, who'd sentenced countless Germans to the guillotine for "defeatist talk," said finally, "We can serve Germany or the Führer—not both."

"There are men on the inside," Schellenberg told the Reichsführer in low tones. "Career military officers—the Wehrmacht..."

Himmler raised one hand, palm out. A look of consternation flickered over his face. "I don't need to know more."

The Führer had lived with assassination threats his entire political life, starting in 1921, when someone fired shots during a rally at the Hofbräuhaus in Munich. Since then, there had been at least thirty other known attempts. Hitler always attributed his survival to "divine intervention." Schellenberg had wondered, with grim humor, if it were more of a deal with the devil. If so, it seemed the bill was going to come due sooner than Hitler had anticipated.

"We must open a new secret line of negotiations with the British," Himmler went on. "We still have friends there, you know. Not just Mosley. Plenty in the House of Lords. And at White's and Boodle's as well. The Duke of Westminster, for one."

"Reichsführer, I've—"

Himmler glanced at the black sun wheel on the floor and then met Schellenberg's eyes. "Follow me." He sniffed. "I want to show you something in my office."

They walked together down a long, narrow, and poorly lit stone corridor. Himmler's private office was more modest than the rest of the castle. A plain oak desk stood in the room's center with an SS-issue Olympia typewriter, specially fitted with its double lightning-flash key. A stack of official-looking papers towered beside it, anchored by a shrunken head paperweight. A polished black stone inkstand was next to a brass reading lamp. Off to one side were small, silver-framed photographs of Himmler's daughter, Puppi, and his dour-faced wife, Marga, both of whom preferred to stay at home on the farm rather than live in Berlin. Not that women were allowed at Wewelsburg Castle.

"These," Himmler said, picking up a manila folder from his

oak desk and handing it to Schellenberg, "are my peace terms for the British."

Schellenberg read the Reichsführer's most current peace terms, written in green ink in a spidery hand. According to them, Germany would surrender to the United Kingdom but be allowed to continue fighting the Soviet Union in the East.

It was a legitimate offer, Schellenberg knew. Britain and Western Europe had suffered terribly under the German conquest and occupation; Himmler's offer to withdraw all German forces from the West, in exchange for retaining a free hand in the East, would be tempting. Still, it wouldn't be easy to convince the British, especially Churchill. And there was more. "There's the Katyn massacre to consider."

"True, true." That past April, the Germans announced via the Katyn Commission they'd discovered the bodies of more than twenty thousand Polish officers who'd been murdered by the Soviets and buried in Katyn Forest, near Smolensk, in the Soviet Union. The already fragile relations between the Soviets and the Polish government in exile had reached their breaking point.

"We do have," Schellenberg ventured, "an additional bargaining chip." Himmler sat in his black leather desk chair. "Something to trade. *If* you agree, of course, sir."

Himmler looked up. "What's that?"

"A suggestion is . . ." Schellenberg wet his lips. "The lives of the remaining Jews."

As the fate of millions of souls hung in the balance, Himmler waved his hand; his gold watch glinted in the firelight. "No one cares about the Jews. The U.S. and Britain—the entire world—made that absolutely clear early on when they wouldn't take in refugees."

"Some care, Reichsführer." Schellenberg chose his words with caution. "Some care very much. And they have friends. Important, powerful friends." He walked in front of the desk and glanced down at his superior. "Friends we'll need to achieve our goals."

Himmler straightened a few papers on his blotter and considered. "But the U.S. and Britain didn't want the Jews at the beginning of the war. Why would they want them now?"

Schellenberg took the seat opposite the Reichsführer. "Alas, news of your—our—'final solution' has reached Allied ears," he said. "Most don't believe what they're hearing, but eventually there will be evidence. By trading the remaining Jews, we could keep Germany from becoming a pariah nation"— Himmler frowned. Schellenberg amended—"*and* save Europe." He finished in honeyed tones: "You'll be seen as a hero!"

"They must never learn we exterminated so many," Himmler murmured. "And even if they do hear something, anything, they'll never allow themselves to believe it. Faced with the alternative of communism, they'll have no choice but to deny it."

"They *have* heard, Reichsführer," Schellenberg insisted. "And they're hearing more and more every day. And even though they've been, and continue to be, slow to believe, at some point they'll accept the truth." He spoke in a flat tone. "They'll see us as monsters."

Himmler's expression hardened. Schellenberg amended, "The Allies are more likely to accept your offer of surrender with three million Jews in our hands as hostages—the ultimate leverage. Churchill and Roosevelt, for political reasons, can't allow them to be killed."

Himmler stood. "Then we must make the British and Americans choose National Socialism over communism. We need to make sure they're more scared of the Reds than of us." He let out a bark of laughter. "So, in the end, the Jews save us."

He shrugged thin shoulders. "Well, at least they won't be our problem anymore." He looked Schellenberg in the eye. "To save Germany, I'll consider pardoning them."

"If we don't," Schellenberg warned, "Germany is dead." The threat of retribution from Allied military tribunals after surrender was inevitable. And even a military tribunal was preferable to Soviet troops invading Germany first. "Although a couple of fission bombs or long-distance rockets could still turn this potential loss into victory." He quirked an eyebrow. Berlin was full of gossip of "wonder weapons."

"No news on that front."

"Then we must plan for the worst while we hope for the best."

Himmler walked around his desk to face Schellenberg. "It's not an easy task to communicate with the enemy at this point."

Schellenberg, never without an endgame in mind, nodded. "I've forces in play, Reichsführer. Contacts." He tried his best not to look smug. "Let's just say . . . I've had an ongoing conversation with a highly unexpected individual. They're connected to high-powered friends in Britain who could be able to negotiate on our behalf. Let me talk to them."

"You can't make a wrong step," Himmler warned. He clapped Schellenberg on the shoulder. "Return to Berlin—and do what needs to be done." He smiled thinly. "I'll take care of the rest from here."

Schellenberg stood. "I'll need money."

"I'll give you what you need." Then, "Don't let me—us—down."

"No, sir." Schellenberg's fingers twitched; he wished desperately for a cigarette. "And I'll need to promote the weapons we have in development. Perhaps a little lecture tour for our brilliant scientists? Switzerland? Perhaps Spain and Portugal, as well?"

"Good idea."

"I'll speak with Professor Heisenberg myself," Schellenberg promised.

Himmler went to the bar cart and poured two snifters of brandy. "Long live the second Germany," he intoned, offering a glass to Schellenberg.

Out of habit, Schellenberg raised his right hand in salute before accepting the proffered glass. "Heil . . ."

Realizing, he grinned as he lowered his arm and accepted the drink. "Looks like we won't have to do that for much longer."

Chapter One

January 1944

Mornings in London were the exact opposite of those in Los Angeles, and Maggie Hope sometimes felt as if she were back in black-and-white Kansas after a whirlwind trip to Technicolor Oz. Yet in her bedroom in Marylebone, she smiled as she took in the length of the sleeping figure lying next to her: John Sterling. Her ex-fiancé. The man with whom she shared a . . . complicated past. And yet, now it seemed so simple, so easy. *And you were there, too,* she thought with amazement. *In Los Angeles. And you're still here, five months later.* The radiator sputtered to life with a hiss and a series of loud clanks. John stirred, but didn't wake.

Sitting up and tossing aside wool blankets, Maggie pulled on her robe and slippers and padded to the window to pull back the blackout curtains. She looked past the crisscrossed strips of gummed paper on the glass panes to glimpse an incandescently pink sunrise. Bare treetops bent in the east wind, and what had once been flower beds were now slumbering victory gardens.

Maggie spotted two boys, twins from the house across the street, who'd finally returned from their evacuation to the countryside. Before working as a typist to Mr. Churchill, she'd tutored them in math to earn money for the never-ending re-pairs her old house needed. Only a few schools had reopened, so they and the rest of the children ran wild from dawn until dusk. There was no traffic, since gasoline was still in short sup-ply. Maggie watched as a young woman, bundled up in a huge coat and scarf, pushed a pram. She could hear the faint chatter of wrens in the bushes, as well as a siren in the far distance.

She remembered the first time she'd slept in this bedroom, after leaving her aunt Edith, her guardian, at Wellesley College in Massachusetts. Maggie pulled her robe tighter around her—how small and alone she'd felt. She had moved to London to try to sell her grandmother's cold and empty house. Now the house was filled with friends, warm and familiar.

Growing up on the campus of a women's college, a mathe-matics major, Maggie had always been surrounded by intelli-gent, thoughtful people who took ideas—and the women who had them—seriously. For Maggie, the cool beauty of mathe-matics had been a balm against the dizzying confusion of life. She'd been drawn to mathematical puzzles, fascinated by the Fibonacci sequence. She'd also always loved word games, doing crosswords in pen.

If she'd never left the United States, she'd probably still be in the ivory tower of academia, studying math. Not Princeton, as they didn't admit women—and had refused to admit her—but at MIT, where she'd been accepted into the doctoral pro-gram in mathematics.

Still, when Maggie thought of herself as a graduate student, a Ph.D., she could only see herself as bookish and closed off. Cold. Living in a black-and-white world of numbers and theo-ries. War was never good, she knew. *Never.* There was no "good" war. But she was proud to be "doing her bit," with her friends and fellow Britons, and now the Allies, to fight a neces-sary war.

She'd worked as a typist for Prime Minister Winston

Churchill in the summer of 1940, as bombs began to rain on London. Initially, she'd been ignored, but in noticing anomalies, asymmetrical patterns, she broke a hidden code. Breaking it, and fighting for the embedded message to be taken seriously, catapulted her into a career in intelligence, with missions in London, then Windsor, Berlin, Edinburgh, Washington, D.C., Paris, and last summer, Los Angeles.

She and John had visited her aunt Edith, a chemistry professor at Wellesley, on their way from Los Angeles back to London. "I approve, darling," Edith had whispered in Maggie's ear late one night after she'd said good night and kissed her on the cheek. It had felt like a blessing from her thoroughly starched English aunt.

Maggie looked around, taking in the details of her bedroom: the wainscoting, the blue-painted walls, the framed cover of a Wonder Woman comic her dear friend David Greene had given her in Washington, after they'd met President Roosevelt. A case full of beloved books. It was good to be home.

She padded back to bed, sitting next to John, who was now snoring softly. She bent down; he smelled faintly of sleep and bay rum aftershave and warm linen. "Good morning," she whispered in his ear. His breathing didn't change. She gazed at him sleeping, his long eyelashes, the dark stubble on his jaw. She kissed him gently on the forehead. "Good morning." A kiss on the cheek and still nothing. One on the lips. "Good morning . . ."

With one arm, he swept her closer so she was on top of him, now giggling madly. "Good morning, you," he murmured. But before they could kiss again, there was a loud banging on the bedroom door.

"*Mimi! Mimi! Mimi!*" called an insistent little voice. It was Griffin, her friends Chuck and Nigel's son, and Maggie's honorary nephew. The energetic toddler still couldn't quite say "Maggie."

"Sleeping, Griff!" Maggie replied.

She heard her friend and flatmate Chuck—really Charlotte Ludlow—say in her lilting Irish accent, "Come along, dear. Let Auntie Maggie be." She could hear Griffin's squealing protests as they made their way slowly and carefully down the creaking stairs. "Feet take turns!" Chuck said to Griff. "Feet take turns!"

When Maggie had moved into her late grandmother's house, she'd had no idea it would become a home to so many displaced by war. And while Chuck pretended to be scandalized by John's staying the night on occasion, Maggie clearly remembered the early days of Chuck's romance with Nigel—and how he'd come traipsing into the kitchen for a cup of tea, often clad only in Chuck's polka-dotted dressing gown.

There had also been Sarah, a ballet dancer for the Vic-Wells Ballet, who was now a Hollywood starlet. She'd recently moved to New York City to dance for the choreographer George Balanchine and audition for roles on Broadway.

And, of course, there had been Paige Kelly, her best friend from Wellesley, a Southern belle who'd worked as a typist for the United States's ambassador to Britain, Joseph Kennedy, before the war. *Oh, Paige,* Maggie thought. It had been enough years that the sharp pain of her friend's betrayal and death had softened, but it was always with her.

Before Maggie and John could resume their embrace, the telephone in the hall rang. John groaned and ran his hands through his curly, dark hair in frustration as Maggie shot out of bed. "Just a second," she called back. "Could be work."

The hall was cold, and she pulled her flannel robe closer around her. "Hello," she said into the black Bakelite receiver.

"Kim Philby." Harold Russell Philby, better known by his nickname, "Kim," was never one to spend time chatting on the telephone.

"Hello, Kim." It felt strange to use the first name of the

head of the Iberian Section of MI-6. But he'd insisted, as he did with all his agents.

"Meet me at St. Ermin's today," he told her in his crisp upper-crust English accent. "Three o'clock."

Maggie's stomach flipped in anticipation at the words. "What's happened?"

"New intel. The bar." By which he meant Caxton.

She felt a tiny flicker of hope run through her like an electrical current. She didn't like to be idle, and wanted to do whatever she could to help the war effort. She'd been promised her own mission, but time and again it had been held up. *Maybe this time I'll have my shot?* "I'll be there."

In Los Angeles, Maggie received news that Chanel, whom she'd met on a mission in Paris in 1941, had requested her "services" as a courier. Since then, she'd been training with SOE. She'd used the time to refresh her spy skills, return to fighting shape, and study Spain's history and politics, but she was more than ready to begin.

Still in bed, John stretched and yawned, letting the sheet fall to his waist, revealing broad shoulders and a lean torso. "Does this mean you have to go?" He gifted Maggie with one of his true smiles, a tender expression that lit up his face and made his brown eyes dance. It was the gentle and protective smile she'd fallen in love with, all those years ago. The look she was still in love with.

She grinned wickedly, then closed and locked the door. "Not *quite* yet."

Chapter Two

Gabrielle Bonheur Chanel, better known by her nickname, "Coco," took a deep breath, closed her eyes, and plunged her face into a sink full of ice. Every morning, her maid brought up shards from the Hôtel Ritz Paris's bar and mixed them with rosewater.

One of the most famous couturieres and perfumers in the world, Coco was renowned for taking women out of heavy, frilly hats and fussy corsets, and dressing them instead in boyish toppers and creations of tailored, streamlined jersey. She'd also designed costumes for stage and screen, working with Jean Cocteau, Sergei Diaghilev, and Pablo Picasso. She had made her fortune by creating Chanel No. 5, named for her lucky number.

Coco counted for ten seconds, twenty, thirty, then finally lifted her head, gasping for air. She reached for her towel—a warm peach shade, which César Ritz believed would best flatter his guests' complexions—and gently blotted her skin. She believed her daily morning ice bath helped her skin's circulation and shrank the bags under her eyes.

Although impeccably elegant now, she'd been born in a charity hospital in Saumur, Maine-et-Loire, in western France. She'd been only twelve when her mother, a laundress, died of tuberculosis. Her street peddler father had abandoned her and her siblings, sending her to live at the orphanage at the Convent of Aubazine. There, the nuns taught her to sew.

At age eighteen, she'd moved to a Catholic boardinghouse in Moulins, where she supported herself as a seamstress. At night, she'd performed in a cabaret frequented by cavalry officers, where she sang "*Ko Ko Ri Ko*" and "*Qui qu'a vu Coco*," earning herself the nickname "Coco."

She met Étienne Balsan, an officer and heir to a textile fortune, at the nightclub. She soon became his mistress, living a life of luxury and decadence at his estates. In time, she also began an affair with one of Balsan's friends, Captain Arthur "Boy" Capel, who eventually gave her a hat shop in Paris.

Her affair with Boy lasted for nine years, until he died in a car accident. Coco turned to work as solace for her grief and created hats and clothing for Paris's most fashionable women, her career exploding into perfume and jewelry design.

However, she'd closed her fashion business after the fall of France in 1940. Reichsmarschall Hermann Göring and the upper echelon of his Luftwaffe officers had forcibly seized the Paris Ritz and taken it over as Nazi headquarters.

For several years prior, Coco had lived at the Ritz, a late Louis XIV building in the city's first arrondissement, occupying a two-bedroom suite with a view of the grand Place Vendôme. When the Nazis invaded, she'd given up her suite and moved to two small maids' bedrooms, which overlooked the narrow cobblestone street in the back, just a block away from her eponymous atelier and shop at 31, rue Cambon. Although she wasn't selling hats or clothing, her shop still did a brisk business hawking bottles of Chanel No. 5 to Nazi soldiers and French collaborators, for both their wives and their mistresses.

Still, ensconced at the Ritz, she enjoyed luxurious and warm surroundings, hot and cold running water, and the best food available served by the hotel's chefs. She'd had to move most of her furnishings—her blackamoor and Jacques Lipchitz sculptures, and the silk divan she'd reclined on for Horst—to the rooms above her atelier down the street. But she'd kept her Coromandel screens: large, burnished panels painted with flowers and exotic birds, precious reminders of her tragic love affair with Boy.

Although the bathroom's lights also had a soft peach cast, Coco was displeased. She leaned forward into the mirror and squinted to see better. At nearly sixty, her face was still beautiful, though hardened by years of war. There were deep lines between her brows from displeasure and around her mouth from smoking. Her thin neck was corded and her skin crepey and sallow from a lifetime spent in the sun—either tanning on the beaches in the South of France, or hunting and fishing in Scotland, with the many rich men she'd befriended over the years. Too many cocktails, cigarettes, and nightly morphine injections didn't help either.

Coco scowled at her reflection as she brushed her dyed coal-black hair into its perfect bob, which highlighted her cheekbones. She applied foundation, rouge, eyeliner, mascara, and thick red lipstick, then anointed herself generously with her own perfume. She touched the crystal stopper to her forehead, between her breasts, and behind each ear—as if making the sign of the cross. Last, she opened a drawer and took out a gold-tooled leather box. Inside was a syringe and an ampoule of morphine-based Sedol.

"*Mon précieux,*" she murmured as she filled the needle, then flicked her fingernail against it, hard, to make sure there were no air bubbles. The couturiere squirted a few drops of the clear fluid into the air before plunging the needle into her upper thigh. Just a little bit, just to keep her nerves in check, she thought, as opposed to the larger doses she took to sleep.

Dropping her creamy silk robe in a puddle on the floor, Coco sauntered naked to her closet, picking out a black suit with white chiffon collar and cuffs, from one of her prewar collections. It suited her taut, gamine figure perfectly. She completed the ensemble with wedge heels, ropes and ropes of superb pearls, and an oversize black velvet beret.

She plucked a thin white Gitane from her platinum cigarette case and lit it, inhaling the heavy, almost spicy smoke, gray tendrils floating above her. Cigarette clamped between two sun-spotted fingers, she stepped back to consider her appearance in the closet's full-length mirror with a gimlet eye. "Not bad for a peasant," she mocked in her gravelly voice.

Her maid had also brought in a breakfast tray. The black coffee and dry toast Coco ignored, but she couldn't help but read *Le Monde*'s front page: FIGHTING CONTINUES ON KIROVO-GRAD. Between the lines, it most probably meant the Soviets had defeated the Germans and were on their way to Poland. She shook her head and walked over to the silk-swagged window, striking her signature pose: hips and one foot forward, one hand holding the cigarette, the other angled in her skirt pocket.

Even though she'd been born a peasant, and had become an orphan, a seamstress, and a singer before becoming a designer, she carried herself like royalty, with her chin up and shoulders back. Today was important. Today of all days she had to look perfect: chic, feminine, aristocratic. And, above all, confident. Because she wasn't, not at all. At odd hours of the night, when the morphine wore off, she was awake, staring at the ceiling. In those moments, she wondered if it would be better to slit her wrists in the bathtub or stick a gun in her mouth, rather than wait for the arrival of the Allies. She could feel them coming for her, sooner or later.

Outside the Ritz, the wind picked up. It blew the bare black branches of the horse chestnut trees, dislodging even the most stubborn crows, who cawed as they flew off. She leaned her forehead against the cold glass and exhaled a long plume of smoke, thinking of all the times she'd looked through the windows, over those trees, since the Occupation had begun.

A key turned in the lock. She startled and turned, breathing a sigh of relief only when she saw it was her lover, Baron Hans Günther von Dincklage.

He was a tall, blond bon vivant, a decade younger than Coco. His friends called him "Spatz," meaning sparrow. He was a German aristocrat, an early supporter of Hitler, and a renowned playboy. He operated undercover as the "special attaché" to the German Embassy in Paris—all the while working as Abwehr Agent F-8680 for the Nazis. When Coco was rebuked by certain friends for her relationship with Spatz, she'd counter, "Really, a woman of my age can't be expected to look at a man's passport."

Coco and Spatz had met sheltering in the Ritz's wine cellars during a raid. She'd loved that Spatz was half English, from a world she was familiar with from her years with another of her lovers, the Duke of Westminster. But while he'd provided Coco protection in Nazi-occupied Paris while Hitler was in ascent, she was keenly aware that the balance of power in the world was once again in flux. The days of "Better Hitler than Stalin" in France were over. Reichsmarschall Hermann Göring and his officers had left the Ritz and were now posted to the battle-torn Soviet Union or Italy. Anyone important was fleeing the city. Coco knew it was time for her to go as well.

Spatz was impeccably dressed as always, but uncharacteristically pale and subdued. He looked at her with foreboding, mouth tight.

"Darling," Coco said with a seductive smile, stabbing out her cigarette in a cut-crystal ashtray. She walked to him and offered up one rouged cheek, then the other, for him to kiss. "It's still happening?" she asked, picking a piece of lint from his lapel. They always spoke together in English.

"Yes," Spatz replied in his burnished baritone. "The meeting's on."

"Thank God." Coco staggered slightly, from relief. She took one last look in the mirror to check her lipstick and correct the angle of her hat, then picked up her quilted alligator purse from the carved rosewood entrance table. Spatz helped her on with her heavy black sable and opened the door.

As they walked to the elevator, she proclaimed with far more confidence than she felt, "Today, darling—today we make history."

Chapter Three

Maggie arrived at St. Ermin's Hotel just before three. A shabby, late Victorian red-brick mansion, set back from Caxton Street in Westminster, St. Ermin's was within walking distance of the abbey, Buckingham Palace, and St. James's Park. More important, however, it was located at the crossroads of all the British intelligence agencies: MI-5, MI-6, and Special Operations Executive were all close by.

It was a glorious winter day with bright, wind-scoured skies. As Maggie walked from the Tube stop, she felt her body tense in anticipation of meeting with Kim. Her shoulders braced as her stomach clenched. She recognized the feeling—excitement with a side of terror—and realized she'd missed it, missed going on missions, what she'd come to think of as work.

She'd dressed carefully for their meeting, in a blue wool suit and white blouse, long navy coat with a patch at the elbows. Her face was schooled in a neutral expression, and she'd pulled back her glossy red hair in a low bun; one of her favorite hats was pinned on at a slant. Chill gusts of wind blew dead leaves on the icy pavement into the gutter, over the curbs painted phosphorescent white to glow in the dark of the blackout. There they collected, along with newspapers, cigarette butts, and a tiny lost pink mitten.

Overhead, a giant barrage balloon loomed, buffeted by the winds. Billboards advertised Wardonia shaving blades and Guinness beer, and displayed a government poster with British, American, and Soviet flags choking a mustached figure: TO-GETHER WE SHALL STRANGLE HITLERISM!

Because of petrol rationing, there were fewer cars, trucks, and buses, and even more cyclists: middle-aged men in suits and fur homburg hats, women in trousers with their hair protected by knit caps. And there were always more Americans, shouting from transport vehicles or walking five abreast on the puddled pavements, cursing loudly and chewing gum. The Yanks were welcomed in London, to be sure, yet also considered with suspicion as "overpaid, oversexed, and Over Here."

A freckle-faced boy, who couldn't have been more than ten, trumpeted the headlines at a corner newspaper stand: RED ARMY SURROUNDS KIROVOGRAD; DRIVE INTO POLAND GAINS 14 MILES; U.S. BOMBERS AGAIN HIT GERMANY. *Finally,* she thought. *Gaining more traction heading into Europe.* She remembered when Churchill made a speech about "the end of the beginning" of the war. Now it seemed as though it could, possibly, be the beginning of the end.

In front of St. Ermin's revolving doors, a man in uniform and a top hat nodded as she passed. Inside, the soaring ceiling of the lobby was a mass of smoke-stained rococo plasterwork, looking to Maggie like wedding cake fondant coated with ash. There were shabby tartan armchairs, drooping potted palms, and dusty chandeliers. A bellhop pushed a cart of battered leather trunks and suitcases to the elevators, and the air smelled of men's cologne, floor wax, and the restaurant's hot mutton and boiled potato special.

The Caxton Bar was British intelligence's not-so-secret annex, cozy and warm, with a low ceiling and a crackling fireplace. It was dim as well—the wartime low-voltage electricity bulbs barely glowed and the air was hazy with a curtain of smoke. As Maggie entered, she was aware of a palpable tension and energy. Most of the patrons surreptitiously took her measure before going back to their conversations and drinks. She gripped her purse; while she'd been to the Caxton many times before, this meeting felt slightly surreal.

A well-muscled bald man behind the counter polishing coupe glasses looked up and smiled. Maggie knew from talking to him he was a former boxer. "Welcome, Miss Hope!"

"Thank you, Mr. Jenkins! Good to see you again—how's your son?"

"Doing well!" He beamed. "Just turned eighteen and joined the RAF. He's at flight school now."

He's so young, she thought. *Just a boy.* But she said, "He'll make a splendid pilot. And when he returns—safe and sound—he can go back to studying maths." She gave a quirky half-smile. "Maybe I'll do that someday, too." *A girl can dream, after all.*

Jenkins nodded. "God willing."

"Indeed."

Maggie scanned the room for Kim and found him in his usual seat: close to the fireplace, with his back against a wall, facing the entrance. It was the perfect place for a spy to keep an eye on everything. She'd first met Kim in her early days with the SOE, the elite group Winston Churchill had created at the start of the war to "set Europe ablaze."

In the fall of 1940, he'd been one of her instructors at Beaulieu, the SOE's "finishing school" for spies in southern England. There she'd learned encryption, wireless communication, how to use invisible ink, disguises, safecracking, and setting explosives, among other skills. She'd also become a skilled marksman.

Kim, a worn camel-hair coat draped from his shoulders,

spotted her immediately. He held up one hand. "Red!" he called. "Over here!" He cut a dashing figure, with his broad shoulders, "old boy" confidence, and an unruly forelock.

Maggie felt warmed by Kim's smile and loosened her scarf as she walked over. "Holding court from your usual table, I see. And I must say, in the immortal words of Anne of Green Gables, the hair's auburn, not red."

Kim rose and pecked her on both cheeks. "I don't know what an 'Anne of Green Gables' is," he said with the slight stammer she found endearing, "but I'll take your word for it." She knew his voice and accent all too well from her time in the corridors of Number 10 Downing Street and Whitehall; they were the kind that had echoed for generations over public school and Oxbridge manicured lawns. The accent of those loyal to King, country, class, and club. She took the seat next to him, also with her back to the wall.

Of course Maggie had investigated Kim Philby; she researched everyone she worked with. Kim was a major figure in British espionage. After Westminster School and then Trinity College at Cambridge University, he'd joined the Anglo-German Fellowship, a pro-fascist society formed in 1935 to foster closer understanding with Germany. He'd traveled regularly to Berlin on behalf of the fellowship, and even met Germany's foreign minister, Joachim von Ribbentrop.

Two years later Kim had become a war correspondent for *The Times* covering Spain's Civil War, reporting directly from the headquarters of Generalísimo Francisco Franco. He'd returned home in July 1939, after the Civil War ended. When Britain declared war on Germany in September, he denounced the Nazis and was recruited for MI-6, eventually emerging as the new head of the section's Iberian Department.

She saw he was drinking his usual martini with three olives, stuffed with red pimentos. "I've requested your pot of tea."

Kim Philby, she thought, *the man who makes a point to always remember everyone's drink.*

"Usually, I'm the one asked to make tea for these meetings," Maggie said as she settled, unbuttoning her coat, pulling off her leather gloves, and tucking them in her purse. The cuff of her dress was starting to fray. Her stomach growled and she thought of ordering the bar's lunch special—a lumpy mince, garnished with soggy beans and mushy potatoes, which suddenly smelled delicious. But there was work to be done.

Kim pushed back the long lock of hair that had fallen in front of his eyes. "Not anymore." Nearly hidden under the coat and his worn Harris tweed jacket, he wore red suspenders, his old-school tie secured by a monogrammed pin. Maggie said thank you as a waiter set down a tea tray in front of her, and placed the thick linen napkin in her lap.

Her lips twisted in a rueful smile as she remembered her days as Mr. Churchill's secretary and then as a rising agent. It had been only three years, but she felt so much older. What she'd seen, what she'd done, all weighed heavily on her. She wasn't the same; when she thought of her old self, it was as if she were gazing through Alice's looking glass. And she knew that when the war was over, she'd finally have to face her demons. She dreaded it. *But not today,* she thought.

"And how's Mr. Sterling?" Kim asked, leaning forward to pour strong black tea.

"John's well." Maggie smiled involuntarily, just saying his name. She accepted the scalding hot teacup and saucer, inhaling the fragrant steam.

"Back at Number Ten?"

Maggie took a sip. "He is." John was supposed to have joined her on this mission to Spain, but he'd received new marching orders from his former employer, the Prime Minister himself.

It wasn't known publicly, but while Winston Churchill had been at the Tehran Conference with President Roosevelt and Joseph Stalin, he'd contracted pneumonia and was currently convalescing in Marrakesh. When John had returned from Los Angeles, he'd been summoned back to Number 10, to manage things while the Boss was "away."

At first, Maggie had been disappointed John wouldn't join her—he'd trained at Camp X in Canada and had his own experiences in espionage. They'd worked well together in Los Angeles. But she knew he was needed in London. And what she would never say aloud was that perhaps he'd be safer at home as well.

She took another sip and looked around to make sure no one was in earshot. "Tell me about the current situation."

"Things are still in flux." Kim spoke softly. "But moving quickly. The key to winning this war—and the subsequent peace—is Spain."

He took a swig of his martini. "On the surface, Spain's neutral. But it's always been aligned with Hitler, under Franco. Right now, with the way things are going, the country's direction's volatile. With the Allied advance from southern Italy, the partisans are changing sides. The worm's turning in our favor."

Maggie set down her teacup. "But at the Casablanca Conference, the Big Three stated outright they'd only accept unconditional surrender."

Kim plucked an olive from his glass and popped it in his mouth. "People say a lot of things in war."

It was the Allies' clearly stated goal that the Axis powers be fought to their total defeat and surrender. But, in certain circles, it was felt the war had already gone on too long, and it was high time for peace. In addition, many believed it would be disastrous for Britain—and the United States—if western Europe fell into Soviet hands. Which was more than possible, depending on the Allied invasion. Would the United States or the Soviet Union reach Berlin first? The very future of all Europe turned on the answer.

"Our mutual Parisian friend," he said, "has heard from her sources Hitler will be removed soon." Given the mission she'd been preparing for, Maggie read between the lines: he meant Coco Chanel.

"Mr. Churchill would never accept a separate peace deal with the Nazis," Maggie stated flatly.

"No . . ." Kim's low voice was now almost a whisper. Usually he spoke in a precise manner, understated, dripping with irony. But now he was deadly serious. "But there *are* those here who'd like to see Britain make this separate peace. They think it'll keep the Soviet Union from taking over Germany, France, and the rest as well. They're betting most people, like them, would rather see a fascist post-Hitler Europe than a communist one."

Maggie shook her head. "The Soviets are our allies. The Nazis are our enemies."

Kim smiled, a real smile. "I never asked you about your politics—you know, back when you were a student."

"You mean, did I ever dabble in communism?" She laughed. "No, but it was certainly in the air. My aunt used to say, 'Communism in youth is like measles—best to have it young and out of your system.'" Kim chortled.

"I remember quite a few professors and students who were enamored of Marx and Lenin. I even had a brief . . . fascination. But it didn't last long." She shook her head at the memories. "What about you?"

"When I was an undergraduate, I had a good look around and reached the simple conclusion that the rich had had it too damn good for too long, and the poor had had it too damn bad, and it was time it was all changed. I thought capitalism was worse than communism or fascism."

"What happened?"

"Ah." He lit a cigarette. "Then I grew up. Right now, the safety of our troops in North Africa and Italy depends upon Spain's continued neutrality," Kim told her, inhaling. "As well as any invasions of the Continent."

He blew out a stream of blue smoke. "I don't need to tell you the outcome of the war hinges on the invasion of France. And our French friend asked for you specifically. Or, rather, for 'Paige Kelly,' as she knew you in Paris two years ago."

Last July, Chanel had, through contacts at MI-5, requested "Paige Kelly" be present at her upcoming meeting with the British ambassador in Spain. And to personally hand-deliver her message to the P.M.

"Apparently," Kim said, raising his eyebrows, "you 'owe' her?"

Maggie thought back to her time undercover in Paris in 1942. "Chanel did help me," she admitted. "I don't trust her, but still." She leaned back in her chair. "She probably saved my life."

"We're still in discussions with British Ambassador Samuel Hoare's office in Madrid for you and Chanel to meet with him. Of course, that's not the only reason you'll be in Spain."

Maggie certainly knew of Lord Samuel, a onetime appeaser and senior Conservative politician. He'd been First Lord of the Admiralty, then served as home secretary. Winston Churchill had appointed him Britain's ambassador to Spain in 1940. She knew Kim wasn't a fan of Ambassador Hoare; he believed under the ambassador British Catholics had been given too great a role in influencing British policy toward Spain.

"Your partner will help you pierce some of the diplomatic social circles," he said. "In addition to the bit with Chanel, and information gathering, you'll have another assignment in Madrid." Kim leaned in and whispered in her ear. "Have you ever killed a man?"

Maggie managed to keep her face neutral. "You've read my files." The memories, though mostly repressed, were painful. "You know I have."

"We have eyes on a target." *A target?* Maggie thought. Was that the reason for all the shooting drills she'd recently done at Beaulieu? An assassination?

He finished his martini, swallowing the last olive. "Come," he said, picking up his black leather briefcase and standing. "Let's go upstairs. There's someone I want you to meet."

Chapter Four

Coco and Spatz were silent as her chauffeured Rolls-Royce wound its way through the streets of Paris to the Hôtel Lutetia. It was a cold and bleak day, with a raw wind blowing off the Seine.

The so-called City of Light was now known as *la capitale de la faim*—the capital of hunger. There were few cars or trucks, as petrol was rationed to all but the most elite. The streets, which once bustled with German officers and soldiers—and the French collaborators who flirted with them—were now nearly deserted. The Nazis who remained, too aged or infirm to be sent to the Soviet front, kept to their heated offices. Most shops were closed and boarded, and trash and rotting leaves collected in the gutters.

There were no Jews left in Paris—at least none who weren't in hiding. Occupied France had adopted all the Third Reich's laws against Jews "and other vermin." Throughout France, and in Paris at the Vél d'Hiv, around thirty thousand people had been deported to Germany's concentration camps.

Coco fingered her pearls absently as she glanced out the car's window. They passed two people dressed in ragged coats, shoes resoled with cardboard, heads bent low against the wind. A sign warned in block letters that eating stray cats could bring disease and death. A man only in shirtsleeves fished in the gutter, pulling out a half-smoked cigarette in triumph.

For a moment, the couturiere met the resentful glare of a young girl. She was maybe thirteen, maybe older, her cheekbones sharp from hunger. She was wearing an ill-fitting, oversize man's coat. Coco knew in an instant it must have belonged to a male relative or friend of the family, taken from Paris and made to work in mines and weapons factories in eastern Europe. Or to the dead.

The girl thrust a fist in the air and, with her other hand, slapped her biceps. It was the *bras d'honneur,* an explicit expression of hatred. Coco stared back as the girl's eyes burned into hers. Hostility to the Nazis and the collaborators was palpable now, overt. Coco knew those in the Resistance and those cheering them; they all hoped for an Allied invasion and victory in the coming year. Once that happened, she knew she'd be one of the first rounded up for retribution for years of collaboration with the Occupation.

She dropped her string of pearls and looked away, shuddering. A purge was undoubtedly coming. Women who slept with Nazis—"horizonal collaborators," as they were called—were told they'd be rounded up and marched naked through the streets, their heads shaved, their foreheads branded with swastikas. There would be imprisonment, trials, tribunals. And then, finally, the guillotine.

Coco glanced sideways at Spatz. He, too, gazed disconsolately out the car window, also living on borrowed time. She realized the British and Free French secret agents must have an ongoing record of his work with the Gestapo. A record they'd use against him. If he were caught.

She reached over to grasp his hand. *I've already endured so much. I'll make it through this as well. That's what I do: I survive.*

. . .

The Hôtel Lutetia, with its belle époque flourishes, was located at 45 Boulevard Raspail, in Saint-Germain-des-Prés, in the sixth arrondissement of Paris. Just as the Hôtel Ritz had been commandeered by Göring and the Luftwaffe, the Lutetia had been appropriated by the Abwehr, German intelligence.

Coco's driver pulled up to the sandbagged entrance and rolled to a stop. An SS guard in uniform approached the car and opened the door for her. Head high, she entered the grand lobby, blinking away memories of times past: cocktails, dinners, and dancing with Picasso, Stravinsky, and Diaghilev. That time was long gone, along with the fragrant bouquets of roses that used to fill the lobby. It was eerily silent now, with no piano music or chatter, just men in uniform walking quickly with downcast eyes. Above, the glittering cut-crystal chandeliers flickered unsteadily.

Spatz led her to the mahogany counter. An officer with a large patch of white burn-scarred skin on his left cheek raised an arm in a salute. "Heil Hitler!"

"We have an appointment with Count Joseph von Ledebur," Coco told him. She had both hands on her purse in front of her, trying not to stare at his shiny scars.

"I'll let Major Ledebur know you've both arrived, sir," he told them, picking up a black telephone receiver.

Coco and Spatz were silent on the elevator ride to the fourteenth floor. The car arrived with a thud, and the gloved attendant slid the door open for them. At the end of the long hall, in front of two grand double doors, a uniformed guard stood at attention. He rapped at the door.

A young bleached-blond secretary let them into what once must have been the suite's parlor. "Major Ledebur knows you're here," she told them, her accent revealing she was a na-

tive Parisian. Coco noted she was wearing a knockoff Schiaparelli dress from Printemps and sniffed in disapproval of the
Italian designer, her rival. "Please, follow me."

Coco raised her chin as the secretary opened another set of
double doors. Inside, Ledebur's office was plain and business-
like. A formal portrait of Adolf Hitler was the room's only
decoration. "The major will be with you shortly. Would you
like coffee? Tea?"

"No." Coco's nostrils flared with displeasure at being made
to wait as she took one of the seats in front of the desk; the
secretary scurried away. Spatz put a large hand on Coco's
dainty gloved one. "Patience, my darling," he murmured.

She pulled her hand away to rummage through her purse
for her platinum cigarette case, opened it, then pulled out a
Gitane.

"No smoking in here, my love."

"If he's going to make me wait," she said acidly, waiting for
Spatz to light it for her, "I'm going to be comfortable." He
looked uneasy, but was quick with his gold lighter. She took a
sharp drag.

At last, Ledebur entered. He was in his mid-forties, with
remarkably dark and bushy eyebrows streaked with gray and
set at extreme angles, and a deeply cleft chin. He was also in
uniform.

"Heil Hitler!" he exclaimed, saluting. "Spatz—good to see
you! Madame Chanel, thank you for coming." He spoke in
Austrian-inflected French.

Coco ground out her cigarette in a paper clip tray and extended a gloved hand. "It's Mademoiselle," she corrected.

He took her hand and bent to kiss it. "My apologies, Mademoiselle. It's a true pleasure—indeed an honor—to finally meet
you." He slipped into the black leather chair behind the massive desk. "I'm pleased to tell you both that Operation Modelhut's officially been approved. Not just by our man in Paris

but also by General Walter Schellenberg, in Berlin." Spatz's jaw relaxed almost imperceptibly. Coco knew how hard he'd worked, using all his connections, to secure Schellenberg's authorization.

"On the basis of your relationship with Churchill," Ledebur continued, steepling short, hairy fingers, "and other high-ranking British citizens, we're allowing you to proceed with your proposed plan, to travel to Spain and meet with the British ambassador in Madrid."

Coco nodded, pleased. Her long-standing friendships with members of the British aristocracy, through her lover the Duke of Westminster, were her calling card in this mission. "I'll make a great fuss about looking for a location for a new boutique. Has the meeting with Ambassador Hoare and Paige Kelly already been set up, or will I receive those details in Madrid?"

Ledebur cleared his throat and met Spatz's eyes. They'd obviously discussed this detail without her. "In regard to Miss Kelly, we're doing our best," he said to Coco, "but can make no promises."

"The young woman is a British spy I once met in Paris. She's the *key* to this mission," Coco insisted. "She can *hand-deliver* our missive to Winston Churchill. My name on the cover letter, of course, will guarantee he sees it and takes it seriously—but it's imperative it reaches him. I don't trust Hoare. I don't trust the diplomatic mail. But Miss Kelly will see to it."

"What makes you trust this Miss Kelly?" Ledebur asked, impressive eyebrows raised. "She's on the other side, after all."

"I *don't* trust her. I don't trust anyone!" She took a moment to collect herself. "But once upon a time I did her a favor, a rather large favor. . . . And let's just say—she owes me."

"Ambassador Hoare in Madrid would surely forward your message."

"Sam, yes," Coco said airily, waving a hand. "Sir Sam. I

know him well. We've stalked deer and fished for salmon together in Scotland, at the Duke of Westminster's estate, many
times. Sam's a terrible shot but a decent angler. And he always
loses at Ascot." She smiled, relishing his surprised expression.
"But I have no confidence in him. Not as I do in Paige Kelly."

She saw with annoyance Ledebur didn't understand how
many people—the right people—she knew, and how influential
she could be. He didn't understand how the worlds of fashion
and diplomacy intersected, as she did.

"We're putting you both up at the Madrid Ritz." He tilted
his head. "You should feel right at home."

She looked to Spatz and then back to Ledebur. "Spatz will
accompany me?" She didn't want to travel to Madrid alone.
And she trusted only her lover.

"Yes, Major Schellenberg has ordered Baron von Dincklage
to accompany you."

"It wouldn't be a bad thing if I actually did open a House of
Chanel in Madrid," Coco mused. "Introduce Number Five to
the Spanish market. Perhaps Lisbon, as well." Spatz nodded.

"While there, you'll socialize as befits your station," Ledebur continued. "While Spain's been technically neutral in this
war, General Franco always leaned our way. With the winds of
war changing, we want to make sure the Allies don't gain any
advantage. You, Mademoiselle, can be quite helpful in per-
suading General Franco to continue to support Germany. After
all, the general isn't just a Spaniard but a Catholic. He surely
wants no part of the atheism communism would bring."

Coco raised penciled eyebrows. "I'll be meeting with General Franco?"

"We're working on it. There's a dinner party we want you
to attend for one of our German physicists, Werner Heisenberg. General Franco will most likely be there as well."

"A physicist?" She wrinkled her nose. She associated with
artists and aristocrats. World leaders. Not scientists.

"A Nobel Prize winner," he assured her, smiling fondly, as though at a wayward child. "I admit, Mademoiselle, I'm astonished at the mission you've proposed. How can we trust that someone like Churchill, even if you were friends with him at one time, will take you—and us—seriously?"

"One word." Coco raised a gloved finger. "Blackmail."

Ledebur's eyebrows rose. "On whom?"

She chose not to tip her hand. "People," she said shortly. "Important people. People high up enough to cause trouble if certain facts . . . came to light."

"Where do we go from here?" Spatz interjected. "Straight to Madrid?"

"No," Ledebur told the pair. "First you'll go to Berlin, to meet Major Schellenberg in person," he said. "He wants to speak with you," he said to Coco, "before you travel to Madrid—just one last bit of red tape. After all, only he can produce your passports to Spain."

"You can't do that?" Coco asked with her most charming smile. She had no desire to go to Berlin.

"No." Ledebur was adamant. "You will meet the Major."

"When?" Spatz asked.

"Tomorrow." Ledebur reached into his desk drawer and pulled out an envelope. "Here are your tickets for the overnight train. Your affairs are in order?"

"Of—of course," Coco replied. For just a moment, her confidence was shaken. So much was riding on this mission.

"It's happening quickly, isn't it, darling?" Spatz said, placing a hand on hers. "But that's diplomacy for you—hurry up and wait, then wait and hurry up." She didn't return his smile.

Ledebur went back to the drawer and pulled out a folder full of documents. "You must also sign a few things. Nondisclosure agreements."

Coco bristled at his tone. "Or else . . ."

He handed her papers. "It would be in your best interest,

Mademoiselle." Spatz smiled as Ledebur passed Coco a black fountain pen. She took a deep breath, signing document after document.

Ledebur went through all the pages, then grinned like a Cheshire cat. "I now christen you Mademoiselle Coco Chanel, Abwehr Agent F-7124. What shall your code name be?"

"She chooses?" Spatz asked, genuinely surprised.

"Of course."

Coco thought about the operation name, German for "model hat," a nod to her past career in haberdashery, and wondered if she should choose the name of a perfume or some other piece of clothing.

But then she recalled her former lover Bendor, Duke of Westminster. He was the man who'd introduced her to British society. Who'd introduced her to Churchill. Who'd gifted her La Pausa, her beloved home in the South of France. Even though they'd never married, and ultimately parted ways, she still held him in high regard. Like so many of the British upper class, he feared the spread of communism throughout Europe. And also like so many, he thought fascism was the antidote.

" 'Westminster.' " She squared her slight shoulders. "My code name's 'Westminster.' "

Chapter Five

The fourth floor of St. Ermin's Hotel had been taken over by SOE. Maggie could see through open doors that the former hotel bedrooms were now dingy offices, filled by various men in suits at desks. Sometimes there were four or more to a room, their faces obscured by blue clouds of cigarette smoke. She could hear the ringing of telephones, the clack of typewriters, and men speaking softly to one another over plywood partitions.

In a chilly former suite with a dusty carpet, now used as a conference room, Kim introduced Maggie to a tall man with a lanky frame. He had a long thin face, wide at the balding forehead, narrowing to a pointy chin. His baggy herringbone suit was rumpled and his blue striped tie slipping from its knot. He was smoking a wooden pipe, and the room was redolent with sweet tobacco.

Maggie recognized him immediately. "James Chadwick!" she exclaimed, brightening and offering her hand. He shook it without enthusiasm.

"You know this man?" Kim sounded surprised as he set down his leather briefcase.

"Professor James Chadwick," she repeated, eyes wide. "British physicist—awarded the Nobel Prize in 1935 for the discovery of the neutron in 'thirty-two. It's—it's an honor to meet you, sir."

Chadwick merely nodded. "Thank you, Miss Hope. Let's have a chat, shall we?" Maggie and Kim sat across from the physicist at a metal conference table.

Kim began. "I'm glad you're already familiar with Professor Chadwick's work. It's been instrumental in the Allies developing what we're calling a . . . fission bomb." Outside the window, a row of long icicles dripped like daggers. Maggie did her best not to gasp. She knew what a fission bomb was—or rather, could be.

"Professor Chadwick's MAUD Report from 1941 provided the British government with the scientific basis to begin its research," Kim explained. "Since then, we've joined with a group of top American physicists to develop the world's first atomic bomb. We're calling it the 'Manhattan Project.' "

Maggie had read Max Born's *Experiment and Theory in Physics* and accounts of Chadwick's work with neutrons. She'd studied quantum theory and matrix mechanics. *If British and U.S. physicists are involved, then surely . . .* "You're working with Professor Albert Einstein?"

Chadwick looked to Kim and jabbed toward Maggie with his pipe. "You're sure she's allowed access to this information?"

I may not have to make tea anymore, but will I always and forever be underestimated? she thought, while keeping her expression bland.

"*Major* Hope has a higher security clearance than you do, Professor."

Ha! she thought, secretly enjoying the professor's expression of surprise.

"Never liked the idea of women in war," said Chadwick. "What about capture? Interrogation?"

"Let me assure you," Maggie told him, "I've stood up to both capture and interrogation by the Gestapo. And not only did I escape, but I'm back here, preparing to return to undercover work."

Kim cleared his throat. "And the major asked you a question."

"Yes," Chadwick admitted. "Einstein's involved."

"Who else?" Maggie asked.

The physicist glanced to Kim, who nodded permission. "J. Robert Oppenheimer, Leo Szilard, Ernest Lawrence, Enrico Fermi . . . A few more."

Her heartbeat quickened. She knew these men, followed their research religiously. These were indeed the scientists who could create a fission bomb for the Allies.

An atomic bomb changes everything—not just the war, but life on the planet in perpetuity. We are now in a dark new age. "The war's now the battle of the laboratories," she said slowly, realizing. "Isn't it?"

She looked to Kim. "Why are you telling me this?" The world seemed to be spinning off its axis.

"The Battle of the Laboratories, I like that—and you're exactly right." Kim leaned back in his folding chair and lit a cigarette. "And we need to win this battle, just as we've won the others. The Germans began the *Uranprojekt,* known informally as the *Uranverein*—"

"The Uranium Club," Maggie finished.

"Yes." Kim exhaled blue smoke. "To the best of our knowledge, the Uranium Club's goal is to build an atomic reactor and a fission bomb. They began in earnest in September of 'thirty-nine."

Maggie nodded, not surprised. "After the invasion of Poland."

"The Germans had already conquered Czechoslovakia,"

Kim continued, "home to Europe's only uranium mines. They had the heavy-water plant in Norway, too. But we've . . . taken that out of the equation, as it were."

Maggie thought back to the Norwegian SOE agents she'd trained with in Scotland. And suddenly realized what their mission had been. She exhaled in awe and admiration, as well as a feeling of relief. *If the Nazis had access to heavy water . . .*

Chadwick picked a stray piece of pipe tobacco from his mouth. "We physicists have placed rather macabre bets on when the Germans might finish. If we're . . . where we are now with our bomb, and they've had a three-year head start . . ."

It's the stuff of nightmares, Maggie thought.

"Well, I don't sleep much anymore," he finished.

"Werner Heisenberg," Maggie said suddenly. Both men turned and stared.

"How the hell do *you* know about Heisenberg?" Chadwick asked sharply. Then, "Excuse my language, Miss Hope."

"Major Hope," Kim reminded.

"Werner Heisenberg's a pioneer in the study of subatomic particles," she replied without blinking. "Winner of the 1932 Nobel Prize in Physics, for the creation of quantum mechanics."

Chadwick sniffed and placed his pipe in a ceramic ashtray, regarding her coldly. "And what's that?" He obviously didn't believe she knew.

"Heisenberg's principle of uncertainty," Maggie told him, covering her annoyance. "It shows you can't observe both the position *and* the velocity of a particle at the same time—you can't be sure of where something is simultaneously with its velocity. In other words—eternal uncertainty."

Kim laughed, a harsh chortle. "A perfect principle for the world at this time—when no one truly knows anything."

"It's more . . . we can't know everything, all at the same time," Maggie amended.

"During your recent retraining at Arisaig House and Beaulieu," Kim said, "you practiced target shooting. And refreshed your already excellent German." He leaned forward. "I know you're willing to die for your country, Major Hope. You've proved that on numerous occasions."

Kim looked her in the eyes. "Now, our question is—are you willing to kill?"

What sort of mission is this? she thought. "Kill?" Maggie leaned back and appraised him. "I . . . suppose it depends on the target."

Kim stubbed out his cigarette. "We know you have killed. On various missions, over the years. But it's always in the moment, never as part of a plan. Would you," he said, with his cut-glass consonants, "be prepared to kill the enemy—in a planned assassination?"

She was at a loss for words. *I'm an intelligence agent. A code breaker. A secret agent. A spy,* she thought. *But an assassin?*

"We need to find out how close Heisenberg and the Germans are to having a bomb," Chadwick told her. "He's going to be in Madrid soon, giving a lecture at the university."

"Why would Professor Heisenberg take the time to travel to Spain, if he's allegedly hard at work on an atomic weapon?" she asked, stalling for time, attempting to process the enormity of what she was being asked to do.

"Heinrich Himmler is rolling out a propaganda tour for German weapons, disguised as a lecture circuit," Kim told her. "Going to neutral countries' universities. Promising a 'super-weapon' to bolster patronage—especially with people like General Franco, whose support for the Nazis may be wavering."

"How far along is Heisenberg?" Maggie asked the men. *How big of a threat is he, really?* she thought. "Surely you've had word? From other scientists?"

"We have intel from an Italian physicist that Heisenberg's working on fission energy," Chadwick said.

"Fission energy could power a battleship or a submarine. That's different from a bomb," Maggie countered. *Maybe I won't have to be part of this mission.*

"By this point in the war, he *must* have thought of creating a bomb," Kim stated. "Hitler would have left him no choice."

Maggie swallowed. "Professor Chadwick, do *you* think Heisenberg's capable of building an atomic bomb?"

The physicist picked up his pipe and stuck it back in his mouth. "Yes."

Think, Hope! "Do you think Heisenberg *would* create such a weapon? For Hitler?" she managed.

"Could he? Yes. Would he? I don't know." Chadwick placed his hands on the table and spread his fingers. "I've met him a few times. He's a complicated man. Cagey. Competitive. Thinks of himself as the best—that German scientists are all the best. But he's a good egg. Or so I thought. We were . . ." he finished sadly, "friends. At one time. Or at least, I thought so."

"What happened?"

Chadwick leaned back and put his hands in his pockets. "Heisenberg sold out his better angels when Hitler took power. He chose to stay with Nazi Germany, even when he had every opportunity to leave. So, no, I do *not* consider us friends any longer." He took a few puffs. "I know at one point he considered himself 'a German, and not a Nazi.' But war changes all of us—and who knows who he is now, and what he believes, at this point."

Maggie leaned forward. "The question is, would he scuttle a project of such magnitude, to save the planet from Hitler's insanity? Secretly sabotage the effort? Would his ego allow him?"

Chadwick sighed. "I don't know if Heisenberg could resist influence from the top at this point. From everything the media are reporting, it certainly seems plausible that they're close to having the bomb."

He handed Maggie a folder of international newspaper and magazine clippings. She glanced through *The Washington Post*. Ernest K. Lindley's quote was underlined in red pencil: "The Berlin radio's reference to blowing up half the globe would seem, to a layman, to hint at progress in the release of atomic energy."

Three London papers carried a United Press report out of Lisbon that reported the "latest travelers to arrive here from the Reich said today that Germany's long-vaunted 'secret weapon' is based upon the principle of energy released from split atoms."

And the *Newsweek* article titled "Can the Nazis Blow Up Half the Globe?" imagined a single high-flying airplane dropping bombs "so tremendous and all-inclusive that in a fraction of a second the entire community had been wiped from the face of the earth."

Maggie forced herself to focus back on Chadwick, who was saying, ". . . but the truth is, we don't know anything for certain."

"Schrödinger's bomb," she said finally. Chadwick nodded, but Kim seemed confused. "Until we know for absolutely certain," she explained to the spymaster, "the Nazis simultaneously do and do not have a fission bomb." She felt light-headed. One bomb could wipe out an entire city and decide the war. She tried to picture the world with no London, no Washington, no Boston and Aunt Edith, and had to close her eyes for a moment.

"Would Germany," she asked finally, "at this point in the war, choose to spend their now-limited resources on a theoretical weapon? Do they even have the money at this point?"

"We don't know," Kim said. "But I have verified intelligence Hitler's pinning his last hopes on what they're calling a 'wonder weapon.'"

"The *Wunderwaffe*," Maggie murmured, lost in thought.

Some of the rumors of Nazi weapons in development were out-landish, such as earthquake generators and death rays. Others, like bacterial and viral weapons and new deadly gases, were entirely feasible. But the possibility Germans would manufacture—and detonate—an atomic bomb was game-changing. *We've now entered the world of post-humanity,* she thought.

"We just don't know exactly what the so-called wonder weapons are," Kim said. "There's also been chatter about rockets—long-range, unmanned rockets carrying bombs. Not as awesome as an atomic weapon, but still terrifying and dangerous if enough are pointed at Blighty."

He cleared his throat. "This opportunity for you to go to Madrid—for the Chanel business—makes you the perfect person to assassinate Heisenberg. We fly you in, you do it, we fly you out. No one will know anything. You'd be the last person suspected. So . . ." He paused. "Are you willing? To kill Heisenberg?"

Maggie opened her mouth and closed it. She was speechless.

"Think of the consequences of inaction," Chadwick urged. "Think of the exponential. What would you prefer? The death of a single scientist—or the death of hundreds of thousands of civilians?"

Maggie pictured Hitler with fission bombs. What he could do. What he *would* do. *With nuclear science, one person's capable of killing millions, with a bomb probably the size of a teapot. So it's the death of Heisenberg—or the possibility of everyone you love vaporized in an instant.*

"The German philosopher Karl Engisch discussed a similar decision," Chadwick mused. "Do we kill one person to save a large number?"

"That's the utilitarian way to look at it," Maggie countered. "The mathematical way. But what about empathy? Who should decide who lives and who dies? If anyone?"

"And that, Major Hope, is our dilemma," Chadwick said,

resting his pipe in the ashtray. "And now *your* dilemma, as well."

Maggie took a long moment to think about what she was being asked. Soon after she'd arrived in London, she'd uncovered and stopped Winston Churchill's would-be assassin. That was her introduction to a life of spying. Now she was being asked to become an assassin herself. *The wheel's come full circle,* she thought and shivered.

"Yes," she said finally. "I'll do it." She raised one hand, palm out. "*But* . . . only if I'm sure—absolutely sure—Professor Heisenberg and his team actually have the bomb or are close."

Chadwick shook his head. "There's no way to know for certain. As you've said, it's Schrödinger's bomb."

"I'll go to Professor Heisenberg's lecture in Madrid," she told him. "And I'll listen. Afterward, I'll talk to him—and again, listen. And—then and only then—I'll make an informed decision."

"There might be one moment where he has a tell," Kim mused, "something that'll reveal if Germany has the bomb or not. In that moment, you'll have to choose whether to take him out."

"In the end, I must know if Heisenberg's a giant, or a windmill," Maggie told the men.

"Cervantes—*Don Quixote*—how appropriate." Kim opened his briefcase and reached inside. He took out a tiny Beretta .25, which he handed to Maggie.

"I suggest you become accustomed to carrying this at all times." The silver pistol was less than five inches long. Its handle was made of burled wood with delicate silver inlay.

"It's tiny," she said, weighing it in her palm. "Light."

"It needs to be, if you're going to keep it hidden. But the size means it's deadly at short range. You'll have to be close. And you have only two bullets before you need to reload. You can make only one mistake."

The gun in Maggie's hand was cold and small. She checked to make sure the safety was on, then opened her purse and slipped it inside. Although it was light, she felt it weigh heavily on her lap.

"They call a post to Madrid the 'gravy train,'" Kim was saying. "In Spain, while half the country's paying the price for being on the wrong side of the Civil War, the other one's enjoying the fruits of victory."

Maggie followed what he was saying but also couldn't get the Bing Crosby and the Andrews Sisters' song out of her head: *Oh, lay that pistol down, babe, lay that pistol down, pistol packin' mama, lay that thing down before it goes off, and hurts somebody . . .*

"It's a big city in a neutral country," he continued, "with food, wine, freedom. That is, until an agent is made. Franco has no mercy for spies—especially Allied spies. He's been known to torture spies in ways . . . Well, I'm sure you can imagine."

Maggie *could* imagine. She still had the occasional nightmare about being held by the Gestapo in Paris. "You still in, Red?" he asked.

The question hung over the three of them, as a man's life, the end of the war, and Maggie's soul hung in the balance.

She thought for a moment. "I thought the SOE decided against assassination after Reinhard Heydrich's. Too much 'collateral damage.' When Heydrich was killed in Czechoslovakia in 1942, the Nazis wiped out two villages in retaliation. That put an end to all elimination attempts."

"They won't be able to trace this one to us," Kim said. "A woman? A random 'Irish' woman? In neutral Madrid?" He shook his head. "No one will ever know. And you'll have backup. Agent Connor Sullivan."

Maggie was still, processing everything she'd just learned.

She remembered Connor Sullivan from training at Arisaig. She'd always been impressed with his intelligence, strength, and good humor. When John had gone back to work for the P.M., Sullivan had been her next choice for the mission.

Kim seemed to sense her paralysis. "There's something we'd like to show you." He stood and went to a film projector in the corner of the room.

Chadwick rose and drew the shades, then turned off the overhead lights. As the machine whirred into life, Kim adjusted the focus. The black-and-white footage, flickering on a bare wall, was jumpy and occasionally distorted.

"This film was smuggled out of Europe by our agents," Kim said in a grave voice, his face shadowed. "A few paid with their lives." He flipped a switch. "The public's never seen this—it's all top secret."

The first shaky images showed a city being destroyed by German Heinkels. "Rotterdam," Kim told them, "bombed in revenge for Dutch resistance."

The next spluttering images showed a mass execution by firing squad. "Poles," Kim explained. "Intellectuals, scholars, artists—heroes all. Rounded up and killed by Nazis."

Subsequent scenes showed Nazi roundups of Jews with yellow stars on their sleeves, in Vienna, Bucharest, too many places to count. Murder by firing squads in Stalingrad. Then a series of executions, by firing squad, guillotine, and hanging.

"These, I'm sorry to say, are our own agents," Kim said. Maggie swallowed hard. Any of the blurred figures might have been someone she'd trained with.

When the secret films were finished, Kim turned off the projector and flipped on the lights. Chadwick rubbed at his eyes with his fists, then cleared his throat.

Maggie was shaken, but not surprised. Not after all she'd been through, all she'd witnessed with her own eyes. She saw

Kim was taking her measure. "The people who committed these atrocities might someday have—or might already have—a fission bomb. They won't hesitate to use it."

She nodded, numb—the stakes were high beyond comprehension—and said only "I understand."

Chapter Six

The bell tolled four as the sun slipped below the horizon, the sky growing ever more scarlet. A siren pulsed in the distance as Maggie and Kim circled St. James's Park's small lake, their footsteps crunching on the frosty path.

They stopped to gaze at a pair of pelicans grooming on the shore. The Russian ambassador had donated a pair to Charles II in 1664, and their descendants had lived there since.

Finally, away from the path, they sat on a bench overlooking sandbagged trenches. Kim buttoned up his coat and tightened his scarf against the wind as Maggie shivered.

The park's bleak landscape seemed appropriate to Maggie. "What else is in play? What couldn't you say in front of Professor Chadwick?"

"Mr. Churchill is ill. Quite ill." Kim exhaled, the wind catching a gust of his cloudy breath, which smelled of smoke and sour gin. "It's more serious than people know."

The P.M. had been ill before, but he'd always pulled through. Maggie hadn't seen him in person in years, though, and wondered about the toll the war was taking on his health. "No!"

"I'm afraid so. If Churchill were to . . . die . . . there're all sorts of people in Britain who could be persuaded to negotiate a separate peace. Many of them well connected."

" 'A separate peace.' Which is what Coco Chanel wants to use me to broker. But if the P.M. is gone, so is her personal advantage. Who else could she deal with?"

"There are British fascists," Kim suggested.

"The Duke of Westminster." Maggie glanced up as two ducks flew overhead, landing with a splash in the bottle-green lake. "Her former lover."

"There are others. Many others. Oh, and one more thing," Kim warned. "There's a man named Tom Burns who works with Ambassador Hoare in Madrid, as a press attaché. He might be pro-British and loathe Hitler, but he's also Catholic and sided with the Nationalists. Supports the clergy and the monarchy—and Franco. Watch out for him." He rubbed at his nose. "A good Catholic is, by definition, a bad Englishman."

Maggie wasn't so sure she agreed. "When do I leave?"

"Soon. You'll need to pack all the clothing you can from that former flatmate of yours, to look like 'Paige Kelly' again."

"I left the summer clothes in Paris, but there're still some winter pieces I can go through."

"Now, young lady, get back to John!" Kim told her, standing. "And best to Chuck and little Griffin. And that cat of yours, what's his name?"

"K," Maggie told him, rising. *Of course, Kim knows I have a cat. He knows bloody everything.*

"Perfect name for an agent's cat, just perfect," Kim mused. "Oh, and there's this." From his coat pocket he pulled out a small box and handed it to Maggie. She opened it, revealing a blue silk lining. Inside was a gold tube of lipstick. She'd been part of SOE long enough to know what the object really was— and that a cyanide pill was hidden in the base. She hesitated for a moment.

"I don't think you'll need it," Kim reassured her. "But . . ."

"Of course." She accepted it, slipping it into her purse.

He then handed her an envelope with a thick wad of Spanish currency, which she also took. "*Buena suerte,* Red."

"Good night, Kim."

The last rays of the blazing sun slipped away, leaving a bleached red sky. Kim walked to the park's Blue Bridge, which spanned the lake, providing an excellent view of Buckingham Palace to the west and the Horse Guards Parade to the east. He stopped in the middle. Not far from him stood another man, who was feeding a group of mallard ducks with bread crumbs from his pocket.

Amid the brown, black, and iridescent green ducks was a solitary red-crested pochard. He had a round orange head, black breast, and scarlet bill. He mixed easily among the ducks, who accepted him as one of their own.

The man was neither tall nor short, young nor old, fat nor thin. His alert eyes were hazel and his light brown hair receding and graying at the temples. He wore an unremarkable gray overcoat and a bowler hat pulled low, obscuring his features. Kim had stopped a few feet away.

Kim reached into the breast pocket of his camel-hair coat and pulled out a glass bottle of Rennie tablets, poured a few into his hand, then popped them into his mouth, crunching down hard.

"If you didn't drink so much, you wouldn't need antacids," the man said in a neutral English accent, impossible to place.

Kim swallowed. "But without a drink in my hand, how would I pass as a loyal Englishman?" His lips twisted into a smile.

The man didn't acknowledge the joke. "Your girl—we can trust her?"

"No," Kim said. "She's not one of us. But I do have a plan. For when she lands in Lisbon."

"Good." The man emptied his pockets and the ducks and red-crested pochard dove for crumbs.

"Our *comrade,*" Kim continued, "is acutely aware of the possibility of a separate peace in these precarious times. He believes the Anglo-Americans are delaying the second front for that very reason. This clothing designer—and her peace offer—may sound like a joke, but it's deadly serious business."

The man shook his head. "We'll meet next week. You'll tell me how it's going."

"Have you ever heard of the uncertainty principle?" Kim asked.

A frown cut the man's face. "In my line of work there's only life or death—no uncertainty."

Kim popped a few more antacids into his mouth as shadows of twilight fell. "Until next week."

Chapter Seven

As Maggie walked home from the Great Portland Street Tube stop, a sharp wind picked up, rattling the bare branches of the plane trees. The darkness of the blackout was lit by a blaze of stars and a crescent moon. There were also pinpricks of light from traffic signals, now just faint red and green crosses, the slatted headlights on cars and bicycles, and the battery-powered flashlights people carried.

No one paid her any mind except for a spindly man driving a knife-sharpening wagon. As he passed, his thick-legged Clydesdale snorted and whinnied. The man touched a hand to his cap and called, "Smile, darlin'! It's not the end of the world!"

Maggie walked by, unseeing and unhearing, like someone dazed by an explosion, unable to process the enormity of what she'd just learned. She'd defused unexploded bombs herself, when she'd worked with the 107th. But those could only take out a house, perhaps part of a city block.

And while that was horrible, what the scientists were working on now could wipe out an entire city. A planet-changing weapon, which either existed or was soon to exist. With the inevitability of the fission bomb, the world was already plunged into a new dark age—irrevocably changed. The only thing that mattered now was which side would have the bomb first. *The Battle of the Laboratories, indeed.*

And now she had been asked to assassinate, to kill—to murder—the person who might be creating the bomb for the Nazi side. *We're on the edge of a precipice, about to fall into an abyss, and no one knows, no one can guess what's to come.* How could she possibly make small talk tonight? The tiny gun in her purse suddenly felt unbearably heavy. Her insides cramped with fear and dread. She thought back to the beginning of the war, the London Blitz. Her righteous anger. Her certainty in good and evil. Her innocence of death. *How simple it all seemed. How young I was,* she thought. *And how very naïve.*

By the time Maggie opened the back door to her house, she'd at least begun to process the shock. She was determined to carry on fighting, for the Allies. She'd lived through too much already to see the world as she knew it disappear with the drop of a new Nazi "wonder weapon." She felt anger, but now also profound sadness when she thought of the Nazi leaders and the destruction they craved. And she knew she would do anything—absolutely anything—to rid the world of Hitler and his ilk.

When she entered the kitchen, she schooled her face into something resembling a neutral expression, but evidently not well enough. "Hail, Knight of the Woeful Countenance!" David Greene called in greeting.

She smiled blandly as she said her hellos to David; his partner, Freddie Wright; Chuck, and Griff. As she went to kiss John on the cheek, she pushed the afternoon's conversations from her mind. She tried her best to appear normal, but the effort was—almost—too much.

Chuck had already drawn the blackout shades, and while the electric lights were dim, she'd also lit beeswax candles she'd made herself from the new hives she kept alongside the chicken coop and the victory garden. The air was wonderfully warm from the oven and scented with the aroma of browning potatoes.

The flickering flames shone rose-gold light on everyone's faces. Sarah was there, too, at least in spirit. On the icebox was a postcard showing the Statue of Liberty, which she'd sent from New York City.

John took Maggie's coat. *It's all right not to think tonight,* she told herself.

"*For neither good nor evil can last forever; and so it follows that as evil has lasted a long time, good must now be close at hand,*" David quoted.

"He's been reading Cervantes," said Freddie by way of explanation as Maggie took a seat, "and wants *everyone* to know." The back door rattled in the wind and the lights flickered.

David, looking cherubic in the candlelight, turned to Freddie and quoted: "*It's up to brave hearts, sir, to be patient when things are going badly, as well as being happy when they're going well.*"

As Freddie rolled his eyes with affection, John countered: "*Finally, from so little sleeping and so much reading, his brain dried up and he went completely out of his mind.*" Freddie snorted as David glared at John.

"You mean *Don Quixote*?" Maggie asked. John nodded.

"Have you ever read it?" Freddie asked.

"Not in the original. In a lit class, in translation." She had a dim recollection of the tales of the idealistic knight, Don Quixote, and his trusty page, Sancho Panza. "And just selected readings."

Chuck, chestnut hair pulled back in a scarf, apron over her dress, was at the stove stirring a saucepan of gravy. "Welcome home, love," she called to Maggie. "Glad you made it through that wind. Supper'll be ready in two shakes."

Maggie's stomach grumbled. "Thank you." Even if it was the end of the world, she was hungry. *I've been hungry all the time lately,* she thought.

She leaned in to press her lips to the top of Griffin's head, catching a whiff of his spun-sugar baby hair—which she and Chuck had dubbed "the Most Wonderful Smell on Earth, Ever."

The toddler sat in his high chair, flanked by David and Freddie, hugging a well-loved plush toy. *Very* few people knew David and Freddie were a couple; and the men kept it quiet, for obvious reasons. But they could be themselves in the privacy of the candlelit kitchen.

Maggie gazed at their beloved, glowing faces with newfound appreciation. And fear. It coursed through her veins. She wanted to shield them from, well, everything. Then the intrusive thought—*just one bomb, the size of a teapot . . .*

When John leaned in to kiss Maggie again, David put his hand in front of Griffin's eyes. "Merciful Minerva! Not in front of the child!"

Maggie and John broke apart, as Griff shook his toy and called, "Mimi, Mimi, Mimi!"

She was happy to be distracted by the toddler. "Yes, it's Auntie Mimi—can you say Maggie?"

"Mimi!"

"Say 'mag.' "

" 'Mag.' "

"Say 'gee.' "

" 'Gee.' "

"Say 'Mag-gie.' "

"Mimi!"

They laughed as Chuck stopped short at the sink, piled high with dirty dishes. "Jeepers creepers!" she exclaimed. Now that Griffin was learning to talk, she was trying her best not to swear in front of him.

"May I help?" Maggie asked.

Chuck waved a hand. "Later. I'll put up my feet and you lot can do the pots and pans." She opened the oven door to check on a Woolton pie, a motley assortment of root vegetables baked in a mashed potato crust. Maggie's stomach rumbled loudly.

"Pour yourself a drink," Chuck told her. "You've just missed a *fascinating* discussion on burst pipes."

"Ours?" Maggie asked, heart sinking. Although the house had been hit by a bomb only once, and rebuilt, it still was prone to all the maladies of an old pile.

"Ours, actually," David specified. He and Freddie lived together in David's flat, in Knightsbridge on Cadogan Square, where they pretended they were roommates. "It's all the freezing and thawing this winter. Loo ceiling's a terrible mess. Gin, Mags?" he asked, picking up a bottle. "We have bitters, so I can make it pink, if you'd like."

"Tea, please," Maggie told him, still feeling cold. "Chuck, sure you don't need a hand?"

"We're almost there, just have a nice cuppa," Chuck said, as John poured Maggie a mug of tea. She took a sip. It was hot, strong, and perfect, especially given the company and setting.

In his high chair, Griff played with his plush "Gus the Gremlin" doll, produced by the Walt Disney Company for John's book, which ultimately never turned into the promised film. "Gus hungy!" Griff announced, shaking the toy.

David raised his glass of pink gin. "David hungy, too."

Freddie reached over and put a hand on David's shoulder. "Yes, but you're not a two-year-old, darling."

Griffin pointed at David and chortled. "Twoo!" the toddler cried. "Twoo twoo twoo!"

"Yes, I *am* two," David admitted. "In my heart of hearts, I'm still a Lost Boy from Neverland, brought back to London and forced to grow up and act like an adult. At least most of the time." He looked to Griffin with a serious expression. "Never grow up, young man. Never. Completely overrated."

Griff blinked and waved Gus again. "Hungy!"

"Yes, I know, my love—all my loves," Chuck said, using

potholders to take the Woolton pie out of the oven. "Mummy's hungy—hungry—too. We're just waiting for the pie to cool. And the gravy to heat."

"How're things at Number Ten?" Maggie asked David and John. It was a loaded question; she didn't know how much they were allowed to answer.

"Better!" David assured her brightly, although he didn't sound convinced. "And John's doing all right—picking things right back up. Not bad for a Hollywood player."

John raised an eyebrow. "He's just rubbing it in because now he's *principal* private secretary."

"The PPS," David said proudly, reveling in the official-sounding initials. At this, John grimaced, and Maggie smothered a giggle.

Chuck brought the pie to the table. "Just cauliflower, carrots, and turnips under the mashed potatoes," she told them. "No meat, I'm afraid. But it's hot and I added dried sage from last summer's garden, so there's that."

Freddie scooted one seat over, so Chuck could sit next to Griffin's high chair. "Here!" she said, picking up her mug. "Cheers! To us—together again!"

They all picked up their various drinks and Griffin his bottle. "Cheers!" they said, clinking glasses and looking one another in the eye in the golden candlelight.

"Together again," David said softly.

"And cheers to Sarah," Maggie added, as they helped themselves to pie. Chuck gave Griffin a bowl of some of the cooled mashed potato crust and soft mashed vegetables.

Maggie took a large bite. The pie was warm and delicious, with just the right hint of sage. "Thanks so much."

"My pleasure." Now that dinner was on the table, Chuck could relax. "It's lovely to be together again. Griff and Freddie and I missed all of you—what with you two," she said to Maggie and John, "in Los Angeles. And our David in Tehran. The glamour of it all!" she exclaimed. "Freddie was here to keep us company, thank goodness. But it's a marvel you lot can come home and eat mashed potatoes in the kitchen—after everything you've done!"

"We *love* mashed potatoes in the kitchen—mushy peas as well," David said, attacking his plate. "No mashed potatoes or mushy peas in Persia, let me tell you." He made a funny face and Griff giggled.

"And the tea in Los Angeles is inexcusable," John muttered.

Maggie gave him a look. "Nice to see you've let that go. Please, John, tell us: how was the tea in Boston?"

"In our largest colony, you mean?"

"Oh, ha ha ha . . ."

"Your aunt Edith, an Englishwoman, made a perfectly proper cup of tea."

"Well, thank goodness!" They ate, talked, and laughed as the candles burned down to stubs and the baby began to fuss. Maggie had two helpings and wished she could undo the waist button of her skirt without anyone noticing.

"I'll take this one to bed," Chuck said, picking Griff up and shifting him to one hip. "Maggie, Aunt Edith sent another care package, so there're canned peaches and milk chocolate bars if anyone wants pudding."

Maggie watched Chuck as she held her son and nuzzled the top of his head. Maggie had always loved Griffin, but looking at the scene, she realized—*maybe this could be me someday.* She and John, married, with a baby . . . She blinked. *There's a lot to go through first, Hope,* she thought. *There's a war on, you know. . . .* She shuddered. *And a possible assassination.*

"Let's clean up," she said, rising and smoothing her skirt. The candles had burned out completely, leaving a last puff of smoke.

"I'll help put Griff down," Freddie told Chuck. They exchanged a long-suffering glance. "So our own 'Big Three' can have their secrets."

As Freddie, Chuck, and Griff left, K sauntered in. "Meh!" he meowed in his peculiar way.

"He's been fed," Chuck called back. "Ignore him!"

"*Meh!*"

Maggie put her hand down, and K came to her, purring loudly and rubbing his cheek against her fingers.

When K finally went to his food bowl, Maggie stood and began stacking dishes to take to the sink. "Well, come on, boys!" she chided. "Chip in." They did, forming an assembly line of washing, rinsing, and drying pots, pans, dishes, and silverware.

As they worked, David spoke in a low voice. "Truth is, the Boss *isn't* doing well. Not well at all. He puts on a good show, of course," he continued, almost letting a wet dish slip through his fingers but catching it at the last moment, "but we hear he's at the end of his tether."

Maggie swallowed as she cleaned another plate in soapy water. "What do the doctors say?"

"That he has pneumonia," David said. "And he's exhausted from the strain of the conferences and all the travel. He can't even dry himself after his baths."

"How's his heart?" Maggie remembered Churchill's heart attack in Washington, D.C., in the winter of 1941.

"Two instances of atrial fibrillation," David told them, as John dried plates and stacked them in the dish rack. "But they say the old ticker's fine now." He stopped and looked at Maggie. "We've all signed the Official Secrets Act, so this won't go any farther than this kitchen." Maggie and John nodded as they finished up. "Still," David added, "he's doing everything—directing affairs of state—from his sickbed."

Maggie had a sudden memory of Churchill, in bed at the

Annexe over the underground War Rooms, wearing his green silk dragon robe, yelling for her to take dictation. How long ago it seemed now. A different world.

"He planned to visit the Italian front after the Cairo and Tehran conferences were over," David continued, "but . . ."

"He's been doing a lot," Maggie said. "Too much, probably. But—"

The three chimed in together, "*there's a war on.*"

"At least he feels good about the Tehran conference—'the plans for victory have been laid,'" John said in his best Churchillian tones.

Once done with the dishes, they sat at the table and K deigned to join them once again. K, whom Maggie had adopted—or who'd adopted her—in Scotland, sprang into John's arms. "I hate cats," John said through K's furry tail, which created the impression of a mustache. "Why does he always do this to me?"

Maggie laughed. "Because he knows you loathe it."

"And he takes great pleasure in it," David added. "Cats are tiny sadists with a questionable sense of humor, don't you know?"

As John dutifully rubbed K under the chin, the telephone rang. "Excuse me," Maggie said, walking to the hall.

It was Kim. "It's on for tomorrow," he said shortly. "You'll be picked up at noon. The car will take you to the Bristol airport, where you'll leave for Lisbon. You'll spend one night there with Connor—or, rather, Francis Mullaney—then together you'll fly to Madrid."

"Anything else?" she asked.

"Bring the gun. And the lipstick."

"When I return I might just have that embroidered on a cushion."

When Maggie went back to the kitchen, her face was pale. "Leaving tomorrow morning," she told them.

"Tomorrow?" John blinked. "It's on?"

"Tilting at windmills?" David asked.

"Yes"—Maggie raised an eyebrow—"but they may actually be giants."

"Ah, this is my cue to exit," David said, shrugging into his coat. "I'll collect Freddie and give you two time to say your goodbyes." He kissed Maggie on both cheeks. "Break a leg and all that." It was a joke, but they both knew the stakes.

"Thank you," she said, hugging him close, inhaling the scent of his sandalwood cologne.

David left. John—still holding K—turned to Maggie. "Well, that was fast."

"Kim explained a few things at the meeting today. There's a . . ." *How to phrase it?* "A new reason to travel now."

"Sorry I can't go with you, the way we planned."

"I'm sorry, too," she told him. "But it's not a holiday. It's work." She met his gaze in the dim light. All she wanted was to keep him safe. "And the Boss needs you."

"I'll worry while you're away."

"I know. But I'll be back as soon as I can," she said with false bravado. She put her hand on his.

"Maggie Hope—" John gently set K on the tiled floor and dropped to one knee. He took her hand. "Marry me." K blinked three times in shock, then ran out of the kitchen.

Maggie was gobsmacked by the proposal. She didn't know how to feel or what to say. *Time, what I need is time.* She finally managed, "John Sterling! Get up off the floor!"

He rose and she tried to pull her hand away, but he held on. "No," he insisted, dark eyes serious. "Marry me."

"This is ridiculous," she said, flustered, cheeks pink. *I can't let this be my engagement day.* "I'm walking you out." She felt panicked and could barely think. It was one thing to picture marriage and babies—the reality was another. *On top of the beginning of a dark nuclear age,* she thought.

At the back door, John put on his wool overcoat in silence as Maggie wrapped his black-and-white-striped Magdalen College scarf around his neck, as if it could protect him. He lifted her chin with one finger. "At least think about it."

"I will." She meant it. There was just too much darkness at the moment. It was gentle, sweet, melancholy. She knew that, whatever happened, he was her true love. He slipped out, into the darkness of the blackout.

When he was gone, she closed and locked the door, leaning against it to catch her breath.

Finally, having packed the last of Paige's designer clothes from before the war, as well as the silk scarf Chanel had impulsively given to her in Paris, Maggie changed into her nightgown and washed up.

Tucked in bed, she set the alarm clock. She saw her door push open by a few inches and fall closed. There was a pause, the sound of padding feet, and then K jumped up on the bed, purring loudly. "I'm leaving again, Fur Face," Maggie told him, reaching out to scratch him behind the ears.

K blinked orange eyes. "*Meh,*" he meowed in his odd way. He flopped down and rolled over to expose his soft, white furry belly.

"I just hope you can forgive me—again," Maggie murmured, cuddling him close, his glossy fur fragrant and warm.

There was a loud bang. She started and raised her head in alarm. *Is it outside or inside?* K tensed, too, his pupils dilated, his ears back and muscles taut.

But it was only a blustery gust, banging a loose shutter. "Shhh," Maggie whispered, as she stroked his fur, her heart racing. "It's just the wind," she assured him. She was grateful that, at least for a moment, it was true.

Chapter Eight

Coco and Spatz's train had left Paris's Gare du Nord the previous afternoon; now they watched the sun rise from their luxurious private compartment, reserved for high-ranking Nazi officers. They drank scalding black coffee from bone china cups as the train sped through the German countryside.

Coco had dressed carefully for her meeting with Walter Schellenberg: all black with just hints of white and a slash of red lipstick, deliberately echoing the colors of the SS. Even her jacket's buttons, with their interlocking double Cs, evoked the SS's insignia.

"I grew up in an orphanage," she said to Spatz, pushing aside a plate of dry toast. "And now I'm brokering peace deals with the most powerful men in the world." She glanced out the window at the sepia landscape speeding by. "Peace in our time!"

"That didn't work out too well for Chamberlain, darling," Spatz warned her. "Let's not get ahead of ourselves." He was also dressed for the day, wearing his formal black SS uniform. They were perfectly matched.

The train began to slow as it approached Berlin's Zoologischer Garten Station in Charlottenburg, and the whistle blew. The brakes shrieked, and, finally, the train lurched to a halt.

Spatz dealt with porters to send their Goyard trunks and suitcases ahead to their hotel, while Coco dabbed herself again with her namesake perfume, and gave her appearance in her compact mirror one last, hard look.

As the couturiere exited the train into clouds of steam, Spatz offered her a gloved hand. She took it. Coco had visited Berlin many times before and admired the design of the Zoologischer Garten station, with its iron-and-glass arched roof, modernized for the 1936 Olympics. She looked up, expecting to see the glorious design.

But the roof was gone. She stared at the remnants of steel beams, mouth open. A cold wind sliced through the station, causing trash and newspapers on the platform to scuttle. She turned her gaze to Spatz.

"Bomb damage. Late November." His mouth twisted. "Americans."

Only one track was running, and there were endless lines of people with threadbare clothes and blank eyes waiting to board, their faces drawn from hunger. Coco was shocked. Usually Berliners massing in the train station were loud and demanding, complaining and joking, something she had always detested. But now everyone was uncharacteristically silent. It was disconcerting. Frightening, even.

The censored news in Paris hadn't mentioned heavy bomb damage to Berlin. "My God," she said, one hand to her black hat in the bitter wind, taking in the station's destruction.

Dirty snow blew sideways as a squadron of British planes flew overhead. Coco watched through the open ceiling as they passed, feeling the vibrations rattle her breastbone, body frozen in fear.

"Their target's farther north," Spatz reassured her, eyeing their speed and direction. "Come."

On Jebensstrasse, a black Mercedes SS limousine was waiting for them. As the driver traveled the cold, nearly empty streets, Coco peered out through the window, horrified at the bomb damage. Even the neo-Romanesque Kaiser Wilhelm Church was gutted, its once proud spire a blackened stump.

She caught Spatz's eye and raised a tweezed brow. "Also late November. Now they call it 'the hollow tooth.'" Coco swallowed. "There's still time to change your mind, you know," he said in a softer voice. "No one's forcing you to do this."

Coco peered out the window again, taking in Berlin's extensive damage and destruction, appearing more like a Doré hellscape than the city she loved. For a moment, she was afraid, truly afraid, picturing Paris looking the same. . . . No excuse would suffice. She would be seen as a collaborator. She *was* a collaborator. But there was still time to save herself.

This mission to Madrid was her only hope—for herself, her empire, her fortune, her reputation, her very survival. She turned to him and lifted her chin. "No," she told him. "We keep to the plan."

The Mercedes pulled up in front of the SS Reich Security Main Office, home to the Gestapo and SS Security, on Prinz-Albrecht-Strasse. "Walter Schellenberg's a fine fellow, darling," Spatz reassured her as they exited the car. "Not your usual Nazi. He has charm, style, sophistication. You'll like him." She took his arm.

The entrance was flanked by soldiers carrying automatic rifles. They passed through security without incident. Upstairs, a middle-aged secretary with a tightly scraped-back gray bun greeted them outside Schellenberg's office. She escorted them to a large closed double door.

"Welcome!" Schellenberg exclaimed with a beaming smile. Coco noticed he didn't say "Heil Hitler" or raise his arm in salute. "So good to see you again, old friend," he said to Spatz in German, shaking his hand warmly.

And then, in perfect French, with just the hint of an Alsatian accent, "And you, of course, you must be the inimitable Mademoiselle Coco Chanel." He clicked the heels of his polished boots together and bowed deeply, kissing her gloved hand. "It's an honor to have you with us, Mademoiselle—or, should I say, Agent Westminster?"

As Coco allowed herself to smile in response, Schellenberg turned to the retreating secretary. "Coffee! And some of those delicious *Lebkuchen*!" She ducked her head and left. "Come, come—have a seat. How was your journey?"

The office was freezing, and Coco kept her fur around her shoulders. As they exchanged pleasantries, she placed her purse in her lap, crossed her ankles, and glanced about the spacious room. Gray light seeped in from silk-draped windows. There was an enormous globe in one corner. An official portrait of Hitler hung above an oversize walnut desk; she noted the photograph was slightly crooked.

"The desk is quite . . . large," she managed tactfully as she pulled at her pearl necklace.

"I call it my 'office fortress' desk," Schellenberg said proudly. "It has two automatic guns built right in—guns I can fire with just the touch of a button. I can press another, and a siren will summon guards to surround the building."

Coco recrossed her ankles. "I promise, neither will be necessary."

"And there are microphones everywhere, darling," Spatz told her with a half-smile that contained a warning.

"Of course, Mademoiselle is our honored guest here," Schellenberg said disarmingly. "I only mention these things so you're assured of your own safety."

His bright eyes danced with what looked to be merriment,

and Coco again forced herself to smile in response. "Thank you," she told him with as much charm as she could muster. "I—we—do appreciate it."

"You can't see, but all the windows are covered with mesh. Wires act as sensors, which alert guards if anyone approaches."

"What a brilliant idea," she commented through a fixed smile. "I should design dresses with them for ladies whose escorts become too . . . friendly."

As Schellenberg and Spatz chuckled, the secretary entered, carrying a tray. She set it down on the low mahogany table and began to pour coffee from a silver pot.

"I hear you and Mademoiselle had a good talk with Major Ledebur, in Paris," Schellenberg said, as though it were a social call. He dropped two lumps of sugar in his steaming coffee with silver tongs, and helped himself to a large glazed *Lebkuchen*. Coco accepted her steaming cup black.

"Yes," Spatz said, taking his, "and the major directed us to meet with you." By rote, the couturiere took a sip.

Spatz placed his cup on the table, as though they were at the Mad Hatter's tea party. "Mademoiselle," he said to Schellenberg, "with her formidable list of English connections, has graciously offered to assist us with our Spanish concerns."

"I hear you're 'friends' with Bendor, Duke of Westminster, Mademoiselle," Schellenberg said to Coco through a mouthful of pastry. "A good ally to us here in Germany—one of the great British patriots."

Coco nodded. Bendor had joined the anti-Semitic Right Club and the Parliamentary Peace Aims Group in 1939, claiming to be in touch with "Nazi moderates." He'd made speeches for the groups, asserting Britain was fighting the war only to make money for Jews and international finance, or words to that effect. However, after bombs had begun falling on London, the Duke kept his opinions to his inner circle and disbanded the clubs. Still, he hadn't changed his mind about anything, just become more careful.

Schellenberg dabbed at his lips with a swastika-embroidered linen napkin. "And you and the Duke went shooting with Winston Churchill?"

"Many times," she replied truthfully.

"When was the last time you saw Churchill?"

Coco knew this was a test. It was true she had been an acquaintance of Winston Churchill's. When she'd been Bendor's lover, Churchill had been good friends with the Duke, and she'd seen him socially. However, when she and the Duke had broken off their affair, and he'd married a more "suitable" British debutante, she'd seen Churchill less frequently. But they did keep up their friendship and met each other at social events in London, the South of France, and Paris, until the beginning of the war.

"The last time I saw Winnie in person," Coco said, deliberately dropping the Prime Minister's nickname, "was in Paris, in the spring of 'forty. When David—that is, the Duke of Windsor—left Lisbon for the Bahamas, Winnie came to my suite at the Ritz for a drink. He was terribly disappointed in the former King." She plucked at her iridescent pearls with red lacquered nails. "As was I. Wallis—Simpson, Duchess of Windsor—was a client and a good friend. I spent many happy times with her and David. I was sorry to see them go."

"We were all disappointed," Schellenberg said darkly. Then he smiled again. "We want a certain message from you delivered to Winston Churchill through Sir Samuel Hoare at the British Embassy in Madrid—and for you to spend time with those there, in particular, those who're friendly to Churchill."

"Sam and I are also old friends," she assured him. "We've also been shooting and fishing together in Scotland—with Bendor and Winnie."

"You see, they're all old friends," Spatz asserted. "Which is why we suggested Mademoiselle as the courier for the peace proposal."

Schellenberg rose and walked back to his enormous desk, taking an envelope from the blotter. He lifted it up. "This is what we need delivered to Churchill." The paper was bone-colored and heavy, pressed with a large red wax seal.

"Many of the details are, of course, private," Schellenberg stated, his eyes hardening. He handed the envelope to Spatz. "You'll carry it, sealed, until it's time for Mademoiselle to give it to Ambassador Hoare, with her own personal cover note."

Spatz slipped the envelope into his breast pocket. "Of course."

"And you, Mademoiselle," Schellenberg said, "will pen your most charming missive to Churchill, as an introduction, and include it in a larger envelope—showing that you origi-nated this idea of a separate peace. You'll emphasize you have it on good authority that senior German commanders really are at odds with Hitler, seeking an end to the war. That you trust us. And that it would be best for Britain if she agrees to the separate peace settlement. Be sure to mention something about the Red threat."

Coco swallowed. She knew what was implied for Hitler: assassination. "I've a special contact who's coming, Miss Paige Kelly—or at least that's her *nom de guerre,*" she said. "She's with British intelligence. And she can courier the envelope di-rectly from the ambassador's office to Churchill. I trust her more than Hoare and his 'diplomatic pouch.' "

Schellenberg appraised her through narrowed eyes. "Why don't you trust normal diplomatic channels?"

"That wax seal on any letter would be easy to break and remelt," she said. "And I'd be disappointed if no one tried it. With Miss Kelly, there's only one person involved. And she'll be discreet."

"What's your hold on this Miss Kelly?"

"Let's just say," Coco said with her most Gallic shrug, "she owes me—for my assistance with a certain . . . situation . . . that happened in Paris during the summer of 'forty-one."

"Fine." Schellenberg retook his seat. "In addition, we're hoping for a closer alliance with General Franco. He's always been on our side, unofficially, but things have become increasingly"—he steepled his fingers—"challenging, shall we say, as the war drags on."

Coco assured him, "In the fashion world, I'm considered a master diplomat."

Schellenberg raised an eyebrow. "Well, in Madrid we expect you to socialize with supporters of General Franco, most of them titled Spanish aristocrats. It's quite fitting—these are the people who'd buy your clothes."

"I already know many of them."

"There will be a special gala at the Palacio Real, Madrid's Royal Palace. It's for one of our most important scientists, Werner Heisenberg. General Franco will be there. We expect you to attend, as well."

"Galas are Mademoiselle's natural element," Spatz told him. "And you mustn't underestimate diplomacy in the fashion world—the barbarity, sadism, and power plays I've observed over the years at ateliers and runway shows in Paris would make Himmler himself look like a rank amateur."

"What would you like me to say to these Spanish aristocrats?" Coco asked.

"We want you to put forward the idea of Germany making a separate peace with Britain. But casually. Make sure people know your opinion—that you'd be in favor of it. And you'll—again, casually—ask them their thoughts. We want to know how certain high-ranking individuals in Madrid feel. Every evening, you'll debrief to von Dincklage, and he'll report to me, through the German Embassy."

While Coco was displeased with the idea of France remaining under Germany's boot—it was treason, after all, to sell out her homeland—it was a far better option for her than the alternative. "I do sincerely wish for German victory," she said. "Without it, Bolshevism will run rampant through France."

"Germany and France are cousins, after all," Schellenberg said, washing down the last of his pastry with a gulp of sweet coffee. "Germany and England, as well. And while England and France haven't always been friendly, we will protect the French. We will protect *you*," he said, looking hard at both. "Germany won't forget her friends in peacetime."

Coco nodded, relieved. "And the negotiation for my company?" she asked. "Any word?"

The Nazi seizure of all Jewish-owned property and businesses in France had provided the couturiere with the opportunity to regain control of Parfums Chanel. The current directors and majority share owners of Parfums Chanel, the Wertheimers, were Jews who'd fled to the United States before the Occupation. As an "Aryan," Chanel was keen to have German officials legalize her claim to sole ownership—and before the war officially ended.

"Let's deliver this letter to Churchill first, shall we?" Schellenberg told her. "We can deal with your company later."

Coco drew herself up. "Just remember, I'm doing *you* a tremendous favor."

"By the way," Schellenberg said, "you never mentioned to Major Ledebur what exactly you have on Winston Churchill."

She smiled. "Let's just say it's good—good enough to obtain and hold the Prime Minister's attention."

"Well then, Agent Westminster," the general told Chanel as he rose, "Operation Modelhut may officially begin. I'll take care of both your passports and provide the necessary Spanish money. Everything will be delivered to your suite at the Adlon, including your train tickets. You'll leave for Madrid first thing tomorrow morning."

"But my company—"

"When your mission's complete and we've evaluated your services in Madrid, we'll continue this discussion." He offered his hand to Coco, who took it and stood.

The meeting was over.

As they walked out of Schellenberg's office, Coco held her head high. But as soon as the door was closed, she grasped her companion's arm, holding herself up as her knees almost buckled. "Quick, Spatz, take me to the Adlon. I need a martini." He looked at her, usually so cool, so composed, so very French.

"*Now.*"

Chapter Nine

Maggie ran to greet a man on the tarmac of Bristol's Whitchurch Airport in the last red rays of the setting sun.

"My darling fiancée!" a young man called in a lilting Irish tenor, his words blown sideways by the wind. He was sandy-haired and freckled, slim and slight, with bright blue eyes and an infectious grin. "Give your sweetheart a kiss!"

"Connor!" she exclaimed. They embraced; his lean frame belied his strength.

"Not as handsome as that John Sterling fellow, I realize," he declared as they drew apart, "but I'll do in a pinch, I suppose."

"Good to see you again," she told him, clapping him on the shoulder. "Glad to be working together."

They watched as their plane, a Douglas DC-3-194 from the British Overseas Airways Corporation, taxied closer and rolled to a stop. When war had broken out in Europe, the British Air Ministry had prohibited private flights and most domestic air travel. The only allowed destinations for British flights were a few of the neutral countries. Even then, the British government restricted flights to diplomats, military personnel, and those with government approval—which Maggie and Connor had, thanks to Kim Philby. The U.K.–Lisbon flights operated four times a week, but since *Gone with the Wind* actor Leslie Howard's plane from Lisbon to Britain had been shot down in June 1943 by the Luftwaffe, they flew only at night.

Workmen in coveralls rushed to push portable stairs to the plane's door as Maggie walked over. "Ready?" she called to Connor.

"Ready!" He grinned and gestured for her to go first. "After you, my lovely fiancée."

There were nine other passengers on the flight; including the crew they were thirteen. Maggie and Connor sat together in the last row, separated from the others. Maggie heard all about Connor's wife, their nine-month-old baby, and their new flat in Greenwich in whispers, practically lip-reading over the noise of the engines. "It kills me to leave them," he told her as they flew over the English Channel to the Bay of Biscay. "They're my life."

Maggie thought again with a shudder of what a Nazi nuclear bomb could do to the city of London. To Connor's family. To all their loved ones. And what she was being asked to do to stop it.

"I know you've a beau and all, but you don't know love— real love—until you have a wee one," he told her.

Maggie thought about her own late father and estranged mother and how familial relationships could be . . . complicated. "If you say so."

"I'd show you a photo," he continued, "but they won't let me travel with one. You know how it goes."

Maggie nodded, then gazed out the plane window, seeing the bright lights of Lisbon come into focus as they approached. Because the so-called White City was neutral, with excellent ports, it had become one of the major centers of world affairs during the war. For the same reasons, Lisbon was a glittering

city of spies, with Allied and Axis agents monitoring one another's countries' every move.

The plane circled, finally landing at Portela Airport. "Well,
this is much nicer than parachute drops by moonlight," she
said to Connor as the plane hit the runway and bounced three
times. She remembered all too well the fear, the panic, and the
rough landings she'd had on past missions.

"Nothing but the best for my girl!" Connor smiled as the
plane taxied to a stop. He stood and offered her a hand. "Welcome to Lisbon!"

On the tarmac, a car provided by SOE was waiting for them.
After the proper coded phrases were exchanged, the driver
took the curving road hugging the Bay of Cascais, along the
Tamariz Beach, to the nearby town of Estoril. "I wish we could
have continued straight on to Madrid tonight," Maggie told
Connor as the car bumped along.

"Just a quick overnight and then we'll go tomorrow," he
assured her. "I've made this trip quite a few times now. Best to
have a night of good sleep first, and arrive in Madrid refreshed."

"Not sure if I'll be sleeping tonight."

As the car crept through the darkness, Maggie saw illuminated billboards advertising Sandeman port wine and Omega
watches—how long had it been since she'd seen bright lights
like this at night in London?

"Lots of royal families are living in exile at the Palácio Hotel
in Estoril—plenty of spies, as well," Connor said. "And then
there's the infamous casino. It all seems like fun and games, but
the stakes are deadly."

"I've heard of the casino." Casino Estoril was Portugal's
top attraction, with gaming, a fine restaurant, a cinema, and
the WonderBar—a massive nightclub with a live orchestra, en-

tertainment, and dancing. It was the preferred meeting place for every spy, of every nationality, in Lisbon.

"Someday, when the war's over," she told him, "you'll have to come back with your family and enjoy the beach."

"Amen to that. And maybe, someday, you and John could stay at the hotel on your honeymoon." Maggie turned her face to the window, but her lips curled up in a secret smile.

The Palácio Hotel's grand white deco façade was spotlit by glaring bright lights. Bellboys in caps dove for their luggage while Maggie and Connor walked past the doormen. Huge bouquets of flowers perfumed the air. The hotel's lobby, decorated with French antiques, was filled with exquisitely dressed guests. As they made their way over the polished floor, Maggie heard people speaking Portuguese and Spanish, but also English, French, Polish, German, and Japanese.

Maggie and Connor approached the mahogany front desk. They presented their fake passports to a man with too-white false teeth, his silver-streaked hair parted in the center and held with copious amounts of brilliantine. "Mr. Mullaney, good to see you again—congratulations on your upcoming marriage," he said, smiling widely, exposing even more white teeth. "And, Miss Kelly, welcome to the Palácio. We hope your first visit will be memorable."

I'm sure it will be.

He accepted their passports and examined them. They filled out special forms, including the registration required by the Polícia de Vigilância e Defesa do Estado, the secret police. Portugal had been at the espionage game since 1939, watching over countless "diplomats" from around the globe, and required a paper trail for every potential spy.

Maggie's heart beat loudly as her pen scratched the paper, but her hands were steady. The man handed back their passports. "Have a wonderful stay."

"*Obrigado,*" Maggie answered, with as much cheer as she could manage.

The bellhop brought their bags to their handsomely appointed adjoining rooms, and Connor gave the boy a generous tip.

Maggie went to the bathroom and considered her reflection in the beveled mirror. She released her hair from its pins and clips. "I'm going to change and head to the casino," Connor called through the door. She could hear him dressing. "Just a bit of business, before we're on our way tomorrow. You all right alone?" It was almost eight o'clock. "I'm sure you're exhausted and want to rest."

But Maggie wasn't tired at all, and she wanted to see everything she could. Also, her stomach was growling. She opened the door. "I'm starving."

He clicked his tongue. "You'll provide excellent cover . . . Paige," he admitted.

"Delighted to assist . . . *Francis.*"

He grimaced. "I didn't pick my cover name."

"It's lovely. Very Catholic. Like St. Francis of Assisi."

"Can you be ready in ten minutes?" He sounded doubtful.

I'm trained to jump from planes—of course I can manage a gown and heels. But Maggie only smiled serenely. "Absolutely!"

Dressed in evening wear, they left the hotel and strolled down spotlit paths through the rose gardens from the Palácio to the Casino Estoril. The casino was a large, white, modern building. *A world away from war,* Maggie noted. *Or, at least, so it seems.*

They passed through bronze-embossed mahogany doors and Connor paid for their *cartes d'entrée.* He offered Maggie his arm, and they entered the windowless main salon. It was smoky, loud, and hot. Glittering crystal chandeliers hung from high ceilings and the floors were covered in thick red carpets.

Men in black tie and ladies in gowns with massive jewels and elbow-length kid gloves glanced up at the handsome couple before turning their attention back to the gaming tables. Maggie could hear excited conversation and "Ladies and gentlemen, please place your bets," in multiple languages against the click-clack of chips and the purr of roulette wheels. Gloved waiters circulated with silver trays of complimentary champagne, while staff in livery changed out dirty ashtrays.

The casino fizzed with adrenaline. Throngs of people mixed and mingled, holding cocktails and cigarettes. "*Kakete kudasai shinshi, shokun!*" a dealer in a green visor called to a group of eight Japanese men playing chemin de fer. He bowed respectfully. The gamblers were probably transmitting messages through numbers at the roulette tables, she presumed.

Maggie accepted a coupe of champagne and scanned the room. The undercover security guards, wearing poorly tailored dinner jackets and sporting bad haircuts, stood out. *What are the* real *stories happening here?* She watched a Russian man, with a large diamond pinkie ring, call out a series of numbers. A bet—or code?

A tall and slim thirty-something man in white tie sat at the baccarat table. He had silky black hair, long elegant features, and an expression of sophisticated ennui. Both men and women stared with blatant interest, but he seemed impervious. His companion, a lush brunette in scarlet silk, removed a diamond and ruby necklace and handed it to him. It looked heavy. He threw it nonchalantly on the felt-covered table and turned his attention back to the game.

"He's one of ours," Connor whispered in her ear. "Known as Don Miguel Ángel Ramos from Oaxaca, Mexico. His cover is he's the Walt Disney Company's representative to Portugal and Spain. If anything happens here, find him. He'll take care of you."

So he's in the other game, Maggie noted. *The* real *game.*

They passed a group of gray-haired men playing blackjack, speaking perfect English with slight German accents. "They're supposed to be playboys, but really they're keeping track of ships coming in and out of Lisbon for the Kriegsmarine.

"And," Connor added with begrudging respect, "together, the bastards also count cards—although management's never been able to prove anything." He shook his head. "They've probably raked in a few million escudos by now, while keeping their cover *and* taking in a good salary as well."

At the WonderBar, every table was packed and there was a crush at the bar. On a raised stage, an orchestra played "*La Cumparsita*" while a glamorous couple performed the tango. The man wore all black and the woman a close-fitting red sequined dress with an asymmetrical fringed hem, seamed fishnet stockings, and Cuban heels. They held their torsos still as their legs crossed and twisted in the dance's intricate footwork.

Two young women at a table near the dance floor, wearing ersatz designer clothing and paste jewels, were having an argument. As Maggie looked on, it grew louder and more emphatic. One yelled, "*Puta!*" and the other threw a drink. They both ran off in tears.

Connor swooped in to pull out a chair. "What can I fetch you, my darling bride-to-be?"

"Just a tonic, please," she told him as she sat, "no gin." Her stomach growled. "And something to eat? Pretty please?"

"They have wonderful shrimp Mozambique," he assured her. "I'll order that for us." The pair onstage finished their dance, took their bows, then exited. Maggie applauded. As the orchestra segued into "Begin the Beguine," couples filled the floor, dancing slow rumbas.

She lost sight of Connor in the crowd as Miguel Ángel Ramos, the diamond and ruby necklace trailing from his jacket's front pocket, slipped in next to her. His long, elegant build and glowing tan made her think instantly of sports played in white—tennis and cricket, perhaps polo as well. He was drinking a glass of red vermouth on ice with a slice of lemon.

"You must be Señorita Kelly," he said, eyes missing nothing. "Francis Mullaney's fiancée." He leaned in and caught her hand, then kissed it. "I'm Ángel."

"How do you do?" Maggie said, pulling her hand away. "Paige Kelly. Francis tells me you work for Walt Disney." *And British intelligence,* she thought.

He crossed long, slim legs. "Portugal and Spain are my territory."

"What does that mean?"

"I meet with local film industry people," he explained, waving beautifully manicured fingernails. "And secure good coverage for the Walt Disney Company in the papers and magazines."

"Publicity," Maggie said.

"Exactly. What do you think of Estoril?"

"Haven't been here long," she told him. "But it's certainly another world." *An incredibly privileged one,* she thought. *Most people these days can't even imagine.*

"*C'est la guerre.*" The male dancer in black walked past their table and Maggie saw Ángel's hungry gaze follow before he snapped his attention back to her. *Ah,* she thought. *Safe in taxis—not at all a taxi tiger.* He was, as David and Freddie would say, "like that."

"Would you care to dance?" He stood and offered his hand. Maggie didn't particularly want to—she was famished and almost light-headed—but she understood it was best to blend in.

Ángel led her to the dance floor; up close, he exuded the aroma of sharp, citrus-scented pomade. Maggie had only a faint recollection of the rumba, but Ángel was an excellent partner, and she soon fell into the rhythm of *slow-quick-quick, slow-quick-quick.*

As he guided her expertly around the floor, the music changed to "*España Cañi.*" The musicians were now playing guitars and castanets, and the rhythm throbbed a *paso doble,* a double step. Maggie remembered from ballroom dance lessons as a girl that the sensual dance told the story of a matador in a bullfight, with the man dramatically spinning the woman around like a cape.

They had reached the promenade section when a high-pitched scream pierced the music. Maggie froze in place. The musicians stopped playing to stare. She turned, wide-eyed, to see a commotion by the bar. "Come on," she said to Ángel. "We have to help."

"No," he told her, holding her. "No." There was thick silence now. And then shouting and shrieking, and the high-pitched buzz of agitated conversation.

Maggie rose on tiptoes, trying to see what had happened. She searched for Connor in the throng but couldn't find him. "*Chame a polícia!*" a woman's husky voice shrieked.

Another voice, lower and male, responded harshly, "*No— nós temos nossa própria segurança!*"

No police, Maggie could translate. Where was Connor? She pushed Ángel's hand away and maneuvered through the crowd, heart in her throat. By the long bar, she caught sight of a man's body sprawled across the marble floor. The black handle of a knife protruded from his abdomen; blood stained his white linen shirt red, creating a puddle on the floor. *Connor? No, it couldn't be,* she thought. A woman fainted in her partner's arms as Maggie pushed her way closer.

"*¡Yo soy un doctor!*" a man called and knelt, feeling the injured man's neck for a pulse. The doctor closed the eyelids, and then gently placed the man's pale hands on his chest. He then rocked back on his heels, closing his eyes and bowing his head, and made the sign of the cross.

Maggie stopped short. It was Connor. She saw his face was gray, lips turning blue. She clapped a hand over her mouth, pushing back a scream.

She knew, with horrible certainty, he was dead.

Chapter Ten

Ángel grabbed Maggie's arm with a vise-like grip and steered her away from Connor's body and the assembling security guards.

She shook him off and tried to return, but he blocked her path. "You can't be involved," he whispered, fingers digging into the flesh of her upper arm again. "You can't take the risk of being picked up and questioned. You'll never make it to Madrid."

"But—" Connor was her friend. He was a husband. A father. And now he was dead.

"This is Lisbon," Ángel hissed. "They could arrest you on false charges, keep you for months, even years. We need to leave, fast. Come." He put his arm around her and guided her back to the hotel.

The lobby was crowded despite the late hour, and Maggie kept her head down as they made their way to the brass cage elevator. She tried to control the tremors shuddering through her. At the door to his room, Ángel told her, "The police won't look for you here. Lock the door. Try to get some sleep."

As if I'll ever sleep again. "We need to find out what happened to Connor," she whispered. "Who murdered him."

"And we will—I know a man who can radio a message

from the British Embassy here to London. We'll have more information tomorrow. I promise."

Maggie nodded numbly. When he left, she closed the door and locked it, then braced a chair against the knob for safety. Unseeing, she stepped out onto the balcony into the cool, salt-fragranced breeze. She was oblivious to the ocean waves rolling in the dark, and the cold stars glimmering overhead. She watched car headlights in the distance as she tried to take deep breaths, the way she'd been trained.

Shivering, she returned to the room, locked the balcony doors, and began to wash up by rote. It was only in bed, under the covers, her gun beneath her pillow, that she gave in to her feelings and wept. Later, after drying her eyes, she returned to logic. *Who'd want to kill Connor? And why? And in such a public way?* But no answers were forthcoming, and she lay awake until dawn.

The next morning Maggie wore tinted sunglasses to hide her swollen eyes. Ángel procured her suitcase and she changed. Then he drove them up the ocean highway to the dusty, steep hills of Lisbon, the car shuddering in the salty wind. She looked but saw nothing as they passed the docks, turning to wind their way up snaky cobbled streets, nearly colliding with a small red trolley. *Dead,* she thought, over and over again. *Connor is dead.* And then a tiny but shameful feeling of relief. *It could have been John—and it wasn't.*

Finally Ángel stopped and parked on a narrow side street of apartment buildings. Drying laundry pinned to lines on the wrought-iron window railings whipped back and forth in the gusts. Maggie kept the sunglasses on and pulled her coat tighter around her. She was surprised by how quickly the shock was wearing off, how familiar she now was with death, with violence. There was a mission to accomplish, after all. *Always forward, never back.* There would be time to grieve later. She only hoped that when the time came, it wouldn't be too much to bear.

As church bells clanged, they entered a modest gray building. Maggie followed Ángel down a worn stone staircase.

There, in a damp, windowless cellar, five men sat with cigarettes, blue tendrils of smoke curling up to hanging fluorescent bulbs. Maggie recognized two from the plane. The others were a motley crew: one looked like a fisherman in the traditional Portuguese long knit hat, another like a university professor in tweed, and a third dressed as a gigolo in silky shirt and tight trousers.

The room was silent. The man in tweed stood. "We heard what happened to Connor," he said solemnly. "And we're devastated." They bowed their heads and the fisherman and gigolo crossed themselves. "It might have been a random act of violence. Might have been something Connor brought on himself—with his gambling problem—or we may have a double agent here."

Maggie found her voice. "Connor has—had—a gambling problem?" He didn't seem like the type—but then again, who ever really knew about such things?

Ángel nodded as the tweedy man replied, "He was a consummate professional as an on-duty agent, but he used his downtime in Estoril to gamble. 'Having little ones is expensive,' he'd say. We warned him, but . . ."

Maggie looked at the men, her fellow agents, and swallowed. *Always forward.* "Now what?"

"Frank here"—Ángel indicated the man in tweed—"was able to pass a message through late last night, thanks to our contact at the British Embassy."

Cigarette clamped between his lips, Frank said, "And we got word from Sonny early today the mission's still on."

"Sonny" was Kim Philby's code name. Numb, Maggie nodded. "All right, then." She rubbed sweaty palms on her skirt.

"I'll take you to the airport," Ángel told her. "We must hurry."

The man in tight pants rose and brought a brown bottle down from a shelf. "But first let's have a toast."

They stood and passed the bottle around the circle. "To Connor," each said in turn as they took a drink.

"To Connor." Maggie took a swallow and felt the alcohol burn her throat. Then, "And to his family."

"To his family." They clinked glasses again.

"Continue on to Madrid, and check in at the hotel according to plan," Frank told her. "We'll send another agent to you."

Maggie reflexively felt for her gun. It was still in her purse, hard and cold.

"The code is 'The historical way to meet a lady,' " he said. "And then you say—"

"I know the rest," Maggie said, shaking off the effect of the alcohol on an empty stomach. "Let's go," she said to Ángel. "We've got to make it to the airport before the police."

The man in tweed said, "We won't rest until we find out who murdered him."

Maggie gazed at him on her way out the door. "Thank you."

Chapter Eleven

oco and Spatz's train arrived with a cloud of steam and a shrill whistle at Madrid's Atocha Station the next morning, at exactly five minutes to nine.

The waiting car took them to the Hotel Ritz, located in the exclusive Retiro district, across from the Prado Museum. The belle époque hotel had been built by King Alfonso XIII and opened in 1910. After General Franco's victory in the Civil War, the hotel was among the first to be restored to its former splendor. It was currently the most expensive hotel in Madrid, in addition to being a well-known haunt for Nazis and other fascists.

Their car slowed to a stop at the Ritz's entrance on the Plaza de la Lealtad. The circular drive bustled with the arrival of antique Rolls-Royces, as well as some equally old Hispano-Suizas, Peugeots, and Citroëns. The discomfort from the trip to Berlin, and now Madrid, was catching up with her. As was her anxiety. The mission to Madrid was no longer theoretical. She was here. And she needed to perform.

As Spatz managed the bellhops and luggage in decent enough Spanish, Coco took the moment to strike a regal pose and look about. The pale January sunshine came and went as clouds scudded across the sky. She put a hand to her hat in the stiff breeze and glanced up at the façade: it was classically

French, and white with a black roof. She smiled; it could have been inspired by one of her own designs.

Nodding to the doorman, she glided past, pausing in the airy white marble lobby. A clear glass ceiling vaulted upward, and Coco could see the sun momentarily as it broke from behind the heavy clouds, then hid again. Huge vases of spicy-sweet red carnations, the national flower of Spain, filled the room with their fragrance. Her heart was in her throat and there was a slight tremor in her hands, but she forced her shoulders down and her chin up.

She eyed the others milling about: aristocrats and royalists in Balenciaga, members of Franco's Falange in uniform, Nazis in Hugo Boss suits. There was no sign the hotel had been used as a military hospital during the Spanish Civil War, and she overheard no talk of the current war. Still, she knew she was surrounded by spies; her every move would be noted and reported back.

Although the Madrid Ritz's unwritten rule was not to admit NTRs—*no tipo Ritz,* "not the Ritz type"—she saw several film stars from Joseph Goebbels's UFA, which produced and distributed Nazi-approved motion pictures. Coco assumed some kind of joint project was going on, with a Spanish director and a production company. Of course they were staying at the Ritz.

"You speak Spanish!" she cooed to Spatz when he caught up. She didn't want him to sense her fear. "You never cease to amaze me." She picked an imaginary piece of lint from his coat's lapel.

"Not as well as French," he told her. "But passable. Wait here and I'll check in."

Coco took a seat on a red brocade sofa in the atrium, under a huge fragrant display of yellow roses and even more red carnations; her wobbly knees required it. The harpist played Gabriel Fauré's "Impromptu," and she distracted herself by taking in the marble floors, potted palms, and Ionic columns as well as the hotel's stylish guests. She forced herself to smile when she saw several women wearing silhouettes from her past collections. A man in black scribbled notes in red pen at a table, while two dignified graying Spanish men in dark sunglasses and cashmere coats drank champagne.

When Coco and Spatz arrived in their suite, they found a maid in a starched black-and-white uniform already unpacking their luggage. "Later," Coco told the slight young woman, who bobbed her head and slipped out.

Coco was glad to be somewhere at least relatively safe. The suite was large, elegant, and ornate, with a sitting room and separate bedroom. The walls were papered in red watered silk and the sofas and chairs were covered in charcoal linen. Every surface sported vases of gold and red flowers, and a platter of freshly cut orange persimmons and plate of round *rosquillas de Alcalá,* the Spanish puff pastry, waited for them on the coffee table.

Coco went to the windows, pushed apart the sheer curtains, and gazed down over the Plaza de Cánovas del Castillo, a roundabout in the Paseo del Prado. A splashing fountain featured a marble statue of Neptune, the Roman god of the sea. He wielded a trident in one hand and a sea snake in the other as he kept watch over the traffic circle. There were only a few cars circling, along with a rusted bus, a skinny donkey pulling an ice cart, and plenty of bicyclists. Spatz came up behind her, wrapping her in his arms and kissing her cheek. Beyond the fountain was the Palacio Hotel.

"That's where all the Allied spies stay," he told her, kissing the back of her neck. "We're separated from the enemy by just a fountain."

"Maybe not 'the enemy' for long." She leaned against him, heart beating wildly. "What now?"

"I suggest we order coffee, and you reach out to your contact. And we're scheduled for a late dinner at Edelweiss with the German ambassador."

"How late?"

"Around eleven."

Coco chortled. "You're not serious!"

"Remember, we're on Spanish time now—we'll come back here for a siesta."

"What's the German ambassador's name again?"

"Coco," he admonished, "you must remember these things." She stiffened, not used to his correcting her. But he was right; this was serious business. He seemed to sense her unease, and whispered in her ear, "Did you know, Agent Westminster, that Mata Hari also stayed at the Madrid Ritz?"

"No!" Coco couldn't help but smile, seeing herself next in a grand tradition of female spies.

"Yes! In 1916, I believe. She used the name Countess Maslov. You're in good company. Come," he said, leading her away from the window and through the double doors to the bedroom. "I can tell you're nervous and I know the perfect way to distract you."

"Siesta? Already? It's still morning . . ."

"I can think of far more interesting things to do while we wait."

Chapter Twelve

With a heavy heart, Maggie left Lisbon. The seat next to her on the flight to Madrid was empty; she was painfully alone on the cold and bumpy flight.

She took deep breaths to various counts. From the small window of the plane, she saw the straight lines of fallow fields in Castile below, and in the distance, the snow-dusted mountains of the Sierra de Guadarrama.

Across the aisle, a man in a priest's cassock leered at her, his cheeks and nose the color of rioja wine. "You are English?" he asked.

"Irish," she told him, in character as Paige Kelly.

"Three hundred years before British rule reached its peak, the sun never set on the Spanish empire," he told her in Spanish-accented English. "We Spaniards changed the history of the world," he said. "Brought tomatoes and chocolate and chiles to the Old World, sugar and wheat to the New."

And smallpox, Maggie thought, but didn't say. She smiled at him, but turned back to the window, in no mood to chat. *Was Connor's death really retribution for some kind of gambling debt?* she wondered. *Is there something more sinister at play?* Still, she had to focus on her mission. There would be time for questions—and grief—later.

To steady herself, Maggie reviewed what she knew about

Spain, up to and including the Civil War. She thought of Picasso's nightmarish work *Guernica,* an enormous black-and-white oil painting from 1937. She'd been fortunate enough to see it in New York City when it had toured the United States.

In it, a gored horse, a wide-eyed bull, a screaming woman, a dead baby, and a dismembered soldier showed the destruction wrought when the northern Spanish town had been strafed from the air by planes from Nazi Germany and Fascist Italy—at the request of General Franco and the Spanish Nationalists. *And what if they'd had a fission bomb?* she thought. *What if they do now?*

Finally, they landed at Madrid's Barajas Airport. *This is where it all began,* Maggie thought, her stomach tightening. *The Spanish Civil War. The fight against fascism. Against dictators. The war the rest of the world's battling now.* Except, were they? Was it still all about fascism—or was communism just as much a threat?

The war had begun on July 17, 1936—when conspirators initiated their coup in Spanish Morocco, a day before the Madrid attacks—and ended on April 1, 1939. The Spanish Civil War pitted the fascist Nationalists, composed of monarchists, landowners, most Spanish business owners, much of the Roman Catholic clergy, and most of the Spanish army, against the Republicans, who were backed by those in the army loyal to the Second Spanish Republic, workers, trade unionists, and socialists.

Nazi Germany and Fascist Italy had backed the Republicans, and the Soviet Union had supported the rebels. Volunteers from countless countries including Britain and the United States joined to fight for the republic. The war was covered by journalists in new ways: in print, radio, and photojournalism. She remembered following Martha Gellhorn's strangely intimate reports from the front in *The New Yorker*—in an early piece, the journalist had written about witnessing a convoy of tanks in the dark outside Madrid. She'd described them "as if six boats, with only their harbor lights showing, were tied together, riding a gentle sea." Maggie had never shaken the startling image.

As the plane taxied to the terminal, she saw another aircraft with the red-and-black swastika on its tail—a Ju-52. It was her first time in Spain. And although she'd been prepared, she was still shocked to see Nazi planes parked alongside those from Allied and neutral nations on the tarmac. *But of course,* she thought. The German and British Embassies weren't even far from each other. People from Allied and Axis countries could mingle freely. Operatives were everywhere. After so many years of war, it seemed to Maggie like a world through a looking glass.

With a wave of apprehension, Maggie stepped down from the Iberia aircraft into a harsh wind. She'd transferred her gun to a holster strapped to her thigh and she felt its weight with every step.

She proceeded through customs and was questioned and searched by cold-eyed guards in capes, guns at their belts. The one who patted her down was busy with her breasts and bottom. Her blood turned to ice. She held her breath and bit her lip as he breathed in her ear and pressed himself against her, just missing the tiny gun strapped to her inner thigh. With a lewd wink and a final pat on her backside, he said, "Welcome to Madrid!"

With knees rubbery from relief, she found the taxi queue. Already waiting in line was a German in civilian clothing—he wore the SS death's head pin on his cashmere coat's lapel. He nodded and, when a taxi arrived, asked in English where she was going. *Must be the red hair,* Maggie thought.

"Madrid," she replied. She forced herself to smile. "The Palace Hotel."

"Ah." A regretful look crossed his face. "I'm at the Ritz."

She was from an Allied nation; he was with an Axis one. There would be no sharing a ride. He opened the taxi's door for her with regret. "I'll take the next one."

The rusty taxi made decent time on the frozen dirt roads, as there was hardly any traffic. Maggie noted the landscape was dusty and dry, with only a few scrubby, leafless trees and scraggly pines.

Her stomach clenched in apprehension as she remembered there was no immunity in Spain if she were discovered to be a spy. Maggie checked for the lipstick tube containing her cyanide pill. Her gun still pressed against her thigh.

Someone had left Madrid's newspaper of record, *ABC,* in the backseat. Although Maggie didn't read Spanish, she was fluent in French and could follow along roughly. It was mostly propaganda—the front page was a mix of General Franco, "patriotism," Catholicism, and the dangers of Bolshevism. There were also a few stories about the war, all favorable to Germany and Japan.

Flipping through the pages, she saw numerous photos of the short general: at a bullfight, with a bishop, with a voluptuous female movie star at a premiere, with the higher-ups of the Falange in uniform. Throughout, Franco was presented as a sort of beloved and benevolent father figure. Maggie's lips twisted in disgust.

As her driver lit a hand-rolled black cigarillo, Maggie glanced through stock reports, Real Madrid football scores, and a feature on the star bullfighter Juanito Belmonte. He was photographed in profile in the bullring, nearly bent backward with his cape, narrowly missing the charging bull's horns. *Poor bull,* she thought, remembering reading Munro Leaf's *Ferdinand the Bull* as a child. She flipped the page. The week's weather was anticipated to be cold, cloudy, and even windier. *Fantastic,* she thought.

Her eyebrows rose when she turned more pages and saw

the name Werner Heisenberg. Here it was: official confirmation the Nobel Prize–winning physicist was coming to the University of Madrid, to lecture at the Physics Department. She'd heard about the school's program; they'd tried to recruit Albert Einstein in 1933 with an honorary doctorate and a chair before he turned them down for Princeton. *Good for him,* she thought. *And look at him now, working on a fission bomb for the Allies.*

She folded the paper and pushed it aside, turning to gaze out the taxi's window. She took deep breaths and her heartbeat slowed. The road had few cars, several bicycles, and a couple of lorries drawn by skinny mules. The bullet-pocked buildings were evidence of the recent war.

They passed a colossal circular red-brick building that reminded her of a football stadium. *"La Plaza de Toros de Las Ventas,"* the driver said proudly. Maggie knew what it was, Madrid's famous 24,000-seat bullring. It was where man fought beast to the death—and who would survive was never certain.

As they made their way into the city, she saw apartment buildings with decorative black wrought-iron railings that reminded her of buildings in New Orleans. *More like the buildings in New Orleans resemble the ones in Spain,* she realized with a wry smile.

The slicing wind buffeted the taxi until they turned down a narrow cobblestoned street. There two uniformed police officers with guns had a man pinned against a wall. *"La policía,"* the driver said, his eyes catching Maggie's in the rearview mirror. *"Se cuidado."* *Be careful.* She nodded.

Maggie saw more squares and plazas with dry fountains and statues, bordered by leafless trees. On the Plaza de las Cortes, in front of the Congress of Deputies, Maggie spied a statue of Cervantes. Small children played tag at the novelist's feet, watched by governesses wrapped in heavy black shawls. Maggie stared wistfully at the statue, remembering how she'd once been as idealistic about "doing her bit" as Don Quixote. Back when she was Mr. Churchill's secretary, and still saw things in black and white. How long ago those days seemed, how many shades of gray there were in war. And how she didn't even recognize that girl anymore.

"*¡Hotel Palacio!*" the driver announced proudly as he pulled up to the stately belle époque building's front doors.

A thunderclap of bells chimed the three-quarter hour, and Maggie nearly jumped out of her skin as she paid the driver in the curved entrance. "*Muchas gracias,*" she told him, two of the few words of Spanish she knew, as a bellman took her luggage from the trunk.

"*Vaya con Dios, señorita,*" he told her. "*¡Buena suerte!*"

Maggie understood "good luck." She knew she'd need it.

In the Palace's marble lobby, she found the front desk. A dapper, portly man, with thick, neatly parted black hair and wide-set brown eyes, checked her in. "Where's your fiancé, Señorita Kelly?" he asked in perfect English. "When are you expecting Señor Mullaney? We have a room reserved for him as well."

"He's been . . . detained," she told him, managing to keep her voice steady as she pushed thoughts of Connor away. *Not now.* She signed her cover name to all the paperwork, accepted a polished brass key, and walked to the elevators.

Maggie knew the hotel's beautiful glass-domed lounge with ample natural light had been used as an operating theater during the war. She gazed up. The cupola was a mosaic of stained glass: blue, yellow, and orange. Glass red and fuchsia roses bloomed profusely above, echoing the roses on the plush carpet below.

It was here that she was supposed to meet her new partner— but not until the evening. Still, a man wearing a well-tailored suit was staring at her. He wasn't bad-looking, she noted, somewhere in his late twenties, with brown hair and eyes set in a long olive face. Although he wasn't tall, he was athletic and held himself with grace. Maggie did her best not to stare back, but she watched him in her peripheral vision. He seemed familiar. *Why? Is he the contact? Is he early?*

Also, other people seemed to be staring at him, whispering. *Is he an actor, perhaps? A musician? Flamenco dancer? Soccer star?*

As a pianist played Ravel's *Dulcinée,* she walked slowly toward the elevators, giving him time to approach. When she reached the elevator bank, she noted the man following had her two suitcases in his hands.

Is he a bellboy? she wondered. *But he isn't wearing a uniform—in fact, his suit's quite smart.* But he never said the code, and when she tried to tip him at the door to her room, he seemed offended and even a little dismayed. *Is he a German spy? Do I have a tail already?* Maggie wondered. *But surely no spy would be so bold, so . . . obvious.*

Right?

Nerves jangling, she locked the door, put the chain on, then slid a chair at an angle under the door's handle. She glanced around. It was a spacious room, with dark wood reproduction Empire furniture and a worn but clean carpet.

She sat down on the bed; it was hard and squeaky, but fine. She went to the windows and drew the heavy blue velvet curtains, parting the lace ones. Her room overlooked the Plaza de Cánovas del Castillo, featuring the Neptune Fountain.

As Maggie gazed out the frosted glass, she saw a yellow trolley rattle by a group of men in dark suits riding bicycles. A group of nuns in black-and-white habits waited at a red light. Across the plaza was the Hotel Ritz, where Coco Chanel was no doubt already ensconced, and where the Germans would most likely put Werner Heisenberg up.

Maggie had traveled light, so there wasn't much to unpack.

Once she had hung her clothing in the armoire, she took a hot bath, luxuriating with a large white cake of lavender-scented soap, then put on a cotton nightgown.

She realized she was exhausted—the last twenty-four hours had taken a toll. She lay on the bed, placing her purse with the gun under the pillow. The dread she'd been fighting to control surged back. Was Connor's murder not a random act of violence? Was there a double agent? *What does that mean for the mission?*

Finally, she allowed herself to close her eyes and fell into a fitful siesta.

Chapter Thirteen

Later, Maggie kept her coat around her shoulders in the chilly air of the Palace Hotel's rotunda. She waited at a round velvet banquette, surrounded by huge bouquets of red roses.

The glass-topped rotunda was a glamorous, cosmopolitan, bustling place. Handsome waiters with trays passed gracefully. A string quartet in a far corner played the "Habanera" from Bizet's *Carmen*. Maggie was surrounded by affluent Spanish families having a celebratory vermouth, businessmen in suits deep in serious discussions, men flirting with women who were likely not their wives, and, undoubtedly, any number of undercover agents.

She kept her hand on her purse, feeling the hard edges of the gun, while surreptitiously looking for her contact.

After several false hopes, Maggie saw a tall and elegant man in a well-tailored suit approach; he opened a monogrammed silver cigarette case. "The historical way to meet a lady," he said, bowing deeply, offering her a cigarette.

She was shocked to see Don Miguel Ángel Ramos—the British agent from Lisbon. *Why has he been assigned to this mission?* "How . . . kind of you to invite me," she responded stiffly in turn, declining the cigarette offer. The coded exchange was complete.

"Ángel Ramos," he said, offering a hand. "Would you do me the honor of joining me for a drink in the bar, Miss Kelly?"

Maggie rose and tucked her purse under one arm. She took his hand lightly. "Of course." *And we're off,* she thought.

They sat in a dark, candlelit corner of the Palace's intimate bar and ordered glasses of pale fino sherry. "How do you find Spain?" Ángel opened.

"Haven't been here long." *As you well know,* Maggie thought, but bit her tongue.

"You know, the Spanish empire was larger than the British, at one time," he said, as the waiter set down a bowl of glossy green olives as their complimentary tapa.

"As an Irish citizen who grew up in the United States, you can hardly expect me to be enamored of colonialism," she replied, in character. Then she softened. "But Madrid, at least what I've seen from the ride from the airport, seems an impressive city."

"Miss Kelly, allow me to introduce myself," he said theatrically. "I'm a friend of your fiancé, Francis Mullaney. While Señor Mullaney will be staying in Lisbon—after your breakup—I'm here as your guide to the city." He popped an olive in his mouth.

So that's how we're going to play it, she thought. *That "Francis" is still alive, but we've broken our engagement.* "Where are you from originally, Señor Ramos?" she asked.

"Ángel, please," he said. "And I'm Oaxacan—Mexican. My father was Spanish and my mother an Aztec princess. Grew up in Mexico City and Los Angeles. I do business for the Disney brothers here and in Lisbon, but also keep up with my contacts in the U.S. and London."

A fantastic position for a spy, Maggie thought. "How did you manage that?"

"I'm fluent in Spanish, of course—as well as English, German, French, Italian, and Russian. British and American companies find the combination of languages irresistible."

Maggie was impressed. "Your English is excellent."

"I studied at Cambridge—classmate of Kim Philby's, actually."

"Small world!"

"Indeed. I stayed to pursue a doctorate in medieval languages, then moved to London to teach at King's College."

She tilted her head. "Yes, I know the school."

"Even before the war, though, businesses wanted me for my Spanish. Then, in 1940 or so, the Brits created an agency to distribute media in Latin America. My job was to create material specifically for the Mexican market."

"However did you become involved with Mr. Disney?"

"One of the main contractors on the U.S. end is the Walt Disney Company, who did a 'Good Relations' tour in Central and South America—right before the attack on Pearl Harbor."

Maggie remembered John talking about Disney's South American tour. *No, don't think of John.* They were silent as the waiter set down their small glasses of pale sherry. Ángel raised his. "*Salud,*" he toasted, looking her in the eye.

"*Salud.*"

"Coco Chanel will contact you here," he said in a low voice. "The meeting with her and Ambassador Hoare will most likely be tomorrow. Whatever papers she gives you for the Prime Minister, you'll hand over to me, for safekeeping. Then we'll see about Werner Heisenberg's schedule. So you can . . . finish the job before we fly you home."

Maggie felt her stomach lurch at the name of the German physicist. Still, she had a job to do. "Perhaps Mademoiselle Chanel can make introductions?"

"Maybe." Ángel sounded doubtful. "You aren't naïve enough to consider her a friend, are you?"

Who is he to question me? Maggie thought, bristling. But

she realized he didn't know her at all—just as she didn't know him. "No," she reassured him, as she selected an olive. "Of course not. But she and I do have a certain . . . rapprochement. And obviously she's using it—and me—for my contacts. I see no reason not to do the same."

He quirked a glossy black eyebrow and took a sip of sherry. "Smart." He looked around the room and spied a woman wearing a tweed Chanel suit. "Coco Chanel might be a brilliant clothing designer, but she's a terrible employer."

"Her reputation as a businesswoman didn't come up when I was in Paris," Maggie said drily, recalling the brutal details of that particular mission. She pushed away her glass of sherry, suddenly queasy.

"Before the war, she paid her workforce atrociously—and was outraged if any of them asked for a raise. She was abusive to her staff and horribly anti-Semitic, blaming all her business problems on the Jews. She signed a contract with the Jewish Wertheimers and has tried ever since to take back control of her company by using Aryan law under the Occupation."

He picked up another olive. "When her fed-up, underpaid workers finally went on strike, she gave in. But then the Germans arrived in 1940, and she closed shop completely, leaving them all without jobs. Terrible, just terrible. She used to be a seamstress herself—she should treat her workers with respect. And pay them fairly."

Maggie had no illusions about Mademoiselle. "I'd like to go out tonight," she said, "to try and contact someone from the University of Madrid. Any intel on where they're putting Heisenberg up? The Ritz, I'd assume?"

"Yes." Ángel checked his large gold wristwatch. "It's nine-thirty. You must be starving. We have a reservation at Horcher." He put up a hand, and from across the room, the waiter nodded.

Maggie knew the restaurant. "Horcher?" Her stomach did

a flip. The one in London had a reputation for catering to British Fascist sympathizers.

"Yes, there's one in Madrid, as well as London. Berlin has the original, of course. Göring eats there for free, they say. The German diplomats—and spies—missed the Horcher's German food so much in Madrid they opened another here." He smiled, baring even white teeth. "And then we're going to a reception given by Doña Rosa, the Marquesa of Griñón."

"Good." Maggie had heard of the Marquesa during her training—one of Madrid's foremost socialites. Perhaps there would be people from the university there. *We'll hide in plain sight,* she thought as she pulled her coat around her and gathered her things. She tucked the purse, with the gun, under her arm.

"Earlier today, when I arrived, a man helped me with my bags," she told Ángel as he paid the check. "I'm certain he wasn't a bellhop or in any way an employee of the hotel." She buttoned her coat. "I have to say, it unnerved me."

Ángel looked at her sharply, then shrugged. "An admirer, most likely."

"When I offered him a tip, he seemed offended. He spoke perfect English—I'm thinking he could be German."

"You're new," Ángel said, putting down several pesetas with the bill. Maggie noted they displayed General Franco's unremarkable profile. "You'll be under observation for a while. From all sides."

"Still, I don't like that he knows the number of my hotel room. Especially after . . . Lisbon."

As they left, he whispered in her ear, "The Germans have what they call a 'snatch team'—Ablege Kommandos—experts at making people disappear, if you get my meaning." Maggie swallowed but kept her expression neutral.

"They kidnap their victims," he continued softly. "Drugging them and sneaking them across the border, taking them alive to Germany—or they kill them with a poison added to food or drink. After twenty minutes the substance leaves no trace, and the body can clear any autopsy."

He tilted his fedora at a roguish angle. "The Spanish police look the other way. Believe me, if the Gestapo wanted you out of Madrid, you wouldn't be left wondering. You'd be either in Berlin, or dead."

"I see." They were almost out of the lobby, Maggie's heels clicking on the floor.

"The Nazis have roughly five hundred agents in Madrid, a hundred or so with diplomatic cover, and another four hundred in various phony firms and jobs. They also have a number working at a secret shortwave listening and decoding station," he told her. "The city's teeming with Germans, and any porter, bellman, waiter, concierge, or driver can be an informant. And, just so you know, at Horcher's there are microphones in all the flower arrangements. Assume everything we say will be overheard."

Chapter Fourteen

Dinner at wood-paneled Horcher was pickled partridge and venison with glazed chestnuts served on Austrian porcelain. Maggie and Ángel sat with their feet propped under the table on crimson silk pillows, as was the custom in the finest European restaurants. They found themselves in the company of German film producers, directors, and writers and their Spanish counterparts, including the woman who must have been the production's leading lady. Maggie watched her over her wineglass. Her thick blond hair glinted gold in the candlelight, while her clingy plum dress accentuated her generous curves. Her robust laugh was loud enough to cause diners' heads to turn.

From there, they took a taxi through the tight streets and squares of the Barrio de las Letras, "the neighborhood of literature." Ángel pointed out the birthplace of Don Miguel de Cervantes and Maggie's lips twisted in a wry smile. Don Quixote was full of such hope, such chivalry, such idealism. Just as she'd been, once upon a time. *Of course the Don was mad,* she realized. *No one sane could possibly sustain hope in such darkness for so long.*

Eventually they arrived at a palace on Calle de Ferraz, the home of Doña Rosa. The reception was for the cast and producers of the movie, and Maggie saw many of the Germans and Spaniards she'd seen at Horcher, including the golden-haired actress.

She was talking to a middle-aged man with a long, dour face and greasy mustache, who seemed annoyed at her laugh and unimpressed by her cleavage. "Josef Hans Lazar," Ángel whispered to her. "Press attaché to the German Embassy. His real mission's distributing Nazi propaganda and spies."

Maggie surveyed the crowd, noting Baron von Stohrer, Germany's ambassador to Spain, among other high-ranking Nazis. Ángel's eyes landed on a small, slim woman with a cigarette in a long ivory holder. "And of course you know who *that* is."

Maggie did her best not to gasp when she saw: Coco Chanel, wreathed in a gray cloud of smoke. She looked harder than when Maggie had met her two years earlier, her face creased with deeper lines, her body even more angular. But she was instantly recognizable, with the same black-dyed hair and heavily rouged cheeks.

She was with a man Maggie recognized as her lover, Baron Hans Günther von Dincklage, the special attaché to the German Embassy in Paris. He was attractive, she had to admit, tall and lean, with sandy blond hair brushed back with pomade from a broad, high forehead.

Maggie could see Dincklage's appeal for Chanel; he possessed the arrogant coolness of a German aristocrat. That he was more than a decade younger probably didn't hurt either. The couturiere didn't see her, and Maggie turned her face away to keep her advantage for the moment. She made a mental note to find Chanel later, to break the ice before their official meeting at the embassy.

"The Germans think of the Spanish as animals—and Mexicans as even worse," Ángel whispered in her ear as they passed Germans eagerly helping themselves to a generous buffet. "But it doesn't stop them from wolfing down their Iberian ham and swigging their finest cava."

As they made their way through the grand salon, Maggie noticed the Spanish women wore elegant, long-sleeved wool Balenciaga dresses. She realized her own blue evening dress was woefully thin in the mansion's chill air. She suppressed a shiver and raised her chin, determined not to let her discomfort show.

They strolled through room after room, each dripping in silk, velvet, and gilt. The furniture was a mixture of various French antiques, and the paintings El Grecos and Goyas. Originals, Maggie noted with raised eyebrows. There was a group of trim Spanish men with military bearing surrounded by women draped in significant jewels, who were hanging on to their every word. "*Toreadores,*" Ángel explained to her. "The Frank Sinatras of Spain. And their *aficionadas.*"

One of the bullfighters turned to stare at Maggie. She thought, *He looks familiar.*

Ángel greeted a man with a scar down one cheek. "Friend of mine from the studios," he explained as they walked away. "With his mistress, not his wife. Sorry not to introduce you, but mistresses and 'respectable women' are kept separate in Spain."

"If only they knew," Maggie murmured with a half-smile, grasping her purse with the gun. "Do you think there's any chance of seeing Professor Heisenberg here?"

Ángel shook his head. "My sources say he arrives in Madrid tomorrow."

Maggie nodded, feeling relief wash over her. *It won't be tonight,* she thought. *I still have time.*

In a large salon, waiters in white gloves passed silver trays of hors d'oeuvres and coupes of sparkling wine. Maggie spotted British Ambassador Sir Samuel Hoare holding court in a corner. She'd memorized Hoare's appearance from photographs during training—the high forehead, long nose, and sharp angles all the British aristocrats seemed to have. In person, he was taller and wirier than she'd expected, and seemed older, much older, with thinning white hair.

He was engaged in an animated conversation with a younger, far more handsome man.

"Tom Burns," Ángel told her. "Press attaché to the Spanish Embassy." *The man Kim warned me about,* Maggie remembered.

Ángel murmured, "Hoare always looks terrified away from the embassy—afraid some Spaniard might step on his toes."

"Surely that would be a diplomatic incident," Maggie teased. "At his level, he must be safe."

"Who's safe here, really?" Ángel shrugged. "And Tom Burns, what a joke—a Franco sycophant." He clicked his tongue in disgust.

It seems Mr. Burns doesn't have many friends in British intelligence, she thought.

A tiny frail woman seated at an antique gilt card table glanced over and beckoned to them with a bony finger. Her hair was completely white, and her cheeks were heavily powdered, but in the gentle firelight she was obviously the same person as the imperious young girl who'd posed for the oil painting hanging above the mantel. The woman in the painting and the one in front of the fireplace wore the same heavy blue sapphire necklace.

"Doña Rosa," Ángel said in greeting, bowing deeply. "The Marquesa of Griñón," he said for Maggie's benefit. "You look ravishing as ever." He kissed her hand. "May I introduce Señorita Paige Kelly, originally from Ireland and raised in the United States? A good friend. I'm showing her around the city."

The woman appraised him with a gimlet eye. "How *good* of you, Ángel. Always there to lend a helping hand to pretty young women in Madrid," she said drily in softly accented English, then considered Maggie through a fringe of heavy false eyelashes. "Hollywood?" she asked, reedy voice hopeful.

Maggie knew what the Marquesa was asking—if she were a glamorous American who could gossip about film stars. "Boston," she replied.

Doña Rosa sniffed and looked back to the woman sitting in front of her, wearing a large gold and diamond comb stabbed through her elaborate black bun. She continued reading the woman's fortune, telling her the meanings of the cards arranged in front of her on the inlaid table and what they foretold: more children, more love, more fortune. The woman seemed pleased.

She smiled and told Maggie in passing as she left, "Doña Rosa's readings always come true!"

The Doña gazed up at Maggie with a curious expression. "Señorita Kelly, permit me to read your cards. I feel they're calling us."

While Maggie was a scientist, an atheist, and not at all superstitious, she knew this was all part of the game. She perched on the brocade tuffet in front of the Marquesa and waited respectfully.

Doña Rosa shuffled the worn cards. "Now," she announced, her voice a bit louder than before. People turned and wandered over to watch the show. "This young woman is a stranger to me. All I know is she came to the party with our Ángel." This drew a laugh from the group, apparently used to seeing an assortment of young women with Ángel.

"And she's Irish by way of Boston, the city where they had that little tea party." She shuffled and reshuffled the cards, glancing up at Maggie, who had the sudden feeling the Marquesa knew more than she was letting on.

Doña Rosa laid three cards facedown, then took a dramatic

pause before turning the first one over, revealing the Devil. One of the women, in an emerald necklace, looking on gasped.

The Doña considered Maggie with a somber expression in her dark brown eyes and tapped her finger on the card. "You're in danger here in Madrid."

Maggie glanced at Ángel, who rolled his eyes.

"The Devil is about everything taboo," Doña Rosa said. "But, here, it's reversed—meaning you must have some kind of chaos brewing in you, Miss Kelly. Vengeance, perhaps? Retaliation?"

Assassination, Maggie thought. *My plan to kill Heisenberg.* But it couldn't be. There was no magic, no mystery, no secret knowledge, of course—this tarot reading was all for show. The Marquesa was simply creating open-ended drama, with the audience coming to its own conclusion.

The Doña picked up the second card. It was the World. "There's some kind of plot—an international one." At this, from the corner of her eye, Maggie saw Samuel Hoare stop speaking and look over.

"And you're in the center of it," she told Maggie as the British ambassador approached to listen. "Whatever you do here will cause a death, and a rebirth, in you. There will be endings— and also beginnings. You'll never be the same after this trip."

Interesting, yes, Maggie thought, *but still nothing specific. I'm obviously an international and Madrid's a dangerous city. Travel always changes people. That's all it is.*

The Doña turned over the last card. It was Death. Despite herself, Maggie felt a chill pass through her. "I see a bullfight," the Doña said, gazing intently at the card.

"The poor bull's death, I presume," Maggie quipped, and the onlookers laughed uncomfortably.

"The card doesn't mean the death of a person, or an animal, necessarily," the Doña explained. "You may find yourself with ties to the past cut by Death's scythe. But you'll continue, to fulfill your destiny."

"To spend as many pesetas as possible at Balenciaga?" Maggie joked, her voice merry.

At this, the atmosphere lightened, and the Doña collected her cards and reshuffled, then set them aside. She beckoned for her nurse to fetch her more cava. But before Maggie moved on, the Doña fixed her with a hard stare. She crooked an arthritic finger; Maggie bent down.

"Be careful," Doña Rosa warned in a whisper. "You're in danger." Then, "We'll talk more later tonight, dear. In private."

Maggie was intrigued. "At your service, Doña Rosa."

Chapter Fifteen

On Ángel's arm, Maggie walked to the next marble and gilt room, where one fresh-faced young woman was playing the grand piano, while a man and another young woman, giggling, were attempting to sing a rendition of Cole Porter's duet "You're the Top."

She saw Hoare had followed; he was watching her carefully from his position beside a long window. *Kim must have briefed him,* she thought and made her way over to speak with him. "Good evening, Sir Samuel," she said in greeting. "Please let me introduce myself—"

He raised a hand and cut her off: "Mrs. Francis Mullaney. How do you do?"

"Actually, it's . . . still Miss Paige Kelly, sir."

"That's not what I was expecting."

Me neither, she thought, picturing Connor's wide smile. "I know. But here we are."

"I've heard about you." His tone insinuated none of it was good.

"It's an honor to meet you, Mr. Ambassador."

His expression was sour. "Ah—and look, here's your partner in crime."

Maggie turned to see Chanel. She wore a simple gray gown; ropes of pearl, enamel, and gold necklaces and bracelets rattled as she moved. She regarded Maggie with a basilisk gaze. "You've grown," she said in a raspy voice.

Maggie knew her borrowed dress was a bit tight—all the fish and chips she and John had been enjoying—and the comment stung. "Perhaps you've shrunk," she countered. They kissed each other on both cheeks; Maggie caught the distinctive chilly jasmine scent of No. 5.

Then, to the ambassador, Chanel said, "Good evening, Sam."

Hoare bowed and kissed her gloved hand. "Permit me to introduce Miss Paige Kelly," he said.

Chanel plucked at one of her diamonds. "Oh, Miss Kelly and I are old friends," she told him. "From the Hôtel Ritz in Paris. Isn't that right, Miss Kelly?"

Hoare smiled. "How long has it been now, Coco?"

"Years," she said with a wave of a hand. "Lifetimes—and yet it seems like yesterday. I think the last time we met in person was fly fishing in Scotland."

"Or sailing in the Mediterranean? Or was it the Aegean?" He cleared his throat and shot her a sly look. "At any rate, it was before old Bendor was married."

Chanel's eyes narrowed in displeasure. But in ironic tones she said only "Everyone *marries* the Duke of Westminster." She tilted her head. "But while there may be many duchesses, there will only be one Coco Chanel."

Maggie's heart was thudding in her chest. "Mademoiselle, how good to see you again," she managed. "You seem well."

"Thank you, my dear." She leaned over and whispered in Maggie's ear: "Prado. Ten. Tomorrow. The café. Come alone." And then she was gone, leaving only the scent of jasmine.

"It was lovely to meet you, Miss Kelly," the ambassador said.

Maggie knew she'd been dismissed. *But this isn't over,* she thought. *It hasn't even begun.* "We'll talk again soon, Mr. Ambassador."

As Maggie and Ángel were about to leave, Maggie remembered Doña Rosa had wanted to speak with her in private. "Let's say thank you and good night to our hostess, shall we?" Maggie suggested. "She wanted to have a chat—"

Ángel stifled a yawn. "I'd really rather leave—"

"It would be rude—"

A woman shrieked; the sound reverberated among the rooms. There was a moment of silence, and then absolute mayhem. Maggie picked up her skirts and ran to the large drawing room. A crowd had gathered, silent and still, looking down. "Is she dead?" the woman in emeralds cried.

"Someone call a doctor!" a stout German man with corn-blond hair shouted.

"I'm in medical school." A hulk of a young man knelt by Doña Rosa's tiny, crumpled body and, with his enormous hand, felt her neck for a pulse and put his ear to her mouth to listen for breath. Finally, he placed both her hands gently on her chest. "I'm sorry," he said, his voice cracking slightly, as he gazed up with brown eyes wet with tears, his expression betraying his youth and inexperience. "But our dear Doña Rosa is gone. May she rest in peace." He closed her eyes.

Just like Connor, Maggie thought.

A woman burst into loud sobs, while another went quickly to a sofa, sitting before her legs went out from under her. A few of the onlookers made the sign of the cross and bowed their heads in prayer. Maggie caught sight of Ambassador Hoare, pale and speechless.

Maggie stared down at the frail body, which had been so vivacious, so lively, only a short time before. But there was no knife wound, no injury, as with Connor. Maggie glanced up at the medical student.

"What was the cause of her death?" she asked in the chaos.

"Heart attack, most likely. Or stroke." Maggie bent to pick up the champagne coupe Doña Rosa had dropped. The glass was empty, but inside, at the bottom, was a powdery residue. She lifted it to her nose. It smelled of cyanide, a poison Maggie knew all too well from another death. A murder. She handed the glass to the student.

He sniffed it, made a face, then tested the residue with his finger. When he brought it to his nose, his eyes opened wide. "Or . . . she might have been poisoned. Someone—call the police! Now!"

Later, in a taxi back to the Palace Hotel, Ángel said, "Terrible about Rosa, but at least she died the way she lived—the center of attention."

Maggie was still thinking about the medical student's words. "Do you think Doña Rosa was poisoned?"

He shrugged. "I doubt it."

"The man who examined her seemed pretty sure. There was definitely something at the bottom of the Doña's glass."

"She was an old woman," Ángel said, leaning back and gazing out the window as they passed the spotlit Neptune Fountain. "It was simply her time. Death comes for us all. Sometimes when we least expect."

Maggie looked at him sharply. *Is he that jaded by war and death? Or was there no love lost between Doña Rosa and him?* "She asked to talk to me in private, after she did my reading."

Ángel continued to stare out the window. "Did you have a chance to speak with her?"

"No," Maggie said with regret. "No, I didn't. Now I wonder what she wanted to tell me."

"She probably wanted to do a little matchmaking. An American woman, even an Irish woman, would be catnip to her."

Maggie wasn't convinced. "Maybe." Then, "I think she was trying to pass a message to me with her reading."

He smirked. "She does—did—do a little work for us now and again."

"Wait," Maggie said. "Doña Rosa's a spy? You didn't think to mention that?"

"Oh, almost everyone here's a spy." Ángel shrugged. "With the Marquesa's contacts, she would have heard quite a bit. And no one ever suspects an old woman. Looks like she may have discovered something about an assassination plot." He spread his hands. "The thing is, when people hear assassination here, they think General Franco. We're still safe."

As they pulled up to the Palace Hotel, Maggie wasn't reassured. "Next time we go out, you need to tell me who else is a spy," she told Ángel. "By the way, I'm meeting Chanel at the Prado tomorrow morning. Before my meeting at the embassy."

He nodded. "Good luck."

After Ángel dropped Maggie off, he made his way to the nearby Buen Retiro Park, now bathed in moonlight. The trees destroyed during the war had been replaced by small saplings, the wind in their bare branches making them look like dancing skeletons. He sat on a cold, hard bench near the Puerta de Felipe IV entrance and lit a black cigarillo, the tip glowing red in the shadows.

A dog barked in the distance, and within minutes, a muscular man in a dark coat, fedora pulled low, took a seat at the other end of the bench.

Ángel continued to smoke as the man flipped up his collar against the wind. "She's here," Ángel said finally. His warm breath made clouds in the chill air.

"I'll let the Boss know."

"I can't do anything until she completes her missions."

"Shouldn't take long."

"No."

"So sad about Rosa. She could often be helpful."

"No coroner's office will be able to detect the poison by the time her body reaches the morgue."

"Good."

The wind picked up, making the bare branches of the trees sway violently, and Ángel stood. "*¡No pasarán!*" he said, pronouncing the Communists' Spanish Civil War motto, "They shall not pass."

"*Nosotros pasaremos,*" the man replied, before melting into the darkness of the park.

Chapter Sixteen

Maggie's dreams were webbed with visions of Connor, rolling dice in the casino in Estoril. He was covered in blood, the handle of the knife still protruding from his abdomen as he staggered toward her, red staining his shirt. *Help me,* he mouthed. Doña Rosa was next to him, holding her deck of cards, blood dripping from her ears. *Help us.*

Maggie's heart wrenched in her chest, and she turned over and woke with a cry, soaked in sweat. *Oh, God,* she thought, a hand to her neck. Trying to take deep regular breaths, she heard a sharp knock at the door. She grabbed the gun she'd placed under her pillow. *Maybe the knock's from across the hall? Surely it can't be someone for me.*

But there it was again, now a *rat-a-tat-tat,* like machine gun fire. She peered at the clock on her nightstand. Eight exactly. *But who?* She knew only Ángel and the people she'd met at the party. *Has Coco somehow found my room?* She slipped into her old tartan flannel robe, picked up the gun, and padded to the door.

Maggie struggled to remember the small amount of Spanish she'd learned before she'd left England. "*¿Quién es?*"

She heard shuffling feet and then the muffled reply, "*El mozo de espadas.*"

Man of Swords. Wasn't that a tarot card? Was this someone from the party who'd heard Doña Rosa's reading?

She hid the gun behind her back and slowly unlocked and opened the door. Three well-dressed middle-aged men bowed. One held an enormous bouquet of red roses, while the other two held something made from blue beaded fabric that glittered and sparkled, even in the hall's dim light.

"Señorita Kelly," one of them said, "please allow me to introduce myself. I am the 'man of swords' for Don Juanito Belmonte. I—we—come bearing his presents for you."

Maggie stared, confused. "Belmonte?"

"Yes, Señorita." The three men puffed out their chests, beaming with pride.

She blinked. "Who?"

The men seemed truly shocked. "You don't know the great Belmonte?" one finally ventured.

Another offered, "Don Juanito Belmonte, son of the legendary Don Juan Belmonte?"

She shook her head no, suddenly aware of her tatty robe and uncombed hair. *This señorita needs tea.*

The men stared in disbelief. "The Belmonte dynasty's the greatest in bullfighting," the one with the flowers explained, as though speaking to a small child. "Juanito Belmonte's the most famous bullfighter in Madrid—in all Spain!"

Maggie did her best to smile, while she kept her grip on the gun. *Of course,* she thought, remembering the article in *ABC* she'd found in the taxi from the airport. *Juanito Belmonte.* "And what is a 'man of swords'?"

"We assist the matador in all things. We are like . . . Sancho Panza to the great Don Quixote." Then, "Don Juanito saw you—as you arrived at the hotel. He was struck by your beauty. Like Dulcinea."

"Yes?"

"He carried your luggage." Again, they looked incredulous. "A great honor from Don Juanito."

Oh! Maggie thought, relieved. *So not a Gestapo spy after all.* Then, *Or is he?*

"Don Juanito saw you again last night, at the gathering given by Doña Rosa, the Marquesa of Griñón."

Maggie dimly remembered Ángel pointing out a few famous bullfighters. Was one Don Juanito Belmonte? The man from the article? Who'd carried her luggage? It was a relief to know he wasn't a Nazi. *But is he? Who knows what his alliances may be?*

With her free hand, Maggie accepted the mass of thornless roses, tied in satin ribbons. But when the other men offered the sparkling garment, she refused.

"It's Belmonte's *chaquetilla*—jacket—from his *traje de luces*," one explained. "Don Juanito wore this 'jacket of lights' in Seville, when he won two ears." Maggie raised an eyebrow—the blue satin suit covered with sequins, beads, and tassels seemed more like a costume for a Broadway show.

What on earth am I supposed to do with a matador's jacket? And what exactly do they mean by "ears"? The bull's *ears?* She forced herself to keep a neutral expression on her face, even as her stomach lurched.

"Señorita," one said, "please don't refuse—we could never explain to Don Juanito."

"I'll accept the roses," she told them firmly, "but not the *chaquetilla*. Please thank Don Juanito for me. Now, I must dress." She did her best to smile. "Thank you all."

Maggie closed the door and went to the table, putting down both the bouquet and the gun.

She shook her head and rubbed sleep from her eyes, staring at the two incongruous objects. To become involved, in any way, with a man in the public eye while on a mission was ill-advised at best. Surely accepting the flowers would assuage his dignity, she thought, while refusing the sequins would send the message she wasn't interested. *Problem solved.*

She yawned and stretched and yearned for hot tea. She wasn't quite sure how far she was from the Prado and needed to dress if she was going to meet Chanel on time. But before she could reach the armoire, she had to rush to the bathroom, retching violently over the toilet.

Stress, she thought. *Connor's and Doña Rosa's deaths. And too much cava.*

However much she might look like a tourist enjoying a day of sightseeing in Madrid, Maggie had never felt more wary; she watched constantly to see if she was being tailed. She'd dressed carefully, in a wool day dress—white flowers on a dark blue background—and wool coat. She knotted the silk scarf Coco Chanel had given her in Paris casually around her throat.

Maggie took note of her surroundings: the city moved in a slow, deliberate rhythm, so different from tense and harried London. She walked down a narrow street of well-preserved buildings to the Neptune Fountain and followed the traffic circle around to the museum. Near the crosswalk, she saw a parked black Citroën; the driver, his face hidden by a low-fitting cap, was watching her.

Maggie was well versed in the techniques of espionage. There was a list all agents were trained to memorize. Number One: be alert for the unobtrusive. A shadow could be *anyone,* probably the least likely of suspects. But the driver seemed far more interested in a busty blonde in high heels and a mink coat walking by.

She passed a gnarled man in a ragged cap and coat, waving pieces of paper. "*¡Lotería!*" he called in a hoarse voice. "*¡Lotería!*" She couldn't discount him.

A bloodcurdling wail startled Maggie, and she froze. The noise came from a little gray donkey in the traffic circle. He'd reared on his hind legs, braying loudly, as a gasogene passed, belching foul smoke from its chimney; because of the gasoline rations, some of the cars had been rebuilt to run on burning coal. The donkey's owner tried to calm him, but the animal was shaken by a near miss.

By the fountain, a man slouched, fedora pulled down over his forehead, hands cupping the cigarette in one corner of his mouth, protecting it from the wind. He looked like any *Madrileño,* contemplating the day. But as Maggie glanced in her peripheral vision, she saw his eyes sweep from right to left and back again, keeping watch. She knew the expression all too well. The man was a tail. And not a good one—he had an easily identifiable glass eye that swiveled out of line when he blinked.

Since the tail's looking across the traffic circle and not at me, he might be waiting for another. Working as a pair. In a glance she saw that a second man, trilby tilted over his face, a copy of *ABC* under his arm, was strolling in parallel with her.

She knew that, unlike his teammate next to the fountain, this man wasn't Spanish. For one thing, he was wearing a Burberry trench coat over a well-cut suit. For another, his demeanor, his stride, his bone structure, told her in a single glance he was English.

One of ours? Or a double agent?

She entered a café, asked to use the lavatory, then slipped out the service entrance into a back alley. Instead of continuing to the Prado directly, she took the long way around, watching for either of the men, or a third tail.

Satisfied at last she wasn't followed, Maggie bought a ticket and entered the Prado Museum. Even though Spain was a neutral country, she wasn't surprised to see most of the art was gone—taken down for safekeeping during the Civil War, she assumed, and still not returned. *Probably scattered among General Franco's many palaces,* she thought. Her footsteps echoed on the marble floors as she made her way through the gloomy light.

The building had no heat, and she kept her coat buttoned. There were few visitors. She scanned for shadows, but saw only a young guard taking over from an older one, carrying a copy of *Arriba.* A gray-haired man in a black beret who'd walked in behind her was now making pencil sketches of an El Greco Christ. And a woman with thick glasses and a feathered hat leaned in close to a canvas to peer at the brushstrokes.

A few attendants in black uniforms chatted with one another in entranceways; one paced the length of a long, poorly lit hall, slowly kicking a crumpled ticket like a soccer ball until he reached the end, then kicked it back the other way. It made a faint scuttling sound.

Finally, Maggie found the café. It was chilly and mostly empty—too late for breakfast, too early for lunch. A dour woman wearing a bejeweled turban was in one corner, reading the newspaper and drinking thick coffee with *pan con tomate,* bread rubbed with garlic and topped with grated tomatoes and olive oil.

Despite the detour, Maggie was early, and she took a seat at a table with a single red carnation in the far corner of the room. There she had a perfect view of everything. Her hands were sweaty, and she had to remind herself to breathe.

Finally, Coco Chanel approached. The couturiere was enveloped in a black sable coat, her hair as dark and glossy as her fur, her painted lips red. A white silk camellia was pinned to her collar, and she wore creamy pearl earrings the size of gumdrops.

Maggie put a hand up to her scarf and recalled her last encounter with the designer, at the Ritz in Paris:

She was at the hotel's front desk. "It was left several days ago," she'd insisted. "It's a bag, black. It should have a tag with my name on it." She gave the concierge her most persuasive smile. "Perhaps you could check again?" She tilted her head and widened her eyes. "S'il vous plaît?"

The man sighed but deigned to look again. "Oh, this old thing?" he said. Maggie's heart lifted. Then, reading the label, "I guess this is for you, Mademoiselle. A thousand apologies."

As he passed it over, Coco Chanel had watched the exchange without a word, intrigued. In that instant, she could have blown Maggie's cover, but for whatever reasons, she didn't. Maggie took the bag and slung it over her shoulder. "Thank you," she told the concierge, then nodded in gratitude to Chanel.

As she began walking out to the narrow rue Cambon, the couturiere joined her. Across the street and to the left, Maggie could see Chanel's boutique, with its white awnings and distinctive bold black lettering. "I'm going this way," Chanel said, indicating her shop.

"And I, the other," she told the designer.

As they parted, Chanel leaned in to kiss both of her cheeks. "I don't know what game you're playing, Mademoiselle Kelly—or whatever your name really is—" she murmured, taking the jasmine-scented scarf from around her neck and wrapping it around Maggie's. "But it's been droll to watch." She gave a world-weary smile. "And war is so rarely amusing." She pulled away and turned to go, calling over her shoulder, "Bonne chance!"

"Nice scarf," Chanel purred as she approached. The designer appraised Maggie with an inscrutable expression, taking in both face and body. Since the navy-blue wool coat wasn't Mag-

gie's to begin with—it had belonged to the real Paige Kelly—
the fit was slightly off. Too snug. She knew Chanel would
instantly know it wasn't hers, just as she'd known that summer
in Paris about her borrowed finery.

Maggie reached up and touched the silk. "One of my favorites." She was glad Chanel couldn't tell she was wearing her
rival Elizabeth Arden's Printemps lipstick, and her face was
protected from the cold by the Eight Hour cream. But Maggie
would put nothing past her.

Chanel stood in front of Maggie, dark eyes wary. In the
harsh light of day, the lines between her brows and around her
eyes looked even deeper than they had in the gentle candlelight
of the previous evening, like putty cut with a knife. Foundation
and powder had set in the lines, only highlighting them. She
flipped up the collar of her fur and asked, "Shall we take a turn
around the museum?" It wasn't a question.

"Of course, Mademoiselle."

Chapter Seventeen

Maggie and Chanel walked together through the echoing, cavernous galleries, past the guard still kicking the lost ticket. Maggie kept a close eye on the other visitors, but she couldn't help glancing at the art. The colors of the oil paintings—black, indigo, ocher, maroon, and olive green—practically glowed, as if lit from within like stained glass.

"I saw Pablo Picasso's *Guernica* in New York when it toured the United States," Maggie told the couturiere. "I remember reading that Picasso won't allow the painting back on Spanish soil until fascism is gone."

Chanel flared her nostrils like a racehorse, then one hand went to her necklace, picking at one of the black pearls. In a husky whisper she said, "Pablo and I are old friends, you know. We worked together on Cocteau's *Antigone* and Diaghilev's *Le Train Bleu*. It's all a way to promote the tour, flatter the foreign museum guests. He's always had a flair for the dramatic—*and* for making money."

A woman in a feathered hat and patched chinchilla coat was scrutinizing Goya's *Winter*: a group of peasants made their way through a snowstorm alongside their starving dog. They were juxtaposed against servants from a noble household with a slaughtered pig. The tension between the two groups—the haves and the have-nots—was palpable.

Chanel's eyes slid across the painting, unseeing. "I'm thinking of opening a boutique here in Madrid. To sell Number Five," she continued. "It's been an enormous success for me in Paris."

Maggie tilted her head. "I recall your perfume shop was quite popular." *With Nazis and collaborators,* she left unsaid.

They approached an oil painting: Diego Velázquez's *Queen Mariana of Austria.* Shades and tints of white, black, and red showed the nineteen-year-old queen in a bejeweled and corseted dress, with an enormous skirt and elaborate headdress.

"Just look at her sour expression," Chanel said, gesturing with a gloved hand. "Most likely she can't move in her ridiculous skirt and headpiece. Can you imagine?" She sniffed. "Anyone in a dress like that can't do anything, hasn't done anything, and *will* never do anything," she declared. "*This* is what I fought against, as a designer and a woman, all my life: the corsets, the bustles, the heavy hats. Those things *hobble* women—disfigure them, infantilize them. In my clothes women can move. They're free."

They walked in silence to yet another chilly, cavernous gallery. People passed through and then they were momentarily alone, with only the gray light from the wind-rattled windows. "I don't know if you're aware of this," Chanel began, as they approached another huge oil painting framed in gold, "but I'm close to Winston Churchill, and a number of other Englishmen." Maggie nodded; she'd been briefed.

"Whenever Winston was in Paris, we'd dine at the Ritz," Chanel said, warming to her subject. Maggie had the distinct feeling the couturiere was playing up the relationship. "I remember drinking brandy with him and his son the day the news broke about the Duke of Windsor—how he had chosen to abdicate the throne for Wallis Simpson. Churchill *père et fils* were both dead drunk, of course," Chanel related. "And then Winnie began to cry. He wept. His son wept. And, I remember, he said repeatedly, 'One does not put on someone else's costume.' And here I had always been led to believe the British were emotionless. The Churchills carried on like Italians!"

Maggie, who was glad the pro-Nazi and pro-Hitler Duke had abdicated and made way for King George, bit her lip. They stopped in front of another oil, *The Rape of Europa,* painted by Peter Paul Rubens after an original by Titian. It showed the Phoenician princess after she was abducted by Zeus in the form of a white bull.

Chanel scoffed. "Who'd want anything to do with her?" she queried, narrowing her eyes at the terrified young girl. "All that pasty skin and rolls of fat? Just look at her—pale and chubby. Useless. She needs a summer of tennis and swimming in the South of France to bronze up and slim down."

Chanel turned to appraise Maggie's figure. Maggie felt uncomfortable under the scrutiny, as though spiders were crawling over her. "Last night I thought you'd gone to fat, like Europa," she purred. "But now I realize you're a bit more . . . voluptuous. That dress is hideous—you must go to Balenciaga as soon as possible. You'll need new clothes soon anyway."

"I'm not sure if I'll have time," Maggie said. "And I don't need any new clothes."

"Of course you do—or at least, you will. Because you're starting to show."

Show? "I don't know what you mean. I may have gained some weight but . . ."

Chanel eyed her. "Your bosom is full, your skin is positively glowing, and your veins are wide and prominent. Believe me, I know women's bodies. You're with child." She leaned closer to Maggie, eyebrows raised. "You mean—you didn't know?"

Maggie thought back. She and John had used French letters, mostly. A few times they hadn't. Suddenly, she felt ill and thought back to the vomiting earlier. *Morning sickness?* She forced herself not to gasp.

"If you're not . . . on board . . . I can find you someone," Chanel whispered in her ear. "Not a back-alley doctor, but a real one. A safe one." She shrugged. "Of course, it'll cost you."

In an instant, Maggie knew she wanted the baby. A baby. Hers. Hers and John's. *I need to go back to the hotel.* But she couldn't become distracted. *Not now. Especially not now.*

She forced her mind on the task at hand and cleared her throat. "When I spoke with Ambassador Hoare last night, he didn't specify the time of the meeting."

Chanel straightened. "It's at four." They resumed their walk. "I'll have the letter, with an introduction from me, packaged and ready to go. It's imperative you give it directly—personally—with your very own hands—to Winston Churchill. No one else can see it or take it from you. Is this understood?"

Maggie did understand. She'd give the Prime Minister the package. And he'd throw it in the nearest fireplace. "Yes."

"They'll try to take it from you, but I need him to see my handwriting, my words, with his own eyes. Only then will he read what's inside. Only then do we have a chance of stopping this war, of making a separate peace. . . ."

Maggie kept her face neutral but knew with unshakable certainty no separate peace would ever be negotiated.

Chanel stopped short in front of another Velázquez. "You do owe me a favor, Miss Kelly. Or whatever your name is. I could have had you arrested in Paris, but I didn't, did I?"

"Why didn't you turn me in?" Maggie countered. "I've always wondered."

"I do adore a bit of chaos," the designer admitted. "And I like when people owe me. It comes in handy, as you see now." She smiled. "There absolutely must be a truce between Germany and Britain. Communism must be stopped. The fate of the world depends on it." Chanel linked her arm through Maggie's, and they began strolling once again.

Maggie had had enough. "But surely you know about the

Big Three at the Casablanca Conference," she murmured. "And the Allies' condition of 'no separate peace.'"

Chanel shook her head, her impeccably marcelled hair a stiff unmoving helmet. "The Soviet Union's the *real* enemy of Europe, my dear girl. It's in France's best interest if Germany and Britain make peace—as a Frenchwoman, I'm sure of it. And I'm here to sell that separate peace to the Spanish." She smirked. "And if anyone has the ability to sell, well . . . *c'est moi.*"

They stopped at El Greco's *The Man with a Hand on His Chest.* The man in question was dressed in black, with a frothy white lace collar and cuffs.

"I like this one," Maggie said, still trying to gather her thoughts. "His eyes are kind." She tilted her head and considered. "Sad, but kind."

Chanel dropped Maggie's arm and stood with one hand on her hip. "Now, *this,*" she pronounced, "is *chic.* Do you see the plain black, the contrast of white lace? He's dressed almost like a Jesuit priest," she said approvingly. "I adore the Jesuits— they throw the best parties."

They moved on. "The war is . . . not going well for Germany. An understatement," Chanel added. "I expect the Allies to win, ultimately. Not immediately, of course, but eventually. And that's why there needs to be peace with Germany. Now. So Europe doesn't fall to the Soviets."

"The Soviet Union's one of the Allied nations," Maggie reminded her.

The couturiere sniffed. "Bolshevism will soon be everywhere," she said. "Like the Spanish flu. And Churchill knows all about Stalin's ruthlessness. I do believe he'd be relieved if Germany doesn't turn Communist."

"If and when the Allies invade France, they'll restore General de Gaulle as the leader. France will be France again. You'll realize you're—"

"What?" Chanel spun sharply and took a step toward Maggie. "I'm . . . what?"

"Betraying your country." Maggie didn't mince words. "By trying to broker a separate peace, you're betraying France."

Chanel drew herself up. "I will *save* France," she hissed. "Mark my words, if the Communists reach France first, there'll be a Soviet takeover of western Europe. And then . . . You think *this* is war? This, my girl, is only a preview. The real war is yet to come."

Maggie shivered. War between the Soviet Union and the United States. *With fission bombs. Well, let's win this one first, shall we?*

They said goodbye in front of the museum. "And now we return to our opposing camps." Maggie tried to joke about the hotels.

"*Au revoir*—see you at the embassy at four," Chanel said, starting off.

"Just one thing—" Maggie had to ask. "Who do you know in Britain to request me—'Paige Kelly'?"

Chanel stopped and turned on her heel. "Peter Frain," she said brightly. "He's an old and dear friend. I used to design clothes for his circle."

Maggie had an odd feeling in the pit of her stomach. "Who? Who did you design clothes for?"

"Any number of Englishwomen. Oh—La Hess, the opera singer, was one of them, too—living in London then." She laughed.

"Clara Hess?" Maggie managed. Clara Hess was her mother.

"Oh yes, Clara and Peter and I were close—we saw each other often when I was in London with Bendor." She gazed off into the distance. "I wonder whatever happened to her—Clara." She looked back at Maggie. "Do you know?"

If only . . . Speechless, she shook her head.

"Until this afternoon!" she called over her shoulder.

Maggie raised her hand to wave, but all she wanted to do was go back to the room so her knees could buckle in private. Was she pregnant? Could she be? *Well, I could* . . . And Peter Frain? Friends with Chanel and Clara Hess? Her *mother*?

Remembering the two tails, instead of taking the main street, Maggie slipped down Calle de Cervantes, a narrow cobblestoned street with small shops. One was selling painted fans and ruffled flamenco dresses. A florist shop displayed forced bulbs: snowdrops, paperwhites, and red amaryllis.

Next door was a tobacco shop, with black cigarillos and fat cigars in the windows. Maggie could hear rapid-fire Spanish coming from the shop as an old nag pulling an ice wagon passed. She pretended to contemplate the different brands of tobacco, using the plate-glass window as a mirror to search the street for anyone following her.

Satisfied for the moment, Maggie moved on. The street smelled of horse urine, the thick smoke of a hand-rolled cigarette, and a whiff of orange blossom cologne. A man with dark, slicked-back hair passed, carrying a copy of *Ya,* the pro-Franco and Catholic newspaper, under his arm. She watched as he stopped across the street, opening the paper, ostensibly reading. But she could see his eyes darting, watching the cars and pedestrians.

She decided to enter the next shop, spending an enormous amount of time choosing among a selection of tinned octopus, squid in ink, and sardines. Taking off her coat and holding it inside out over her arm, Chanel's scarf now wrapped around her hair, she slipped out through the shop's back door. She made it unfollowed to the Plaza de Santa Ana, not far from the hotel.

There she sat on a wooden bench, trying to catch her breath and take in everything Chanel had said. A horse-drawn carriage passed, along with carts pulled by bony mules and the odd car. Many of the women wore all black, she noticed, trying to distract herself, fringed scarves protecting their faces from the wind. Just as many men wore capes as overcoats.

But despite the charm the scene presented, she stared at nothing as she contemplated three new facts:

Coco Chanel knew her mother.

Peter Frain had set up Maggie's mission to Spain.

And she herself might be pregnant.

Chapter Eighteen

Another enormous fresh bouquet of red roses awaited Maggie in her room. She pulled the card from the arrangement and opened it: it read, *Saludos de Juanito Belmonte.*

She tossed it on the desk next to the morning's roses, then carefully placed her purse with the gun on the bedside table and threw herself on the bed. The last thing she needed to deal with was a lovesick bullfighter.

Could she be pregnant? She tried to think of her last period and couldn't. *October? Maybe?* Ever since the war had begun, they'd been irregular; she'd put it down to stress and rationing. *Is that why I missed recognizing Belmonte?* she thought.

The telephone rang, interrupting her thoughts. With a groan, Maggie rose and answered.

"Señorita Kelly?" a burnished bass voice asked. It wasn't Ángel.

Maggie's heart beat faster. "Yes."

"I am Juanito Belmonte." There was a protracted silence, as though he expected thunderous applause, or at least a squeal or high-pitched giggle.

Maggie had no time or energy. "Yes?"

"I—" He sounded a bit surprised. "I'd like to take you to buy violet sweets."

"Excuse me?"

"There's a special shop that sells violet sweets in la Plaza de Canalejas. It's one of Madrid's delicacies. You *must* try them."

Well, this is . . . unexpected, she thought. *Perhaps it will work as a cover? To be seen out and about with a bullfighter? Hide in plain sight? It might dissuade any of the tails from following.* "When would you like to shop for these violet sweets, Señor Belmonte?"

"Today. After *la siesta.*"

"I have a meeting," Maggie told him.

There was a long pause, as if he hadn't expected her to have plans of her own. Or not instantly reschedule them. "Then tomorrow?"

Maybe he has some connection to the Heisenberg events? "Yes, tomorrow. What time?"

"I'll pick you up from your hotel at ten in the morning. Please wait for me in the lobby."

"How will I recognize you?"

"Oh . . ." There was a pause, as if he'd stifled a laugh. "You will know."

Typical business hours in Madrid began at ten or eleven in the morning. There was a break for lunch and siesta, and then business again from four to eight in the evening. After that was tapas and, after ten or eleven, dinner.

The British Embassy, however, operated on English time. Maggie was expected to arrive at three, an hour before Chanel. The embassy was in the Castilla neighborhood, an old and dignified diplomatic quarter, on Calle de Fernando el Santo, next door to the residence of the German ambassador. She wondered how that juxtaposition had come about and if the two statesmen glared at each other coming and going or just pretended not to see each other.

When Maggie arrived, she noted the palatial building must

have been shelled during the Civil War. Part of the grand façade was much newer than the rest, which was scarred with bullet holes. Still, there were wrought-iron gates and manicured gardens, along with an enormous Union Jack flag snapping in the brisk wind.

Inside, the offices were noisy, fueled by an arsenal of radios, mimeograph machines, clacking typewriters, and ringing telephones. To Maggie it felt very, very British—and she could easily picture herself back in London for a moment.

A tall and dapper golden-haired young man strode to her, flashing a wide grin. With his Savile Row suit, slightly askew tie, and polished Church's brogues, he was unmistakably *not* Spanish.

"Good afternoon, Miss Kelly. Welcome to the British Embassy. I'm Tom Burns—press attaché and your personal guide to Madrid." He bowed. "At your service."

"How do you do?" Maggie responded.

As Burns led her through chilly, high-ceilinged rooms filled with French and Spanish antiques and tapestries to Ambassador Hoare's office, he kept up a steady patter of conversation. He had an ironic way of speaking, the perfect balance of joking and serious, with a public school accent. Englishmen were often like that—often joking—it helped them cope with their feelings, David had once told her.

Burns excused himself and left her alone on a leather chair in Hoare's office, mentally reviewing everything she knew about the man.

When Churchill had become Prime Minister in 1940, he'd made Hoare ambassador and sent him to Spain; many had speculated it was a way to banish Hoare, an appeaser and Chamberlain supporter. Hoare had lobbied for Viceroy of India, but Churchill had denied him. Still, he'd spent the war doing an admirable job here, especially regarding British Gibraltar.

Taking in the office's massive mahogany desk, she couldn't help but think of a story Kim had told her, about how a bat had once flown into Hoare's office. According to Kim, the ambassador had hidden under his desk, crying for the tiny bat to be taken away.

The office, like the desk, was large and imposing, with a gold-framed portrait of the King on the wall. The tall windows looked down onto a courtyard with a bare garden, rosebushes wrapped in burlap. An old globe was positioned in one corner, all the European countries in their prewar colors and shapes.

When Ambassador Hoare entered, wearing an impeccably tailored striped charcoal suit, he didn't bother with a greeting. "I've done everything humanly possible to keep Spain out of the war—and I *won't* have it jeopardized," he told Maggie in a thin voice, walking around his desk. "And certainly not by two women and their nonsense." He unbuttoned his jacket and took a seat, shuffling papers, obviously displeased.

Maggie had a sudden recollection of how Churchill used to say the ambassador was "descended from a long line of maiden aunts" and bit her lip. It was certainly not the first time she'd been underestimated or dismissed.

She rose and offered her hand across the desk. "I'm Major Margaret Hope, Ambassador Hoare," she said. "With SOE. And as we established last night, my operative name is Paige Kelly. I'd appreciate your remembering that."

Hoare raised pale green eyes to hers and reluctantly reached to grasp her hand, not even standing. She felt his fingers beneath hers, bony and chill.

"SOE," he said disdainfully. He frowned. "This 'Special Operations Executive' madness is one of Winston's harebrained ideas, you know. 'Set Europe ablaze'—indeed!" He snorted. "But who must put out the fires when the games are over? SOE is cheerfully mucking up the fine work MI-Six is doing."

Maggie sat. "Sir, I've no intention of setting anything ablaze, nor muck stirring. I'm here simply to gather information."

He glared. Then his thin face sagged, and he graced her with a wintry smile. "I know it's not you," he admitted. "It's Winston—Winston, with his adventures, and secret missions, and spy toys." He scoffed. "Winston thinks war's like a novel. Or—God help us—a Hollywood film."

Maggie held her tongue.

"And I know what the Communists are like," he continued. "Firsthand! I was in Russia when she fell to the Reds. When they killed the Tsar in 'eighteen." He ran a hand through his thinning hair. "We're in a new phase of the war, Miss Hope. We must be just as careful of Communists as Nazis."

"Miss Kelly, please," Maggie corrected him gently. "I prefer Mademoiselle doesn't learn my real name."

"Of course." In milder tones he continued. "Anyway I don't blame you," he said, "I blame Philby. Obviously, we don't believe in this"—he waved a thin hand—" 'separate peace' nonsense." He still looked peevish.

Well, I'm here to do a job. Which is more than meeting with Coco Chanel, she thought. She knew if Hoare had any idea of her real mission, he'd have her thrown into some sort of Spanish dungeon quicker than she could say "Don Quixote."

"Of course," she said in soothing tones. "But this meeting does give us a chance to learn more about the Germans from Mademoiselle Chanel—what they're thinking, what they might be planning. There's no end to the things she might know, let alone Baron von Dincklage."

"Flatter her and encourage her to talk. . . ." Hoare mused. He sighed. "Would you like tea, Miss Ho— Kelly?" It seemed a peace offering.

Always tea, she thought, but she appreciated the gesture. "No, but thank you, sir." She took a deep breath. "Ambassador Hoare, I know Kim Philby sent you my file. And if you've read it, you know that while I may be female, I'm a professional."

He grunted in acknowledgment. "Spain's vitally important to our winning the war, Miss Kelly. Their economy's in ruins. The Royal Navy controls Gibraltar and lets in just enough oil to keep the country functioning. And enough wheat to feed them through yet another bad harvest. There's no gold reserve to back the currency—Stalin made the republic send all of it to Moscow during the Civil War. Let's just say . . . he isn't eager to give it back."

Maggie folded her hands in her lap.

"And while Franco's always been rather . . . cozy with the Nazis, as long as Spain remains officially neutral, we're satisfied. That's the goal."

"I understand, sir." She decided on a new tactic. "And I'm sure it's not easy for one man to hold everything together."

"Exactly!" He exhaled and thawed considerably. "The regime was divided after the Civil War." He steepled his fingers. "The generals who won are 'good aristocrats,' who're sympathetic to Britain and want to keep Spain out of this war. It's my job—alone—to support them and their influence on Franco. This is how we keep the Falange under control. This is how we will reinstate the King."

"King Alfonso died in 1941," Maggie said. "Do you mean the Count of Barcelona?"

He leaned back. "Infante Juan, Count of Barcelona, *thinks* he'll take the throne as Juan the Third. He hopes."

Maggie knew Juan was the third son and designated heir of King Alfonso XIII of Spain and Victoria Eugenie of Battenberg, but his father had been removed by the Second Spanish Republic in 1931.

Hoare shook his head. "But no, I mean his son—Juan Carlos."

"Skipping over the father?" Maggie had been raised in the United States, but she knew how monarchy worked. *One does not skip a generation of royalty.* She imagined Aunt Edith's expression of horror at the very thought.

"Franco's raising the boy, Juan Carlos, himself. The general might be a fascist, but he's a monarchist at heart. Just like Winston. Even if it means bypassing Juan."

The Bakelite telephone on his desk rang and the ambassador picked up the receiver. "Send her in." He stood, buttoning his jacket. "Showtime, Miss Kelly."

Chapter Nineteen

Coco Chanel burst past Burns, who'd opened the door, and sashayed into the room enveloped in a jasmine-scented cloud of No. 5. She was wearing a gray cashmere suit, with ropes of pearls that dangled and swayed as she walked, and draped in a fox fur stole.

Coco can certainly make an entrance, Maggie had to admit. The couturiere smiled coquettishly at the ambassador. "Sam!" she exclaimed. "How lovely to see you again."

He walked over to kiss her kid-gloved hand. "*Enchanté,* Coco. Madrid agrees with you."

"It's lovely here, thank you." Chanel nodded to Maggie as she took the seat next to her. Maggie felt the fox's glass eyes upon her. They were crossed and glittering, looking a bit mad. "Who'd have thought, back in the day, we'd meet in Madrid—and under these circumstances?"

"Indeed."

"And how's Lady Maud?"

Hoare smiled. "My wife's quite tired of Spain, thank you—wants nothing more than to return to England."

Chanel giggled. "Can you blame her?" she said, fingering her pearls.

"And how's Paris's Hôtel Ritz?" There was an edge in his voice, Maggie noted. He was calling her a collaborator.

"*C'est la guerre*, Sam," she said with her most Gallic shrug. "Of course, that's why I'm here. To end the war."

Maggie could see Hoare struggling to bite his tongue. "I look forward to hearing all you have to say, Coco. Please." He waved his hand and sat back, folding his arms across his chest. "Begin."

Chanel waited as his secretary brought in a tea tray, placing it on the table. Maggie nodded to the woman, who left; she herself began to pour the steaming black tea into porcelain cups. It would keep her hands busy and might put Hoare and Chanel at ease.

"I take lemon," Chanel told her, and Maggie added a glistening yellow slice to the saucer. She handed another cup to the ambassador, then poured one for herself. They all ignored the plum pastries, even though Maggie's stomach was rumbling. *Pregnancy craving or just the sight of nonrationed food?* she wondered. Then, *Stop it! Focus!*

"Sam, I'm reaching out to you as a dear old friend," Chanel began. "And because I think that together we can achieve something important. Historic, even. Something to bring about the end of this ghastly war—and sooner rather than later."

Hoare took a sip of tea. "I'm all ears." He set down his cup and saucer and leaned forward.

Chanel crossed one slender ankle behind the other. "Before we start, I wish to establish that despite living in an occupied country, I'm a Frenchwoman, first and foremost. I watched as France was defeated. It was a cruel blow."

Maggie watched Hoare's face carefully. To his credit, the ambassador gave nothing away, except for a small involuntary twitch under one eye.

"The Occupation's been horrible for France, of course, but there *is* a silver lining. While conditions haven't always been . . . optimal, I *do* believe the Germans have brought a certain order to my country." Maggie stifled a snort. "And I'll say life is tolerable—indeed, more than tolerable—under the Germans."

If you're Coco Chanel, live at the Ritz, and dine at Maxim's, it might seem that way, Maggie thought. *Certainly not if you're Jewish.* She remembered the roundup of the "undesirables" at Paris's Vél d'Hiver, an indoor cycling track in Paris. *Is that what she thinks of as "order"? Rounding people up? Detaining them unlawfully? Sending them to concentration camps and who knows what fate?*

Chanel continued. "And I do believe England making a truce with Germany is the only hope for Europe, as we know it, to survive."

"You believe the Soviets are that dire a threat?" Hoare asked.

"I do," the couturiere said, folding gray-gloved hands. "I believe they're a far greater threat than the Nazis, especially the Nazis with Hitler removed. Oh, yes. I've come to know several of the German generals in Paris—not Nazis, but *Germans,*" she emphasized, "and I believe they have good intentions."

Maggie watched in silence as Coco Chanel sold out France. The enormity of it was breath-stopping.

"And so," Chanel said, opening her handbag and pulling out a thick envelope. *To Prime Minister Winston Churchill* was written on the front in old-fashioned French script. The word *PRIVATE* was underlined three times. "I come bearing good news: a peace offer from Walter Schellenberg. *Not* Hitler, you must understand—let's just say he won't be in play much longer—but *Germany.* I present this letter from Schellenberg, with a cover letter from me, encouraging the Prime Minister to read it and to take the peace offer seriously."

Hoare steepled his fingers. "Coco—"

"Oh, I know," she said, smiling and fluttering spidery mascaraed lashes. "I'm a mere woman. But, given my life abroad,

I'm uniquely connected to various individuals who can bridge this gap between countries. When Winston hears the letter's from me, of course he'll accept it. And when he reads it, I know he'll make the right decision."

Hoare shrugged. "Perhaps."

Bollocks, Maggie thought.

"If only I could go to London to deliver it myself . . ."

Hoare stared at her sharply. "We both know that with your . . . affiliations, that would be unwise. Dangerous, even."

Chanel shrugged thin shoulders. "You of all people know the Soviets are worse than the Nazis," she said. "You were in St. Petersburg for the revolution! When the Bolsheviks killed the royal family! You've remained friends with the White Russians who survived the bloodbath and fled to London. You *know* a peace with Germany would save France from communism."

"You're not wrong in one regard, Coco." He glanced to Maggie. "The Soviets *are* a danger."

"I know." Chanel grinned like a Cheshire cat. "I'm never wrong."

Hoare reached out his hand for the envelope, but instead Chanel handed it to Maggie, who accepted it. "Miss Kelly, you'll personally deliver this letter to the Prime Minister? I have your word?"

"Yes, Mademoiselle. I give you my word."

"I assure you—" Hoare began, annoyed.

"No." Chanel overrode him. "Miss Kelly owes me a favor. She owes me her *life*. And if anyone can tender this peace offer directly to Winston Churchill, it's she." She looked to Maggie. "I trust her."

Maggie carefully placed the envelope in her purse. "I'll deliver this message directly to the P.M.," she told them both. "I promise."

"Winston never could turn down a good dinner invitation," Hoare said drily.

"Which is why I believe he'll be amenable," Chanel added.

He leaned forward and said gently, "Just because you've played bezique with the man doesn't mean—"

"You've no idea of the extent of my friendship with Winston Churchill," Chanel snapped. "And the things I know about him—*especially* regarding his dealings with the Duke of Windsor."

Hoare raised his eyebrows as if surprised, Maggie noted.

"Winston violated his own Trading with the Enemy Act— a criminal offense," the couturiere continued, "to protect the Duke of Windsor's property in Paris. And I know several, shall we say, *unsavory* secrets of the Duke and Duchess of Windsor as well. Secrets the British press could and would use to excoriate the royal family."

So there it is, Maggie thought. *Coco Chanel has something on Mr. Churchill and the royals. Blackmail.* She knew Chanel had been close friends with the Duke and Duchess of Windsor. Could it be something about their relationship with the Nazis? And General Schellenberg and his plot to place them back on the throne when Germany invaded England?

"The Soviet Union's the real enemy of France, and of Britain," she insisted. "And, even if she doesn't know it yet, the United States. This truce *must* come to fruition. If not, Europe as we know it will be a memory, replaced by the horrors of Communism. And I don't need to remind you if France turns Communist, the English Channel's not that wide."

"We've been doing a fine job keeping our enemies out so far," Hoare said lightly. But his face was pale. "I'm particularly interested why you asked for Miss Kelly as your go-between."

"Oh, Sam," she began with a touch of sympathy, "I don't trust you or any of your staff to relay my message. Miss Kelly, however, was working as an undercover agent in Paris a few years ago. I saved her life. She owes me. And I'd like to think the action endeared me, at least a bit, to Peter Frain of MI-Five."

And you knew Peter, and Clara, when you lived in London. . . . But that wasn't relevant now. Maggie and Hoare exchanged a quick glance. They both knew this deal of a separate peace for Germany and Britain, with France subservient, was treason. She was betraying France, selling her out to the Nazis.

"It's true," Maggie told them. "I wouldn't be here today without Mademoiselle's help. But I'm British through and through. I've certainly done my bit and more for the war effort. And despite owing Mademoiselle my life, as well as the success of that mission—which was of utmost importance to the war effort—I would never do anything I thought would compromise my integrity, or Mr. Churchill's."

Chanel angled her chin and began to worry at one of her bracelets.

"However," Maggie continued, "I do sincerely believe the Prime Minister will throw this message in the nearest fireplace without opening it. I'll bet my life on it. No matter what sort of blackmail you may possess."

"We'll see" was all Chanel said.

"Which is why I've agreed to deliver it."

Hoare cleared his throat. "I'm sure you have a full schedule, Coco—with all your contacts here." He picked up the telephone receiver. "Send in Mr. Burns."

Burns materialized and bowed to Chanel. "Mademoiselle, you may know I write a little weekly newspaper for expats here in Madrid. Is there anything you'd like to say to them? Something I can quote you on?"

"You may write I'm thinking of opening a new boutique in Madrid, to sell Chanel Number Five," Chanel said grandly. "In fact, I'm happy to send some bottles to all the women in your office."

"Well, there we have it," Hoare said, rising.

"Good!" Chanel stood as well, then Maggie. "Now that this mission is out of the way, I shall enjoy my time in Madrid, scouting for that new shop location."

"Miss Kelly," the ambassador asked, "when do you return to England?"

Maggie rose. "I have another piece of business to attend to first."

"And what's coming up on your dance card?" Hoare asked Chanel.

"I've been asked to go to an event for someone named Heisenwell . . . Heisenstein?"

Maggie could hear her pulse drumming in her ears. "Professor Werner Heisenberg?"

"Yes, that's it. Day after tomorrow. The German Embassy invited me to attend his lecture at the university—but it sounds deathly boring. But I *am* attending the reception at the Palacio Real Thursday."

"You know," Maggie said carefully, "I'd love to go to the professor's lecture."

Chanel sniffed as she adjusted her fox stole. "I doubt a lecture will be sold out." Her disdain was palpable.

"There's going to be heavy security, I'm sure. Is there a way to put my name on their list?" Maggie asked.

"Miss Kelly, I have a friend at the Irish Embassy," Burns told her. "I'll telephone over and see what I can do. As an Irish citizen, from another neutral nation, you'll most likely be admitted."

The smile froze on Maggie's face. "I never told you I was an Irish citizen, Mr. Burns."

"I make it my business to know these things, Miss Kelly."

"If you'll excuse me," Maggie said to all of them. "I'd like to bring Mademoiselle's letter to the hotel and put it in the safe now."

"Why don't you let me drive you back to your hotel?" Burns said.

"Thank you." *If Kim's so concerned about Burns, here's a great opportunity to learn exactly what I'm dealing with.* Her stomach rumbled. "But first, why don't we have lunch?"

Chapter Twenty

Maggie wanted to learn more about Tom Burns. And she was incredibly hungry. Having lunch with him would solve both problems.

"If Paris is a woman, then Madrid's a man," Burns said as they were seated at the English-style Embassy tearoom in Salamanca, on the Paseo de la Castellana. Only a small Lutheran church stood between its front door and the entrance to the German Embassy, festooned with swastika flags. A waiter in a white shirt and red sash left them with two menus. "But this little corner of the world's all British."

It might look like a typical small and crowded English tearoom, Maggie thought, listening to the ambient conversations over the clink of china and scrape of forks, *but it sounds like the tower of Babel.* There were Spaniards, British, Portuguese, Americans, Germans, Basque, and French together, sipping drinks. *All together, despite the war,* she thought. In the background, a wireless played Vivaldi.

They sat at a small round table near the large square windows, which displayed delicate pastries and candied fruits. On the walls were framed oil paintings of woodland scenes. Maggie was grateful for all the face memorization she'd done in training. In one corner, she noted, Baron von Stohrer was sipping rioja with a bishop, while Ambassador Hoare's wife took tea and picked at a lemon tart with the famous flamenco dancer Carmen Amaya.

"This place's so close to the embassies, it's a de facto meeting place for diplomats," Burns told her. "The owner's Margarita Kearney Taylor, an Irishwoman from France, who brought the concept of British high tea to Madrid."

"Sounds like a good place for an expat, then," Maggie quipped. "Do you come here often?"

"I've been known to stop in for a cucumber sandwich or two when I feel a bit homesick," he admitted. "And the tea's perfect. But for your first time, I recommend hot chocolate and churros. Would you like that?"

Maggie smiled. "I would." Burns waved over a waiter sneaking a glass of beer behind the register and ordered for them.

A fly buzzed in the window's corner, trapped, as Maggie contemplated Burns. "Tell me: How did an Irishwoman come to open an English tearoom in Madrid?"

"Madame Taylor moved to Madrid in the late twenties from Paris," he told her. "She married a Spanish diplomat, José María Linares Rivas, counsel to Spanish dictator Miguel Primo de Rivera, and came here for his work."

"Dictators seem to grow here like weeds," Maggie said, spreading her linen napkin in her lap. She decided to be blunt. "I've heard you're an admirer of General Franco's."

"I think he's . . . a good leader for Spain," Burns said carefully. "At least right now. Considering the alternatives. You know, the Civil War is presented as something almost . . . romantic. Especially by Hemingway. But the Communists, under Stalin, were worse—so much worse—than the general and his supporters." He looked her in the eye. "But you must know something about me."

"What's that?"

"When they played 'Deutschland über Alles' before a

bullfight—in honor of some German dignitaries in attendance—I wouldn't sing. I wouldn't stand. In the end, the police were called. They placed me under arrest and handcuffed me. Dragged me out of the ring. I spent a week in jail."

Maggie nodded with respect. *Good for you,* she thought. *Now* this *is something Kim and Ángel never mentioned.*

"Madame opened the Embassy in the early thirties—a discreet place for the ladies of Madrid to take tea and cakes. And the option of ordering a cocktail." He smiled.

"I must say," Maggie said in a low voice, "that, for me, it's strange to see Nazis and Allies mix together so . . . nonchalantly."

"It takes some getting used to when you first arrive, I know," Burns told her. "But eventually it begins to feel normal. Or at least what passes for normal these days."

A small, delicate-framed woman with dark hair and green eyes arrived at their table. "How are you today, Mr. Burns?" she said in an almost theatrical way. Her English was seasoned with a lilting Irish brogue.

"Well, Madame Taylor," he said, rising and kissing her on both cheeks. "May I present Miss Paige Kelly. She's your countrywoman, from Ireland."

"How do you do?" Maggie said.

"Interesting accent you have," Madame Taylor said with a honey-dipped smile.

"I grew up in Boston."

"Ah. And how do you know Mr. Burns?"

Maggie thought quickly. "I was visiting the British Embassy today. Mr. Burns was kind enough to suggest coming here. It's a beautiful spot."

Madame Taylor didn't seem convinced, but said only, "Don't hesitate to ask if you need anything."

When Madame left, Maggie turned her focus on her companion. "Tell me about yourself, Mr. Burns—how did an Englishman end up at the embassy in Spain?"

"I may be British, but I was born in Chile, actually. My father's Scottish and my mother Chilean, descended from the Basques. That's why I'm bilingual, which has come in handy here. I had a Jesuit education, first at Wimbledon and then at Stonyhurst."

"I worked in book publishing in London," he told her. "Edited Graham Greene's *The Lawless Roads*. That led to *The Power and the Glory*."

"I've read both of them," Maggie said. "About a 'whiskey priest' on the run in Mexico."

"About a saint," Burns countered.

Without warning, the wireless station shifted, and the music stopped. A strong female voice on the radio exhorted, "*Comrades, do not despair. Your brothers in southern France are grouping to retake our beloved motherland!*"

"That's La Pasionaria, speaking from Moscow," Burns told her. "The Soviet woman who inspired the Communists. One of the waiters must have changed the station."

"*Spaniards! Beware the American imperialists!*" she continued. "*When this war ends, the good Soviet people will eliminate the seat of the capitalistic system, the United States of America.*"

"Turn it off!" the German ambassador called, while Mrs. Hoare nodded in agreement. The music resumed and the patrons returned to their conversations.

Burns looked at Maggie as she took in what she had heard. "It's hard to believe the Soviets would broadcast propaganda against their allies—and so blatantly," she said finally. *Maybe the next war really has already begun,* she thought.

"The Allies and the Soviet Union have a mutual enemy, for now," he said as the waiter placed two cups of thick hot chocolate before them, accompanied by a plate of fried churros dusted in powdered sugar. "Here," he said, picking one up in his fingers. "You dip it in the chocolate, like this. . . ." He scooped a generous amount of thick, glistening chocolate on his churro and took a bite, eyes closing in pleasure.

"Are you saying, 'the enemy of my enemy is my friend'?"

"I'm saying all sides are preparing for what comes after the war. And I also believe there're any number of high-powered Communists embedded in the highest ranks of British intelligence."

"You mean fifth columnists?" Maggie also took a bite of churro and chocolate. It *was* delicious. For a moment there was just the bliss of sweetness and pastry. Then dark thoughts intruded. *In MI-5 and MI-6? In SOE?*

"Fifth columnists. Exactly."

It was hard to believe. She dabbed her mouth with a napkin. "What evidence do you have?"

"I can't say—but I'm afraid it's true," he told her. "Please be careful in Madrid," he said. "Not everyone's who they appear to be."

That's funny, she thought, helping herself to another churro. *That's what everyone's saying about you.*

Driving back to the Palace Hotel, Burns told her, "Sorry if Hoare was rough on you in the interview. He doesn't trust anyone from Philby's camp."

"I've endured worse," Maggie told him.

"The ambassador allows intelligence gathering, but no espionage here, nothing that could antagonize the regime."

She felt the statement contained a warning. *Well then, it's a very good thing he doesn't know what's planned.*

Burns pulled up to the entrance of the Palace and Maggie waited until one of the bellboys opened her door. Before she

exited the car, he passed her his card. "In case you need anything in Madrid," he told her. "It's a tricky town. Anything can
happen."

She accepted the card and put it in her purse. "Thank you,
Mr. Burns. I'll keep that in mind."

"Please, call me Tom."

"Good afternoon, Mr. Burns."

Chapter Twenty-one

At the Palace Hotel's reception desk, Maggie stopped in front of the man on duty. Short and rotund, he wore a charcoal flannel suit with a carnation pinned to his lapel. When he saw Maggie he erased the anxious expression on his face and smiled broadly.

Maggie made sure no one else was in earshot, then said, "*Buenos tardes, señor.*" In her best limited Spanish, she continued, "*¿Cómo está? Mi nombre es Paige Kelly.*"

"Good afternoon, Miss Kelly," he replied in perfect English. She was a bit disappointed the basic phrases she'd worked so hard to learn were being ignored. "I have a message for you." He pulled a folded note from the letter boxes behind him and handed it to her. It was from Ángel, asking her to meet him at Cervecería Alemana at Plaza de Santa Ana when she returned. She tucked it into her coat pocket.

"Anything else today, miss?" he asked.

"I'd like to use one of the hotel's safe-deposit boxes, please."

He came from behind the counter, bowing slightly. "Follow me, miss." He took her to the elevators. The hotel's lower level was paneled in dark wood and lit by wall sconces. The man sitting at a large desk looked up. He was older, broader, and more muscular than the first, with a hint of menace. "This young lady would like a safe-deposit box," the round man told him.

Maggie showed her passport and room key, and in return was given a large steel case with a key in its lock. The tall man showed her to a private room. "Here you are, miss," he told her. "This is your key. Keep it safe. The only other way to open the box is to have a locksmith force it open. Please let us know when you're finished."

"Thank you." In the tiny room, with a desk and chair lit by a green banker's light, she opened her purse and took out the envelope. She opened the box, lined with red felt, and placed the document inside, locking it. She gazed at it for a long moment before she picked it up and pulled back the curtain.

"Very good, miss." She placed the locked metal box on the counter. "We'll take care of this for you." He handed her the key, which she placed in an inside pocket of her purse.

"*Gracias,*" she said, trying again with Spanish.

He ignored her effort. "You're welcome, Miss Kelly." He stood and picked the box up, ready to take it to the back. "We'll keep it secure for you, never fear."

Cervecería Alemana was a German beer bar and restaurant not far from the Palacio Hotel. Maggie was relieved to see no Nazi flags or regalia, though there were brightly painted German beer steins lining the wood-paneled walls and a large Bavarian mirror hung over the bar. She slipped onto a bench beside Ángel, who was drinking a beer. There were only a few other patrons. From their position they could see both the front and back doors; no one was close enough to overhear them.

"They say Hemingway loved drinking here," Ángel told her. "Although if you believe all the signs around town saying, 'Hemingway drank here,' you'd think he didn't miss a single bar."

He looked at her. "So—where is it?"

"What?"

"The letter." He scoffed. "From our French friend."

"It's safe," Maggie told him, raising a hand to signal one of the silent and graceful waiters.

" 'It's *safe*'?" He didn't seem to be expecting that. "You're supposed to give it to me!"

"Why?" She asked the waiter for a tonic, no gin.

"Because I can protect it," he said. "Better than any hotel." She could see the anger in his eyes.

"It's fine," she insisted. "It's my mission—and I'll keep track of it. It's not in my room—it's downstairs in one of the hotel's safe-deposit boxes."

Ángel said nothing but stared out the window at the passersby in the Plaza de Santa Ana, eyes dark. Finally, he turned back to her. "And the other part of your mission?"

"He's giving a lecture at the university. Tom Burns said he'd ask someone at the Irish Embassy if he can put my name on the guest list."

"Burns?" he asked, displeased. "You spoke with Tom Burns?"

"Yes, the press attaché. I met him at Ambassador Hoare's office today."

They were silent as the waiter put down Maggie's tonic, garnished with dried orange slices, rosemary sprigs, and juniper berries. Ángel made a face. "Be careful of that one," he warned. "Burns."

"Why?" Maggie took a sip, remembering Kim had told her the same thing. "What do you know about him?"

Ángel swallowed his beer. "He's Catholic."

"So?"

"He's pro-Franco."

"Well, I assume being a diplomat in Franco's Spain requires some fancy footwork."

"No—he's *really* pro-Franco. Pro–Catholic Church, pro-clergy, pro-Falange. And if he had any idea what your real mission with the German scientist is, he'd have you arrested and shot in a heartbeat."

"Well, he doesn't know."

Ángel exhaled through his teeth in frustration. "Keep it that way."

Maggie took another sip of her tonic. It made her nervous stomach feel better. She thought of how Aunt Edith would allow her ginger ale and crackers when she was sick as a girl. Probably not a bad morning sickness cure, either, even though it was late afternoon. "Do you think we could order some tapas?" she asked, glancing up at the day's menu printed neatly in *Fraktur* on a blackboard over the bar. "I'm *starving*."

Later, back in her hotel room, Maggie stripped naked in front of the mirror and inspected her body. Was Chanel right? She'd put on some weight from too many restaurant meals with John. "Happy fat," she'd thought of it, from being blissful and relaxed after such a long time of uncertainty.

But now she wondered. Her breasts were larger, and her abdomen protruded a bit more than usual. And under the fluorescent bathroom light, her veins stood out bright blue against her pale skin, as in a medical diagram. If she were pregnant, Maggie knew, her circulatory system would be the first to grow, to provide oxygen to the baby—hence more prominent veins. She put a hand to her abdomen and cupped it gently. "Bean," she murmured with affection. "Little Bean. We'll make it through this."

She wished, more than anything, she could tell John. See his face as shock dissolved into joy. Have him place his hands on her belly. Finally, they would be a family. Still, it could wait. It had to wait. She had a job to do first.

There was a knock, and she shrugged into her robe. "*Hola,*" she called through the door. "*¿Quién es?*"

"Is this Miss Paige Kelly?" came a voice in plummy English. She recognized the speaker as Tom Burns.

"It is," she replied, shocked. "Mr. Burns?"

"Indeed. I'm awfully sorry to bother you at the hotel, Miss Kelly, but I wanted to deliver the news in person."

Maggie undid the locks on the door and opened it a crack. "What's happened?"

"I'm afraid I've bad news, Miss Kelly," he told her. "My contact at the Irish Embassy can't put you on the approved list for Professor Heisenberg's lecture," he said. "Security's tight, for obvious reasons."

Maggie clenched her hands; she felt sick with frustration. She'd been so close! And Heisenberg—in a physics lecture, not a social setting—might just give something away regarding the status of the Nazi fission program.

"Well, thank you for trying," she said slowly. "Is there anyone else you could ask?"

"Afraid not," he told her. "You're . . . quite keen to meet him," he said delicately. "Why?"

Maggie lifted her head. "I'm a former mathematics student, interested in quantum mechanics," she said. "To hear the professor lecture—why, it's historic. He's brilliant. A voice of his generation."

"I feel there's something you're not telling me."

"No."

He leaned in, placing his foot so she couldn't close the door on him. "Miss Kelly," he asked directly. "Do you plan to assassinate Werner Heisenberg?"

Maggie's heart skipped a beat. "*Assassinate* him?" She feigned shock, even as she felt the cold fear of possible discovery. "How could you think such a thing? He's a groundbreaking physicist! How often in your life have you gotten the opportunity to hear a Nobel Prize winner speak? Do you think people from SOE are just killers for hire, and not trained agents?"

She pulled the robe around her more tightly. "I've no desire to assassinate anyone, Mr. Burns." *That's the truth.*

But she now knew British intelligence—or at least Burns— was on to her. Her ears rang and her vision blurred. *The Gestapo could be next.* "Thank you," she said, increasing the door's pressure on his foot until he removed it. "And good night."

Chapter Twenty-two

Maggie arrived in the lobby of the Palace Hotel the next morning. She checked her wristwatch: ten o'clock, exactly on time. She took a seat under the stained-glass rotunda, keeping a careful lookout, wondering if Juanito Belmonte was going to be late, or even show at all.

The lobby, usually a staid, stately place, was bustling. Maggie could see a crowd gathered by the long receptionist counter, just inside the hotel's front doors. The hum of animated conversation was loud and punctuated with high-pitched giggles. She stood, walked over, then rose on tiptoes on the fringe of the crowd, to see what was going on.

At the center of the storm was a man. He was wearing a dark blue double-breasted suit, with a black wool Seseña cape lined in purple velvet slung elegantly over his shoulders. He was smiling, chatting, and signing autographs. One of the concierge staff was bent over in front of him, offering his back as a sort of desk.

He was signing everything for people—menus, receipts, handkerchiefs, even people's hands and forearms. They exclaimed in gratitude and thanked him profusely. One young woman who received an autograph on her palm turned pale, as if she might faint, and clutched her friend. A gray-haired man in a fedora wiped away a tear.

Must be a celebrity, Maggie thought. *Player from Real Madrid, the city's legendary soccer team?* Then she realized the man was Juanito. Juanito Belmonte, the famous bull slayer. No wonder he'd told her she'd recognize him in the lobby! Maggie was annoyed with herself for missing the connection between the newspaper photo, seeing him at the hotel, and then at the party. *What on earth is wrong with me?* she thought.

He was obviously beloved by the public. She was a bit impressed, despite herself, and watched as he took the time to greet each *aficionado* and speak with them individually, looking them in the eyes and favoring each with a broad smile and bow before moving on to the next.

Juanito caught sight of her in the crowd. "Señorita Kelly!" he called in a resonant, golden voice. "Over here, if you please!"

The crowd parted respectfully as Maggie made her way through; some stopped and stared, mouths agape. Juanito bent low and kissed her gloved hand. His eyes twinkled with mischief, and he winked. "I *told* you you'd recognize me in the lobby."

Joke's on me, she thought. "You did indeed."

To the crowd, in Spanish, he said, "So good to see you all! You must excuse me, I now have a date with this beautiful young lady."

He offered Maggie his arm, and she took it. Underneath his cashmere suit jacket, it was lean and ropy, with hard muscles. Multiple men in hotel livery and white gloves tripped over one another to open the doors for them.

Outside, on the curved driveway, was Juanito's car, a glossy cream-colored Bugatti Royale convertible. Maggie's eyebrows raised. *I'm guessing star bullfighters in Madrid are well paid,* she thought. *Like Hollywood movie stars.*

"May I call you Paige?" he asked when she was settled in the tan leather passenger seat. With a last wave to the crowd, he shifted the car into first gear and pulled out.

"Of course." Maggie smiled as they passed the square with the statue of Cervantes. He shifted into second and then third gear, and the car's engine purred. "How do you do, Señor Belmonte? That was quite an entrance."

He grinned modestly. "Call me Juanito, please." People stopped short on the sidewalks, grinning and flailing madly when they caught sight of the distinctive shiny car. Juanito waved back. Maggie felt almost as if they were in a parade.

The ride was short, less than fifteen minutes. *We could have walked,* she thought. But she realized if he'd been stopped and mobbed on the sidewalks the way he'd been in the hotel, it would have taken them hours to reach their destination.

Maggie's senses felt heightened: she saw everything with immense clarity. People in cafés were eating *pan con tomate,* the red of the tomato bright as rubies. The scent of frying squid wafting from a restaurant window made her mouth water and stomach rumble. They passed bookstores, a fountain pen shop, a shop selling ruffled flamenco dresses and Cuban-heeled shoes, as well as a perfumer whose windows were overflowing with boxes of Dana's Tabu, 20 Carats, and Sirocco Donna.

Juanito rolled to a stop in the Plaza de Canalejas, in front of an elegant shop with a dark wooden façade. The sign above the door read *La Violeta* in a graceful font. The windows were filled with white boxes tied in delicate purple ribbons, topped with bouquets of indigo silk violets.

A well-dressed, mustached man wearing a lavender silk tie greeted Juanito with a low bow as he emerged from the driver's seat, then came around to open the car door for Maggie. "*Señorita,* you honor us with your presence," he said, offering a hand. "I'm the owner of La Violeta—welcome."

She grasped it. "Thank you, *señor.*"

"When you visit Madrid, you *must* have violet sweets," Juanito told her on the sidewalk, again offering his arm. "One of my favorite childhood memories is my nanny taking me here to buy *violetas*—and going to the zoo in Retiro."

Inside were dark-wood walls and glass-covered counters. The air smelled of the rich jammy perfume of violet candy. Juanito pointed out flowers glazed with sugar, purple bags of tea, and round chocolates topped with candied petals. Maggie took a deep inhale as she looked around. "This survived the war?" she asked as they examined different displays.

"It did!" Juanito told her proudly. "Opened in 1915 and never closed, not even during the worst of the fighting. Not even with sugar shortages." He smiled at the owner. "I don't know how you did it, my friend!"

The man bowed, then brought them an open tin of tiny sugar-frosted flower-shaped candies. "Please try, *señorita*," he told Maggie.

She took one of the purple bonbons. It tasted sweet, yes, and perfumy, but also fruity, like blackberry. "Delicious!"

"La Violeta's an icon of the city of Madrid," the man said. "Beloved by everyone, including royalty—King Alfonso bought violet candies both for his wife, Queen Victoria Eugenie, and his mistress, Carmen Ruiz Moragas."

"Mmm," Maggie replied through the candy.

Juanito pointed to delicacies on the glass-covered counters as shopgirls scurried to wrap them in white paper and tie them with dainty satin ribbons. When he was finished, he told the owner, "Thank you, once again, my friend. We'll be in the car."

Maggie followed him out the door, confused. "But what about the candies?"

"In Spain," he said, opening the car door with a flourish, "gentlemen *never* carry packages."

The owner reappeared, carrying a large bag filled with boxes and boxes of candy, which he placed carefully in the car's trunk. "*¡Adiós!*" he said with a wide grin. Then, to Maggie, "Enjoy, *señorita*!"

Maggie settled into the passenger seat as Juanito pulled out. "What now?" she asked, intrigued. She glanced back and checked to make sure they weren't being followed.

"The park!" he said with an impish glint in his eye. She could, in that moment, see him as an adorable boy, one taken by his nanny to the sweet shop.

She instinctively put a hand to her lower abdomen. *What if John and I are having a boy?* She suddenly had an image of pushing a pram through Queen Mary's Rose Gardens, the flowers in bright bloom. *Or a girl? Doesn't matter as long as the Bean's healthy.*

Chapter Twenty-three

Maggie and Juanito walked through the neoclassical arch of La Puerta de Alcalá. They entered Retiro Park, lawns dotted with old chestnut, oak, and acacia trees. Juanito chuckled at her brisk pace. "You Anglos always walk so fast! Why? Are you running from bandits?" He took a deep breath and slowly exhaled. "Here, in Madrid, we stroll."

Maggie thought of the pace in Boston and London, even Los Angeles. It was true: people walked briskly in all those places. In Madrid, she'd noticed people weren't slow, exactly, but they didn't rush either. Their pace was stately and dignified.

She forced herself to relax and take shorter steps as Juanito offered a white paper bag filled with violet candies. "You're right," she agreed, choosing one and then popping it in her mouth, savoring the sweetness of the candy in the fresh air, the sun warming her face. They passed a pair of iridescent black crows pecking in the grass. "This is lovely. Thank you for sharing your Madrid, Juanito."

The day was gorgeous, with a brilliantly blue sky and tattered cirrus clouds. There was a brisk wind from the sierras, but with the bright sun, the day wasn't cold, just chill enough to set both their faces glowing and stir the bare branches of the tall, thin poplar trees and the shorter, wider elms.

As they sauntered along the gravel path in companionable

silence, Maggie kept a sharp lookout out for tails. A group of shouting boys, maybe ten or so, played soccer on the patchy grass. A woman in a wheelchair, blankets over thin legs, was pushed by a rosy-cheeked girl. A man on a bench, his fedora pulled low over his face, read a newspaper. Maggie kept an eye on him. "You came here often as a child?" she asked.

"Almost every day," Juanito told her. "Still love it. It was built by King Felipe the Fourth in the sixteen hundreds—finally opened to the public in the last century."

Maggie could see damage to some of the trees from the shells and explosions of the Civil War. Still, nature was healing itself. As they progressed at a dignified pace, Juanito kept his hat low, so he wouldn't be recognized. Even so, she caught a few passersby trying to see if he were really "El Belmonte." A little boy opened his mouth to shout but then shut it, not wanting to be rude. A priest in a black cape and wide-brimmed hat grinned. Still, they gave him his privacy. The park was a sacred space for all *Madrileños*, even famous *toreros*.

"What were you like as a child?" His question brought her up short. Her childhood seemed a vanished dream of academic quads and banks of rhododendrons and walks around Lake Waban in Wellesley, Massachusetts. Of adventures in the woods with friends, with other faculty brats. Time spent in the library, poring over books. Yet also, she realized in hindsight, childhood had been a time of secrets, of repressed feelings, and hidden emotions. So many things left unsaid. "I suppose I was a typical only child. Self-reliant. Bookish. Reserved."

"Yes." His keen eyes seemed to penetrate her. "I can see that." They walked farther, a red squirrel scampering in front of them. "So why were you reserved, Paige? Were your parents unhappy?"

"I grew up with my aunt, not my parents," she told him. "She was English. Formal. Strict. I was told my parents died in a car accident. . . ." She knew she didn't want to share what she'd learned since. "How did *you* become a bullfighter?" she asked, changing the subject.

He bellowed with laughter. "You're my favorite person now," he told her, still chortling, "because all my life I've been compared—and not always favorably—to my father."

"I'm guessing your father's famous?"

He gave a snort. "Juan Belmonte is the greatest *torero*—bullfighter—who ever lived. Here, they speak of him in the same breath as Cervantes and Goya—he's even more famous than Franco."

"Is that allowed?" Maggie asked.

"Just don't say it too loudly."

"Is he still bullfighting?"

"He retired eight years ago." Juanito popped another violet candy in his mouth. "That's why I, a grown man, am still called 'Juanito.' To this day, he's John and I'm 'little John.'" He sighed. "And I will be, for the rest of my life." He sounded more resigned than bitter.

Certainly a lot to live up to, Maggie thought. She had a sudden vision of her mother, Clara Hess, German opera star and Nazi intelligence agent. Who might or might not still be alive. Who knew both Peter Frain and Coco Chanel. *Not the time, Hope,* she thought.

"Have you ever read Ernest Hemingway?" Juanito was asking.

"I have," Maggie admitted. "Not my favorite author, though. I think he enjoys war a little too much."

"The bullfighters in Hemingway's novels are all inspired by my father." Maggie dimly recalled the character of the aging bullfighter in *The Sun Also Rises*. "When he retired at last, he had killed more than fifteen hundred bulls and been gored scores of times."

"It's a wonder he's still alive!"

Juanito chuckled. "He lives on a ranch in Andalusia now,

just south of Seville. He spends his days with bulls in the fields and nights drinking in the bars, reminiscing about the 'good old days.' "

"Bullfighting sounds a bit like boxing in America."

His expression darkened. "No," he told her, holding up one hand. "*Not* like boxing. Bullfighting's an art, almost a religion here." He made the sign of the cross. "If you look at our newspapers, you won't see the contests in the sports section, but on their own page. The *corrida formal* is much more than the struggle of man against beast. It's art with the danger of death. It's a religious ceremony, a blood sacrifice."

He turned to her. "Would you like to come to the *corrida de toros*, Paige? To see me do battle?"

Watch a bull being flayed alive? Juanito risking his life for no good reason? During a global war? No, no thank you, she thought. But she recognized he was a proud man. And going to the bullfight, as the guest of such a famous *toreador*, might lead to useful information she could bring back to London. "I'd like that, thank you."

He appeared pleased, and she smiled. He probably wasn't used to working so hard for a woman's approval. "It's not just killing a bull," he told her. "It's about honor. Honor's very real in Spain. Honor, integrity, self-respect . . . Courage, yes, but courage with grace, with calm."

"Do you enjoy it?" Maggie asked. She had always considered bullfighting a prolonged execution of the bull, performed before a bloodthirsty crowd. She never saw the point and only found it cruel. "The killing?"

She thought of Heisenberg, of her own assignment. *At least the bull knows what's coming,* she thought. *He can fight back.* But then again, a bull didn't have the knowledge to destroy entire cities with a single bomb.

"That moment for the matador is sacred," he told her. "Doing it cleanly and honorably—that's what's most important. 'Thou shalt not kill' is the Lord's commandment, yes. But when man rebels against death, he takes a certain joy in meting it out, even as we face death ourselves ultimately. I certainly don't enjoy seeing bulls suffer. I do my best to be quick and clean. But, in defeating the bull, I—and by extension the *aficionados*—rise above death. In that one sacred moment, we defeat death itself."

"I'd never thought of it that way." *Quick and clean,* Maggie thought. She shivered.

They walked through a grove of chestnut trees, past a pond rippling in the breeze, and reached a building that to Maggie looked like a fairy castle. It was actually a huge conservatory, constructed from glass plates in a graceful curved cast-iron framework, secured by a base of painted ceramic tiles.

"*El Palacio de Cristal*—the Glass Palace," Juanito said as if reading her mind. "And yes, they had to replace all of the glass after the war."

"Beautiful," Maggie breathed. Inside, and out of the wind, they admired the soaring structure and concentrated warmth of the sun.

Finally they moved on, now approaching Madrid's zoo. *La Casa de Fieras,* the House of Beasts, had been built by King Carlos III in 1774. "Come!" Juanito told her. "This was my favorite when I was a little boy!" Emptied during the war, the zoo was once again home to lions, tigers, and bears—as well as monkeys, ostriches, a crocodile, and even an elephant. Each pavilion was built in the style of the country of the animal's origin, all set around an artificial lake.

Maggie had never liked zoos; she didn't like to see animals in cages. But since Juanito was keen, she acquiesced. "Many animals are from countries now at war," he reassured her. "So it's a good thing they're here. They're safe." *They'd probably rather be free,* Maggie thought but didn't say.

As they walked the gravel paths, Juanito regaled her with

stories about the zoo, such as how the aristocrats would pit the animals against one another to fight; and the time the elephant Pizarro had escaped, fleeing down the central street of Alcalá. And, according to rumor, how prisoners had been thrown to the lions during the Civil War.

Maggie and Juanito approached the crush of people gazing down into the bear pit. The brass plaque proclaimed the two bears were from Germany, evacuees from Berlin's zoo.

She stared down. The pit was small, with rocky ground and a patch of brown grass. People craned their heads over the railings, protected by a filigree of barbed wire. One of the large bears, fur matted, was pacing back and forth, glaring up at the gaping people.

He patrolled the confines of his den, back and forth, as if hoping he could somehow find an escape, only to be disappointed to come up against the stone wall once again. The animal's frustration was palpable. Maggie turned away, unable to watch.

A boy, no more than five, leaned over the iron railing. As the bear reared up on its muscular hind legs and growled, the boy shrieked, turning to press his face into his mother's coat. Someone threw a churro and the bear dropped down to gobble it whole before resuming its manic pacing.

"Can you imagine what would happen if it escaped?" a woman in a rabbit fur coat next to Maggie asked in Spanish.

"Complete chaos!" exclaimed her partner.

On the woman's other side, a priest replied, "But that would never happen."

Maggie couldn't help but think of fission bombs, with all their potential. Even in the hands of the most peace-loving nation on earth, all the power waiting, in danger of escaping. She thought of the next war, between the U.S. and Russia. And she felt the prickle of fear and a wave of nausea. "Let's go back to the park," she said to Juanito.

"Let me take you to lunch."

Maggie thought for a moment. Chanel and Burns couldn't help her, but perhaps Juanito Belmonte could. "I'd like that," she said. "But there's somewhere else I'd like to go, here in Madrid."

"And what's that?" he asked.

"A lecture. The German physicist Werner Heisenberg's speaking at the University of Madrid. Security's tight, so it's by invitation only." She looked up at him. "Would you like to go with me?" Fluttering her eyelashes seemed too much.

He burst out in a roar of laughter. It was obviously not a date he'd ever considered.

"It's difficult to obtain a ticket," she continued. "I asked my friend Coco Chanel, but she had no interest in going." She wasn't sure if the bullfighter knew who the couturiere was, but it was worth a try.

"You know, Paige, most women would be interested in fine dining, perhaps a night at the opera, flamenco, shopping. . . . And you want to go to the university? To see some . . . scientist?"

"An *important* scientist," she told him. "He won a Nobel Prize in physics. It's an incredible opportunity to hear Professor Heisenberg explain the uncertainty principle—" *I must sound like a moron,* she realized, *but Juanito's my only hope.*

He shook his head. "I'm a gentleman, true, but not a scholar."

Maggie remembered how Paige, the real Paige, had handled men, and cast her eyes downward and pouted. "Oh."

Juanito looked at her. "And when is this remarkable lecture?"

"This afternoon."

"Alas, I've a preexisting date—with a bull," he told her. "Can't be rescheduled."

"It's very important to me," she said, touching his arm

lightly. "Do you think there's . . . anything you could do to make it happen? Even if I went without you? I'd make it up to you. . . ."

He relented. "I'll make a call. The chancellor of the University of Madrid's an *aficionado* and I've met him several times. I can't make any guarantees, but I'll see what I can do. And, in return, promise me dinner at Sobrino de Botín, the oldest restaurant in the world. You simply must taste their suckling pig."

Maggie's stomach lurched a bit, but she managed to breathe through it and found a wide smile to give him. "Yes, I'd love to—thank you, Juanito."

Back at the Palace Hotel, Ángel was waiting for her in the lobby, sitting at a small table under the rotunda far from the other guests. He was drinking black coffee from a fragile-looking china cup. In the sunlight, the red stained-glass roses glowed as if on fire.

"Where's the letter?" he asked without preamble.

"I told you—in the hotel's safe," Maggie told him. "Safe in the safe, you might say. And I have good news: while Mademoiselle couldn't get me into Heisenberg's lecture at the university, or Mr. Burns, Juanito Belmonte is going to try."

"Juanito Belmonte? The bullfighter?" He raised black eyebrows. "You move fast."

"*He* moves fast," she clarified. "Would you like a *violeta*?" she asked, pulling out the bag of candy Juanito had given her. "He bought me some this morning."

"No. Look, I must have access to that letter—"

"The letter part of the mission's finished, Ángel," she told him, done with the subject. "Now we need to focus on Heisenberg."

He ran a hand through his hair. "When will you know about getting in?"

"Soon. I think Belmonte has any number of ways to make things happen quickly, if and when he wants. And I think he'll get me in."

"You'll bring your . . . equipment . . . to the lecture?"

She knew what he meant and swallowed. "Of course. But first, I'm going to listen to him, listen very carefully."

"Your mission is to assassinate him," he said in a low tone. "Not take notes."

Maggie whispered, "I'm here to ascertain *if* he has or is close to having a fission bomb."

He pulled back. "It doesn't matter, ultimately. You just need to do it. It's easier that way. It's certain, final, and definitive."

"No," Maggie said firmly. "He's one of the greatest minds of our generation, who may or may not be working for Hitler. For all we know, he's blocking the Nazis' ability to realize a bomb. Killing him might only speed up the project." She thought of bullfighting. "I won't kill for sport."

"You're worse than Don Quixote," he said, "and ten times as crazy!" He rocked back in his chair. "This is what happens when women are involved in war."

Maggie let him stew. A waiter came by and asked if she wanted anything; she demurred.

Finally, Ángel spoke again. "I'm going to assume he'll say something incriminating, and you'll take a shot at him during the lecture."

"If I do, I'll fire from underneath my coat. I'll have the gun in my lap." She'd worked out the details with Kim and gone over the process multiple times. "No one will know who did it. And then, in the confusion, I'll exit. We need to have an escape set up."

"I've had a look at the architectural plans," he told her. "There's a women's lavatory on the first floor, not far from the main lecture hall. After you've taken your shot, go there directly. There's a window—open it and climb out. I'll be waiting for you in the parking lot just outside. We'll be off before the police arrive."

The enormity of her task haunted her. "And if I don't make it?"

"You have the cyanide pill."

Maggie nodded. "He'll have security with him."

"I'm more than aware. Still, I don't think they'll follow you into, what do you call it? The 'loo.' "

"I don't think the ladies' loo would stop the Gestapo."

The same waiter reappeared with a folded note on a silver tray. "For Señorita Paige Kelly." There was also a book: Hemingway's *The Sun Also Rises*.

"Thank you," she said, accepting both. She opened the note. "It's from Juanito." She scanned it.

"You've quite the admirer," Ángel grumbled.

"Yes, and he's gotten me on the list of approved guests for the lecture!" Maggie made sure to keep her voice down. "I even have a special meeting with the head of the Physics Department, Dr. Fernando Martinez. I'll see what he has to say about his colleague."

"And then you'll kill Heisenberg."

"And then I'll ascertain if he has the bomb."

Ángel ground his teeth in frustration. "How?"

Maggie forced a smile. "I'll wave a red cape in front of him and see if he charges."

Chapter Twenty-four

The University of Madrid was founded in 1293, but its current campus was designed during the 1920s, under the reign of Alfonso XIII. Looking around the windswept grounds, Maggie could see buildings in early-twentieth-century Spanish architecture: modern and hopeful, characterized by clean lines.

As she walked the campus paths, her wedge-heeled shoes kicking up dust, Maggie somehow felt at home, even though she'd never been to the university before in her life. It was a college campus, regardless, a place of learning and study. But the gun in her purse, bumping against her as she walked, dispelled any feelings of academic nostalgia, as did the still-visible damage from the Civil War.

Before he'd dropped her off, Ángel had told her, "Remember, concentrate on your target, but always keep your escape plan in mind." *Bathroom window, check,* she thought.

"Always remember why you're doing this mission, why it's so important."

"As if I could ever forget?" she'd muttered as she envisioned teapot-size bombs taking out entire cities in terrible explosions all over the world: the screams, the flames, the devastation. The beginning of the end of the world.

While Maggie was thinking about a new war, the past one, the Civil War, was still obvious. She could see bullet pockmarks marring the brick walls, as well as the remains of a bombed and brutalized landscape: trenches and strongpoints, now covered in crabgrass and foxtails. For a split second, she could clearly picture the soldiers, the guns, the sandbags, the shouting, the blood spilling on sandy soil. She felt for the students of the war years, who'd either gone to battle or had the fight brought to them. She swallowed, overcome for a moment.

Still, the landscape, and the students, seemed to have healed. A young man with a thick black mustache was sitting under a eucalyptus tree, strumming a guitar and singing. Young women perched on a bench nearby exchanged textbooks. A few students had ditched their satchels on the grass to play an impromptu game of soccer. And a pair of professors in tweed suits wandered the gravel paths, heads bent and hands clasped behind their backs, speaking in low, deliberate tones.

She was surprised to see so many male students, but because Spain was neutral, the men weren't all being shipped off to war the way they were in most of the rest of the world. *Of course,* she thought. She just hadn't seen so many young men, out of uniform and carefree, in a long, long time. She thought of so many other young men who'd already sacrificed their lives.

Maggie forced herself to focus on the plan. She was there for Heisenberg. Consulting the map the hotel's concierge had drawn for her, she found her way to the Departamento de Física, where Professor Heisenberg was going to speak. She saw from the difference in brick colors that the Physics Department building must have been bombed and then rebuilt. *In a few years the bricks will be weathered enough to match— incoming students will never even know,* she thought. *It'll be forgotten.*

The doors of the department were hung with red, white, and black Nazi bunting, fluttering in the wind. Two men stood on the steps, smoking. She recognized short and boyish-looking

forty-two-year-old Heisenberg immediately by his pale hair
and eyes, his freckles, and his bald crown. He appeared thinner
than he had in the photographs she'd studied, almost frail. He
wore a black-and-white tattersall suit, gray shirt, silver polka-
dot tie, and a heavy signet ring on his pinkie finger. His smile
was open, disarming even, and he threw his head back in a
hearty laugh. His security detail, she noted, was close and kept
careful watch.

The second man was taller and larger, with broad shoulders
and a round belly. His thick black hair was streaked with silver, which made Maggie think of a large, graying teddy bear.
Was this the department chair, Dr. Fernando Martinez?

She slowed her pace, watching them interact. The two men
were obviously old friends, laughing and joking, Heisenberg
reaching up to clap the larger man on his meaty arm. *This is
the man who could, possibly, destroy the world as we know it,*
Maggie thought with not a small amount of awe, *just joking
and laughing and smoking on a university campus. As if he
didn't have a care in the world.*

Instinctively she felt through her purse's leather for the gun.
It was hard and waiting—along with the lipstick case that contained her cyanide tablet.

Heisenberg threw his cigarette stub into the bushes and
caught Maggie's stare. He held her eyes, and his gaze seemed to
penetrate right through her. She held her breath, half expecting
to be arrested on sight. But she forced herself to move a gloved
hand in a wave, give a thin smile, and walk onward. She made
herself take deep breaths. *Focus. Stick to the plan.*

In the lobby, Maggie gave her name and showed identification at a long table. She kept her coat on as she walked into the
large lecture hall. Wintery sunlight streamed through tall windows over scuffed wood floors. She almost smiled as she slid
into one of the seats—the classroom, a world away from Boston, reminded her of MIT's famous 26-100 lecture hall. It had

the same hard wooden chairs, the same vertical sliding chalk-boards, and the same smell: a mix of floor wax, chalk dust, and stale smoke. She took off her coat and sat, placing her purse in her lap.

Her heart pounded. Still, she rehearsed the shot in her mind, the angle to the podium he'd stand behind, the timing of it. *Never forget to breathe.* She could hear her instructor's words playing in her head. *Aim on the inhale, squeeze the trigger on the exhale.*

Thirteen people were already seated and waiting. As the seconds and minutes ticked by, about thirty or so more professors and students joined to hear the world's greatest physicist. Maggie saw men of all ages and a few women. There was also a lineup of SS guards against the back wall, guns out. She tagged undercover Gestapo agents scattered through the auditorium as well; there were four, one in each quadrant, with short haircuts, ill-fitting civilian suits, and darting eyes.

Heisenberg entered precisely on time and strode to the front of the hall. "Welcome," he said in East Franconia–inflected German as the audience applauded. Maggie understood the professor in his native German, but there was a translator to one side, who presented his remarks in Spanish. "I'm delighted to be back in Madrid. Thank you to my dear friend, Dr. Fernando Martinez." The teddy bear in the first row bowed his head in acknowledgment.

"I'm going to begin with my best physics joke," Heisenberg said. "Although, I must tell you, it's my only physics joke. And that's probably for the best." There were a few snickers from the crowd. "I was speeding down the German Autobahn one day, near Berlin, and I was pulled over by a police officer. The officer said, 'Hey! Do you know how fast you were going?' "

He took a beat, then responded, " 'No, Officer—but I can tell you *where* I am!' "

As the audience dissolved in laughter, Maggie felt light-headed. *He's funny,* she thought with disbelief. *He's not supposed to be* funny.

He picked up a thick piece of yellow chalk and wrote an equation on the blackboard. Maggie was more than familiar with it.

$$\Delta\chi\Delta\rho \geq \frac{\hbar}{2}$$

"In classical Newtonian physics," Heisenberg began, "studying the behavior of a physical system is considered a simple task—because several physical qualities can be measured simultaneously. However, that's impossible in the quantum world of subatomic particles." In 1927, Heisenberg had described these limitations as the uncertainty principle.

"Now," he continued, "our knowledge of particles is always inherently uncertain." *As is the outcome of this mission.*

Heisenberg turned to the board and began to write again, the chalk making that familiar tapping sound she'd almost forgotten. She pulled her suit jacket tighter around her in the drafty room. *Listen for certain words,* she remembered Kim saying. *If anything Heisenberg says leads you to believe he's close to constructing a bomb, shoot him.* She shivered.

The physicist put down the chalk and turned back to the audience, wiping his hand on his trousers, leaving yellow dust on the wool. He kept his left hand in his pocket and paced as he talked.

He continued the lecture in earnest and Maggie listened for certain words. *Heavy water. Fast fission. Uranium.* Anything that might indicate he had a bomb. Or was close to having a bomb. But his lecture was neutral—affable, good-natured, even. He covered material only from before 1940.

Even as Heisenberg joked, she felt the shadow of death move ever closer. If he had or was close to producing the bomb, the Nazis could still win the war. To assassinate him would save the Allies. *And surely,* she thought, *surely, a man this brilliant must be close.*

At the same time, seductive counterarguments whispered in her ear: *What if he could be brought over to the Allies' side? What right do I have to kill another human being? What if the gun fails to fire?* Her heart was beating so hard she worried everyone in the auditorium could hear it. Without warning, the refrain of the Bing Crosby and Andrews Sisters' song popped into her mind: *"Oh, lay that pistol down, babe, lay that pistol down, pistol packin' mama, lay that thing down before it goes off, and hurts somebody . . ."*

She remembered what John, once an RAF pilot, had told her: that being a successful pilot meant being fearless. She thought of the people she had known in her three years of war, the brave men and women who'd resisted the Nazis. Who'd given their lives. They'd made their own choices, but this decision, so hard, was hers alone. She thought of the films Kim had showed her at St. Ermin's—all the death, the violence. Eventually, the murmuring arguments died down, and Maggie felt her fear harden into resolve. She would do what needed to be done—that was all. *Concentrate,* she told herself. She willed her mind still, open, present to the moment.

Heisenberg stopped and pointed directly at her. *"Fräulein,"* he said as people in the audience turned to stare. She jumped in shock. "Yes, you—would you please come up and assist me with a demonstration?"

Maggie swallowed. She left her purse hidden under her coat on her chair as she walked to the front of the hall. Her shoes clicked on the wood as her heart beat erratically. She heard ringing in her ears. She couldn't shake the feeling she was in a dream—or was it a nightmare?

"Now, you see I've chosen a young woman—and *not* Dr. Martinez." He smiled at the teddy bear. "No offense, my friend."

The department head laughed and held up large hands. "None taken, Herr Professor!"

"Even if you don't follow the physics, this young lady will be easy on the eyes, yes?" He opened the top drawer of the desk near him and pulled out a flashlight. He turned it on. "Please, turn off the lights," he called, someone in the back acquiesced. The room was dark.

"Now—" He held the flashlight under his chin, causing his face to glow in an ominous way. "I'm an electron," he whispered in a gravelly voice, and the audience snickered. "I'm here, minding my own business."

He pointed to Maggie with the flashlight. She blinked and squinted as the light hit her eyes. "You—you're a photon sent to find me, the electron." He beckoned, and Maggie took a few steps toward him.

Through a fog of adrenaline, Maggie realized what he was doing. As soon as she found him, he changed direction. He was visually illustrating the uncertainty principle. It was mechanically, and therefore logically, impossible to know both the velocity *and* position of an electron—the two fundamental properties of any particle. If you shine enough light on an electron to see it, the light itself will alter the electron's velocity. It was not *anschaulich,* as Heisenberg put it—not "seeable."

"Come! Find me!"

Maggie walked up to him, blinking in the direct beams of the flashlight. When she reached him, they both stopped, face-to-face. Then they each took a step back. The most important part of Heisenberg's thesis was that people couldn't know the velocity and position of an electron, because observation changed everything. *We interfere with everything we run across,* Maggie thought. *We're changers, corrupters of reality. We infuse, and perhaps pollute, whatever we find. What's my own presence here doing to the time line of fission warfare?*

"And you see, when she meets up with me—we collide!—

and we both change our positions!" He switched off the flash-light and they were engulfed in darkness. "And that, my friends, is the visual description of the uncertainty principle." There was a wave of applause as the overhead lights flickered on, and he turned to Maggie. "Thank you, Miss—"

"Kelly," she said.

"English?" he asked, face creasing in consternation.

She wondered if he felt a flicker of danger, as if his electron were reacting to her light. "Irish," she corrected.

His face relaxed. "Ah, I see." He nodded and she returned to her seat, knees almost buckling beneath her; back in her seat, she grasped the purse with the gun, forcing herself to take regular breaths. The lecture continued without incident. Heisenberg said nothing that would lead her to believe Germany had the bomb.

After, she waited in the long queue to speak with him. "Fascinating talk, Herr Professor," she said in perfect German. "Thank you so much for including me."

"And thank you for indulging me, Miss Kelly. I wonder why such a pretty girl is at a dry, boring physics lecture?"

She swallowed; her mouth was like sandpaper. "Not boring at all." She forced her brightest smile. "I studied physics as an undergraduate. Now I teach high school students. But I enjoy keeping up with what's happening in the field." She tilted her head. "I'm most interested in atomic fission."

Out of the corner of her eye she watched one of the plain-clothes Gestapo take her measure, then turn away, unimpressed. *They think I'm just a fan, an* aficionado. *A girl.*

She leaned closer. "The journals say nuclear fission will someday become a source of energy more powerful than coal or oil."

His eyes widened, surprised at her knowledge. "That's our hope."

"Of course," she said, as casually as she could even though

she felt her heart might explode. "It could also be used to create a bomb."

His eyebrows raised. "Theoretically."

"So, it can be done?" She held her breath. *This was it,* she thought. *This was the moment he'd reveal all.* She felt her ears begin to ring.

He looked at her intently, then his face broke into a grin. "Why would a pretty girl like you want to talk of bombs?"

Because your life depends on it, she thought. Her heart was beating loudly, but Maggie didn't back down. "I live in this world, this fast-changing world," she told him. "I may have a child—at some point." *Little Bean could be born into a world with fission bombs.* "I'm invested."

"It *is* possible, of course," he said enigmatically.

"But it would have a huge effect on the German war effort, a fission bomb." His face gave nothing away and she could tell she'd pushed too far. "Tell me," she tried again, trying to hide the desperation in her voice, "as a scientist, are you more driven by politics or morality?"

"I'm a good German," he countered.

But are you a "good Nazi"? She felt her focus slipping. "Of course." *Keep talking. You must learn what he knows.*

She continued to press. "Would you have any moral qualms about producing such a bomb?" She gazed at his face, looking for any twitch, any blink that might give him away, even as she worried he could hear her thundering heartbeat. "I suppose what I'm trying to say is—does your patriotism demand you produce such a weapon?"

He was silent.

"What's more important to you?" she tried again. "Science or humanity?" *Please choose humanity. . . .*

He opened his mouth to speak, but stopped at the sound of a rich bass voice. "Ah, our lovely photon!" It was Dr. Martinez. Maggie bit her lip in frustration.

"Did you know," he asked Heisenberg, "this young lady is a special friend of Don Juanito Belmonte, the famous bull-fighter?"

"Not that special," Maggie said. "We've only just met."

"Ah—" Martinez chuckled. "That's how it begins!"

"I'm afraid I must be going, Miss Kelly," Heisenberg said. "So nice to meet you. Good day—" *No, you can't go! Not until . . .*

They were interrupted by the guards. "Halt!" They rushed up from behind, and Maggie flinched—but they weren't charging her. Instead, they were speaking to the young man waiting in line behind her—he was suspected of having a weapon. She turned and saw the terror in his eyes.

A moment later, he was surrounded. One guard held his arms while another roughly searched him, pulling out a knife from an ankle holster. *Another assassin?* she thought. *Or just someone carrying a knife for protection?* Maggie averted her gaze and backed away slowly.

It could have been me—still could be. Bile rose from her stomach. She tried to block the man's screams. The doors banged open, and then he was dragged out, no doubt to a prison cell—or worse. The "Pistol Packin' Mama" song's refrain again ran though her mind unbidden.

After his removal there was silence in the hall. "I guess he didn't like the lecture," Heisenberg said with a shrug, and there was a nervous titter in response. Everything seemed to return to normal.

"Just checking you've a decent suit for the gala," she heard Martinez say as the two physicists walked away. "You're the guest of honor! You're a professor, yes, but you're in Madrid now, and you must leave the tweed at home!"

She watched him go, shaking, still holding the purse with her gun clamped under her arm. She didn't know what he knew. *He's Schrödinger's cat,* she thought. *Alive and dead. With a bomb and without.*

They exited the lecture hall. *My electron,* she thought, suddenly nauseated. She knew his location, yes, but certainly not his position.

Maggie went to the ladies' room, small and badly lit, to collect herself. Her blouse was sticking to her sweaty back and her breath was labored. Inside, she noticed the lavatory was under construction; the window she was supposed to escape from was bricked up. She felt the hairs on the back of her neck rise as she realized there was no way out. No escape. *Did Ángel know?* she thought. *He must have scouted this location. Was this on purpose? Are* you *trying to have me killed, too?*

She shook her head to clear it and washed her shaking hands in cold water. *No, it was a mistake, an oversight, he never actually did the legwork to check, just went by architectural plans. . . . But he'd sounded so bloody* confident *about the window.*

Again, she looked at the bricks, her death sentence, then left. *If I'm the electron, who's my photon?*

In the parking lot, she saw a black car covered in red rust. Ángel was slouched in the front seat, smoking. He tossed the cigarette out the window as he caught sight of her. *Surprised I'm alive?* She appraised him. *Did you set me up to fail? Did I put a crimp in your plans?*

"I didn't do it," she said as she got in the passenger seat.

He turned the key in the ignition. "I know." The engine turned over. "I would have heard police sirens by now if you had."

"The lavatory window was bricked up," she said flatly as he shifted into reverse and backed the car out.

He came to a short stop and shifted into first. "Is that why you didn't do it?" He pressed on the gas pedal, and the car lurched forward.

She took a slow, shaky breath. "No. He—he gave nothing away," Maggie admitted. "I still don't know what he knows."

As he left the parking lot, Ángel shifted into second, then third. "How are you going to find out?"

"There's a gala," she told him as they emerged from the campus and onto the street.

"There'll be security," he told her, passing a student on a bicycle, a satchel of books swinging from the handlebars. "These things are exclusive."

Her face hardened. She knew what she had to do. "I'll find a way."

Chapter Twenty-five

When Maggie returned to the Palace Hotel, her room had been searched. She routinely left little traps: a thread deliberately placed on her toiletries, a pile of clothes that seemed haphazard but wasn't, a piece of lint on a jewelry case. But there wasn't anything to find. The letter from Chanel was in the hotel's safe and she had her gun, the key, and the cyanide pill on her.

Maggie sat on the bed. Her entire body was shaking. She wanted to cry, but couldn't—all her feelings were trapped, pushed down so far she couldn't access them. She struggled to breathe, her inhales ragged. She'd had her chance, and she just hadn't taken it. Because she didn't believe he had the bomb? Or because she hadn't been strong enough?

The telephone rang; it was Ángel. "Meet me in the lobby at eleven. We're going dancing at Pasapoga."

As they drove up Gran Vía in a taxi, Maggie told Ángel about her room being searched. He shrugged. "It's Madrid—could be anyone. Franco, the Japanese, the Germans? Maybe even someone from Hoare's office? Then of course, there's always the Americans. . . ." He laughed and put a hand on her knee. "It was probably just the maid."

"And why this club?" She was glad of the distraction; she hadn't wanted to be alone in her room with her thoughts.

"It's a place where lots of high-level people drink to excess and reveal secrets. Confidential matters. It's my job to pass on what I see and hear. You're a good cover."

They entered a canopied doorway and descended a wide, red-carpeted staircase to the music of Guy Lombardo. Below was a glamorous, smoke-filled, low-lit room. It reminded her of the WonderBar in Estoril, and she couldn't help but think of Connor.

Men of a certain age and young women held cocktail glasses and flirted and laughed. Ángel must have read her thoughts: he shook hands with men, sidestepping waiters and cigarette girls. Once they'd ordered, Ángel stood. "May I have this dance?"

Maggie was hungry and tired from her day, and dancing was the last thing she wanted to do, but it would look odd if they didn't. "Of course."

As they tangoed, with Ángel leading expertly, Maggie noticed Juanito at a table set behind velvet ropes. He was patiently signing autographs. When he caught sight of Maggie on the dance floor, he appeared shocked. His face darkened.

Ángel observed the exchange of glances. "You must introduce me to your *matador*."

Maggie was eager to sit. "Come." She led him through the throng of *aficionados* to Juanito's table, and the bullfighter rose and bowed. "Paige," he said in a measured tone. "*Buenas noches*. I did not expect to see you here, of all places."

Maggie smiled. "How were the bulls?"

"Feisty," he replied. "And how was the physicist?"

"Fascinating. Thank you for getting me on the list."

"The great Belmonte!" Ángel said, offering his hand. "It's an honor!"

Maggie made introductions: "Juanito, this is Ángel. A . . .

family friend." Ángel quickly began talking of the big upcoming fight, and Juanito, polite to a fault, was drawn into the conversation. But she could see he was unsettled to see her at the nightclub. When Ángel excused himself to order a bottle of champagne for the table, Juanito frowned. "Are you all right?" she asked him.

"This isn't the place for you."

It was almost midnight, and she still hadn't had dinner—she had to agree. "It seems like a fine spot," she offered.

"A lady doesn't come to a place like this," he said.

"There are many ladies here, Juanito."

"No, no—these are . . . women. Not ladies."

Ah, Maggie realized. *A club for mistresses, not wives.* "*You're* here."

"That's my prerogative." Then, "Shall I see you back to the hotel?"

Maggie glanced around for Ángel. He was enmeshed in an animated conversation with a trio of businessmen in pin-striped suits. "Yes, actually," she told him. "Thank you."

In the hotel's drive, he said, "I'd like to invite you to a bullfight. Tomorrow. At four." She'd seen the posters around town; however, the bloody and protracted death of a bull wasn't high on her list of priorities.

But if I go to the bullfight, will he take me to the gala? "It would be an honor, Juanito," she told him.

He gave her a serious look. "The bullfight is the one thing the Spanish are on time for."

"Understood. Until tomorrow."

Chapter Twenty-six

La Plaza de Toros de Las Ventas was the largest bullfighting ring in Spain. Located in the Guindalera quarter of Salamanca, it was built in 1931 in neo-Moorish style, complete with ceramic heraldic crests of all the Spanish provinces. Columns were plastered with posters of the top matadors: Manolete, Gallito, and Juanito Belmonte. The breeze was cool but not cold, and a warm sun shone. A band played a spritely *paso doble*.

The crowd of nearly twenty thousand was buzzing with excitement. People in their finest clothes and hats laughed and called to one another, many drinking. Men chomped on cigars and women pulled out tins of *violetas*. There was palpable tension in the air as men in black pants and colored shirts with cummerbunds raked the golden sand to prepare for the fight.

"Excellent seat!" Ángel exclaimed. They were in the front row of the tenth section. Their slice had a roof, as well as access to an elevator, and lavatories. At the top, set apart, was the Royal Box. "*Barreras de sombra*," he told her with satisfaction as they settled in their seats. "It's best to be in one of the *tendidos* in the shade."

A front-row seat to Ferdinand the Bull's death, Maggie thought, crossing her ankles and placing her purse on her lap. Despite the warm sun, she kept her wool coat on. "Terrific!"

she exclaimed, with all the enthusiasm she could muster. All she could think about was how to get to the gala.

"Since it's your first fight, I'm glad it's Belmonte," Ángel told her. "He's not just a superlative fighter, he's also consistent. And, also, just so you know, this isn't the actual bullfighting season but an exhibition, in honor of Madrid's German guests." He looked down the row, and Maggie followed his gaze. There, in a twill suit, dark wool coat, and trilby hat was Werner Heisenberg, laughing affably with the German ambassador, surrounded by his entourage of Nazis.

Once again, Professor Heisenberg, Maggie thought, *I've found your location, but not your position.* As Maggie glanced around, she spotted Chanel and Dincklage in the same row as Heisenberg. The couturiere was wearing a sable cape, with ropes of iridescent black pearls around her neck, and a red-tipped fur hat. Maggie caught her eye and raised one hand in greeting.

Chanel rose and sauntered over. "You're supposed to be on your way back to England," she whispered in Maggie's ear with her harsh voice. "With *my* letter."

"I have one more . . . errand to do in Madrid first," Maggie told her. *An errand. If only.* "Don't worry. Your letter's safe."

"Mademoiselle!" Ángel stood, removed his fedora, and bowed deeply. "*Enchanté!*"

Chanel allowed her black-gloved hand to be kissed. "And who are you?"

"Don Miguel Ángel Ramos, Mademoiselle—at your service."

Chanel smiled seductively. "You do look rather angelic," she purred. "And how did you obtain these tickets? They're hard to come by."

"From Juanito," Maggie told her. "Belmonte, that is."

"Ah, just like the bulls, the famous bullfighter likes red, I see." She waved Dincklage over. "We'll sit with you, if you don't mind."

It was a statement, not a question. "Of course." Chanel and Dincklage might be good sources of intelligence.

Dincklage arrived, smiling and smelling of lime aftershave, the picture of charm, and Chanel made introductions. "Your first bullfight, Miss Kelly?" he asked, after kissing Maggie's hand.

"Yes, Baron von Dincklage." *Two can play this game.*

"Spatz, please." As they settled, he opined, "Belmonte's a star, of course, but sometimes the success of the match is due to the bull. If the bull isn't aggressive, if he doesn't attack, there's no way the bullfighter can do a good *faena*."

"And what's that?"

"The series of passes the matador does with the bull to wear him down, before he kills him."

Like me with Heisenberg? She looked around at the sea of faces in the stands. The physicist, pale and drawn, stood out in the crowd. He caught her gaze. *Who's the electron and who's the photon here?* she thought.

"The bullring has five gates," Dincklage was explaining. "Plus three *toriles*, for the bulls to go into the arena. The gate of the *cuadrillas*, between the third and fourth *tendidos*, has access to the horse yard. Inside is where the *paseíllo* starts and the *picadores* enter. They're the ones who stab the bull with the lances." Maggie pulled her focus from Heisenberg and nodded.

"The dragging gate, which leads to the skinning room, is between the first and second *tendidos*. And the famous Puerta Grande—the Big Gate, the 'Gate of Madrid'—is between *tendidos* seven and eight. It's where Belmonte will enter," he told her. "Appearing from there is every bullfighter's ambition. Manolete's also one of my favorites. Manolete and Belmonte are the only two who consistently enter and exit from the Puerta Grande."

"What happens if there's a . . . mishap?" Maggie asked.

"They have a fully equipped operating room in the infirmary," Dincklage told her. "And a chapel, as well. With a priest on duty, to hear confession and give last rites, should the worst happen."

Good grief. And all for "sport." "Good to know."

Maggie heard the crowd's noise rise in volume and turned to see General Franco and his wife entering the Royal Box, surrounded by civil guards and police. *He's short* was her first thought. *And . . . ordinary. He could be a bank manager, a waiter, or the owner of a corner shop.*

However, Maggie knew better than to be taken in by his amiable appearance. Franco believed in the "Jewish-Masonic-Bolshevik conspiracy" and was convinced Judaism was the ally of both American capitalism and Soviet Communism. He'd banned public Jewish religious services, along with Protestant Christian ones, since the Civil War. And he'd ordered his director of security to compile a list of Jews and foreigners in Spain in May 1941, and had Jewish status marked on Spanish identity papers for the first time.

While General Franco kept the German military out of Spain, he had made countless concessions to Hitler. Still, as the tables of the war turned, he seemed to be drawing slowly closer to the Allies. He still allowed shipments of wolfram, a mineral needed for Nazi weapons, to pass through his country. But he also sold wolfram to the Allies. She quickly turned away.

Horns sounded and men in embroidered satin costumes led a procession. The audience began clapping and shouting. Many stood. She and Ángel did as well.

"Those are the *alguaciles,* the constables," Ángel told her. "They're here to ask the president of the *corrida*—today, General Franco—for the key to release the bull."

The men were followed by three matadors: Manolete, Gallito, and, yes, Juanito. They wore even grander brightly colored satin suits with elaborate gold and silver embroidery and beading, coral-colored stockings, and black silk slippers. "*Los trajes de luces*," Ángel told her. "Suits of lights." They sat again.

So this is what el traje *looks like in the ring, instead of a hotel corridor.* Maggie noticed that while Juanito's turquoise suit sparkled in the sun, his face underneath his black hat was serious, as if he were going into actual battle. "Juanito's blue *traje de luces* is the same one his father wore in Toledo, when he won two ears."

"Ah," Maggie replied. "And what does it mean if a bull-fighter sends a woman his *traje de luces*?"

Ángel glanced at her sharply. "It's the highest compliment."

Oh dear, she thought.

Chanel leaned over Dincklage to touch Maggie's knee. "Talk about 'dressed to kill,' hmm?"

"Indeed." *Or to die.*

Behind the three bullfighters were nine men carrying their capes. And yet more men, with colored sticks. "The *banderilleros*," Ángel explained. "They'll stab the daggers in the bull's neck to weaken it. It'll be harder for the bull to raise his head."

"Hardly seems fair," Maggie murmured.

He ignored her. "Following them on horseback are the *picadores,* with lances."

For yet more stabbing, Maggie thought, her stomach lurching.

A mule team brought up the rear. They all stopped in front of the Royal Box, removed their black hats, and bowed to General Franco and his guests.

Juanito saw Maggie in the stands and made eye contact. He lifted his chin, then handed his cape to one of the *banderilleros.* Ángel perked up. "Maybe he'll place his cape on our railing!"

"What does that mean?" Maggie asked.

"It's a high honor bullfighters bestow on a dignitary—or lucky young woman—at the beginning of a performance."

The *banderillero* spread the cape on the barrier before Maggie, causing a murmur from the audience. She tried to catch Juanito's eye again, but he was completely focused on the procession, now heading back to the gate.

"Amazing!" Ángel crowed. "What an honor!" Even Chanel beamed her approval.

The men then exited to the sound of drumbeats. After a suspenseful moment, a trumpet blared and an enormous glossy bull with long pointed horns burst into the ring. "That's a Miura, from Seville," Ángel told Maggie. "They're bred for their muscle, aggression, and intelligence." The black bull was running, turning, stamping, snorting. He was furious, looking for something, anything, to charge.

Poor Ferdinand was all Maggie could think.

Manolete, sallow and gaunt, appeared to great applause. Despite the danger, his expression was placid, almost serene. The bull charged and was killed quickly and easily, without too many passes. Maggie forced herself to stand and applaud as two men with mules dragged the body out.

"Not a good bull," Ángel explained. "Manolete didn't have a chance to really show his skill and courage."

Maggie found it all horrible. She took gulps of cold air to keep from being sick.

More drums and trumpets as another bull, this one white, entered the ring. He snorted and tore across the golden sand. Then Juanito appeared. Unlike Manolete, he began on his knees.

"To start the fight on one's knees is dangerous," Ángel told her. He whistled between his teeth and applauded.

The white bull, easily four times Juanito's size, snorted and pawed the sand. Maggie felt a moment of terror, for the beautiful white bull and for Juanito, too. Whatever madness this was, he was brave. Cruel, perhaps, but brave. She swallowed down the sour, gritty taste of fear mixed with acidic coffee, orange juice, and *tomate* from breakfast.

The bull circled the ring, stamping and snorting, then

stopped, turned, and charged. Juanito lifted his glittering cape and swung. Maggie saw the man and bull in the *paso doble,* realizing the real meaning of the dance she'd performed back in Estoril. Juanito continued to work his cape, graceful as a ballet cavalier. The animal lunged and Juanito pivoted, arching his back, as the sharp horns came within inches of him.

As many in the crowd called "*Olé!*" Juanito and the bull continued their passes. The cheers grew louder, but Juanito kept a calm expression on his face, as though he were choosing candy in La Violeta or birdwatching in Retiro Park. Yet Maggie could feel his absolute concentration and saw dark patches spreading on the blue satin under his arms and in the small of his back.

The bull was panting, sweat dripping down its neck, white fur turning red. He charged again, and pierced Juanito's side with a horn. Maggie gasped. Juanito was thrown to the ground as the crowd cried out. Somewhere, a woman screamed. Maggie could see the dark bloom of blood on turquoise satin as Juanito rose, brushing off the sand.

He didn't stop. With the same insouciant grace, he once again waved his cape, twisting and turning it so it glittered in the sun. The *banderilleros* entered, stabbing three pairs of spiked sticks into the bull's neck. The pale fur was further stained with a deluge of red blood.

With elegance, grace, and precision, Juanito drew the bull toward him again and again, twirling his cape in seemingly effortless fashion. Only the dark stains spreading on his *traje* belied his coolness.

Maggie felt much as she had during her friend Sarah's performance of *Swan Lake,* when the Swan Queen was about to die—except instead of a stage and spotlights there was sand and sun. And at least one of the souls on the stage, if not both, was literally going to die.

Adrenaline rose in the stands, the murmuring reached a crescendo, and the two in the ring continued their tragic *pas de deux*. When Maggie heard Chanel shriek, "Kill him! Kill him!" she wondered, *Is she rooting for the man or the beast? Or just for death, regardless of who it may be?*

Juanito finally executed the bull with a stab of his long silver sword, the white fur almost entirely covered in slick red blood. The animal twitched three times, then lay still. The crowd rose and erupted into applause, shouts, and whistles. "It was a fast kill, a clean kill," Maggie heard people saying. *Whatever that means.* The bullring appeared as a Goya painting brought to horrific life.

Assassinated. Just like Heisenberg will be. Might be. Maggie glanced over at the physicist. He applauded weakly. She could sense the performance of death and celebration of victory was too much for him, as well. His eyes met hers; they nodded to each other in mutual understanding.

As the mules dragged out the bloody carcass, the *aficionados* showered the ring with flowers, hats, cigars, and brightly colored candies wrapped in shiny cellophane. Juanito bowed first to General Franco, then to the general's wife. Then to Maggie, and finally all sections of the ring. People screamed and stomped their feet in appreciation.

Juanito cut off the bull's ear with his dagger, then threw it. Maggie stretched her arm into the air instinctively and caught it, the still-warm blood running down her hand to her wrist and staining the cuff of her dress. Her stomach lurched.

"I think—" she said to Ángel, feeling nauseated—from morning sickness, witnessing the death, or catching the dead creature's ear, she didn't know. She handed him the bloody piece of cartilage and fur. "—I need to find the ladies' loo."

After Maggie vomited in the toilet, she washed the bull's blood from her hand, wrist, and sleeve. She emerged from the lavatory to find Belmonte's man of swords, the same one who'd brought the flowers and the suit of lights to the hotel, waiting to escort her backstage to the matador.

She took a deep breath as she entered the dressing room. "You showed great courage," she told Juanito. He had already washed, been bandaged, and changed into a well-tailored wool gabardine suit, looking a world apart from the bullfighter in satin on the golden, bloodstained sand.

"What did you think?" he asked.

"I'm just glad you're all right. You are all right, aren't you?"

"Only a scratch," he reassured her.

"I still don't understand why anyone would voluntarily do what you do."

"When you understand bullfighting, you'll understand Spain," he told her, now surrounded by men clapping him on the shoulders and congratulating him. "It was a way for our ancestors to defend themselves against the attack of wild bulls who always existed here. It's in our blood."

The contest seems a bit fairer for bulls in the wild, not in a ring, but all right, she thought.

He sent the men away and turned back to Maggie. "General Franco's hosting a gala tonight at the Royal Palace. I've been invited." His face flickered. "It's in honor of that German scientist you find so fascinating."

She forced herself not to let her mouth drop open. "Professor Heisenberg?"

"The very one. Would you like to go with me? As my special guest?"

"Thank you, Juanito." *My own bullfight.* Then she regarded him closely. Could he be an agent himself? Somehow setting her up? He had found her the first day in the hotel, she remembered. *Is he somehow in league with the Nazis?*

Regardless, she thought, *I'll risk it—it's worth being able to speak with Heisenberg again.* "I'd—I'd love to."

Chapter Twenty-seven

That evening, Maggie dressed for the gala as carefully as any bullfighter for the ring. Around the top of her thigh, above the silk stocking, she fastened a calfskin holder with the gun inside. It fit snugly against her leg, and she marched up and down the room to ensure it wouldn't slip as she walked.

When she donned Paige's—the real Paige's—black velvet Schiaparelli gown from before the war, it worked exactly as she had guessed, the voluminous skirt giving no hint of the metallic bulge beneath.

The dress was dramatic and not Maggie's style at all—the sleeves and décolletage, as well as the hem, were trimmed in coal-black ostrich plumes. She brushed her hair until it gleamed, pinned it up, then painted Elizabeth Arden's Printemps on her lips, using her fingertips to transfer a bit to her pale cheeks. Another bunch of feathers on a comb in her hair, long white gloves, pearl earrings—her own, this time, a graduation gift from Aunt Edith long ago—and she was finished.

She picked up her clutch, checked for the lipstick tube containing the suicide pill, then stood back and gazed in the mirror. *You look like a crow with all those feathers,* she thought. *Is that good or bad luck?*

Downstairs in the lobby, she approached the hotel's reception desk. *If this is my last night on earth . . .* "I'd like to make a long-distance call," she told the man on duty.

He looked up from his papers. "Of course, Señorita Kelly. I'm happy to assist." He came from behind the desk and led her to a telephone cubicle. It was larger than a phone booth, with wood paneling, a mullioned glass door, and a small desk and chair.

She gave the man a slip of paper with a long string of numbers, and he indicated the desk, with a black Bakelite telephone. "This phone will ring when your call's connected," he told her.

She sat and turned on the banker's lamp, which cast a small circle of golden light. She wasn't supposed to make any telephone calls. Not on a mission. But she had a bad feeling about the night. And in case things didn't go as planned, she wanted to say her goodbyes.

The telephone rang and she picked up the receiver, twisting the metallic cord around her fingers. She heard John's faint voice against the static. "Hello?"

She opened her mouth to speak, and nothing came out.

Again, louder, he said, "Hello?"

Finally, she found her voice. "It's me."

"How are you?"

"I'm fine," she told him. "Peachy—with a side of keen, in fact." That was one of their private jokes.

"Are you home?"

"Not yet. I really must go." She wiped away a tear. "But I wanted to hear your voice." This wasn't the right time to tell him about Bean, she knew. That talk would have to wait. "I'm thinking of you."

"And I'm thinking of you. Come back as soon as you can."

"I'll try." For a long moment, they each listened to the other breathe across the many miles. Tears ran down Maggie's cheeks.

"I love you," he said.

She wiped her eyes and managed "I love you, too," then forced herself to hang up.

As Juanito's long limousine passed through the Opera district, Maggie caught a glimpse of the moonlit white palace. Juanito saw her gaze. "It's not the Royal Palace anymore, but the National Palace, you know."

Maggie nodded, acutely aware of the tiny gun strapped to her thigh, the steel burning her flesh. "Under Franco."

"You must call him Generalísimo Franco, *querida*. And it's built on the remains of an ancient Muslim fortress. It was eventually rebuilt as the Real Alcázar. They say it's haunted."

"Haunted?"

"Legend has it that you can still hear the cries of the Moors whom the Christian kings slaughtered in battle." Their driver skirted the building, turning into a cobbled courtyard with magnificent illuminated wrought-iron gates. "They also say it's where Carlos the Second was possessed by a demon who forced the King to drink a man's brain, dissolved in hot chocolate." Maggie made a face, and Juanito smiled, amused. "Allegedly, there was an exorcism."

"Thank goodness." Maggie tried to imagine something similar happening to the British royal family. No demon would dare possess *them*. And they certainly wouldn't drink brains in chocolate. *Tea, maybe, but not chocolate.*

"It's also said that the Duke of Alba met a beautiful lady in the chapel of the palace, and she turned into Death, with a scythe."

Death with a scythe, not a gun, you say? "Is it where Generalísimo Franco lives?" she asked. Her heart was beginning to beat faster.

"No, he lives a bit outside the city, at the Pardo. But he uses this for official events in town. You'll see why. It's impressive. Twice the size of Buckingham Palace or Versailles."

The palace looked like something out of a fairy tale. *A fairy tale with ghosts, demons, chocolate brains—and now machine guns,* Maggie amended as she saw the stone walls were guarded by armed soldiers. The driver handed over their identification to be checked, the gates opened, and they drove slowly through. As they passed, more Falange guards gave the car the Fascist salute.

Civiles, the Civil Guard who kept General Franco in power, stood at intervals along the road, some cradling submachine guns. At the entrance to the grand staircase, a parade of Falange Youth lined the curb, waving little Spanish and swastika flags. The car stopped, and more soldiers in uniform opened the doors for her and Juanito in front of a statue of King Carlos III dressed as a Roman emperor.

Winds gusted and Maggie shivered in the cold night air. Juanito, handsome in white tie, offered her his arm. They ascended the staircase, lined with even more gun-holding guards.

Halberdiers Hall was a grand, high-ceilinged room. The walls were covered in enormous Cuenco tapestries, ceilings in frescoes, and it was only slightly warmer than outside. Dim electric light tried to sparkle from the chandeliers. Long tapered candles in silver candelabras flickered from massive side tables. The guests were a heady mix of celebrities: German UFA film stars and their Spanish counterparts, bullfighters, and society women. They mixed, like exotic birds, among the studio executives, politicians, and aristocrats. *And—somewhere—Werner Heisenberg.*

Maggie could feel the gun strapped to her thigh as she walked the expanse of plush Aubusson carpets. She didn't think she'd be subjected to a body search, but she was terrified of discovery, nonetheless. Faint strings played Bach's Double Violin Concerto as she accepted a coupe of champagne from a waiter's silver tray. She could swear her heart was beating loud enough for anyone to hear, but took comfort in the fact no one noticed her beside Juanito.

People tried not to stare at the bullfighter, but couldn't help it, she noticed. She was more than happy to be overlooked. *Does this make me the Scythe of Death?* She giggled almost hysterically. *Or a Pistol Packin' Mama?*

Yet more doors opened to reveal the party already in full swing, studded with even more people in white tie and glistening gowns, air-kissing and sipping cocktails. Juanito put his hand on her bare back and guided her in.

She walked carefully on the marble floor, excruciatingly aware of the gun, staring at enormous oil paintings but not really seeing them. She felt almost outside her own body. She was alone, without even Ángel. She had only this one last chance to ascertain the truth about Germany's fission bomb program.

"Are you cold, Paige?" Juanito asked. "Would you like my jacket?"

"No." Maggie rubbed goose bumps on her arms. "I'm fine."

"It's nerves, isn't it?"

Her head snapped around. *Does he suspect anything?* "Nerves?"

"Please forgive me for saying it, but it's quite normal. That's how everyone is when they meet the General for the first time."

The click of heels rang out like pistol shots, followed by a volley of "¡*Viva Franco!*" The General entered, with his balding head, double chin, and little gray moustache.

He was wearing a general's uniform, with a broad slash of red across his plump torso, gold-fringed epaulettes on his shoulders, and rows of medals on colorful ribbons. Here he was, in the flesh, the face on the currency, the postage stamps, endless placards and posters that hung in every shop window.

And he looked mundane, forgettable. Except for the immense power he held.

The air was now charged, electric. All eyes were turned to Franco, every expression deferential. He appeared haughty, as if he'd rather be anywhere else. But then he spotted the German ambassador, who approached him, and they began to converse. People glanced away; the tension in the room dispersed, like a held breath exhaled.

The next room Maggie and Juanito entered was larger, grander, and colder. Across the room, the smooth, rich tones of Spanish were juxtaposed against the jagged consonants of German. There was no need for Nazi uniforms here; the German men wore impeccable Hugo Boss suits and swastika pins. She noted several of them deep in conversation with a cardinal in red robes. A group of Spanish women in Balenciaga, glittering with gold and jewels, stood close to the warmth of the fireplace.

Maggie tried to find Heisenberg in the crowd. People were clustered in small groups, laughing and chatting, the sound of their voices mingling with the clink of crystal. Waiters in white gloves were passing trays of hors d'oeuvres. When one offered glistening charred octopus on a toast point to Maggie, she raised a gloved hand and swallowed back nausea.

Juanito immediately became the center of attention, from both male and female Spanish aristocrats. He grimaced apologetically to Maggie, and she gave him a reassuring smile. She took the opportunity to find a corner where she could keep an eye on the entrance and wait for her quarry.

She exchanged small talk in a mix of Spanish and English with a few of the tiara-wearing women and their partners. Heisenberg hadn't arrived yet, apparently. *I know his eventual location, but not his current one,* Maggie thought, setting her glass of sparkling wine down on a side table with legs carved into beast claws. She didn't want any alcohol tonight. She noticed several undercover security guards prowling through the crowd, their darting eyes, badly fitting suits, and fast walk giving them away.

At last she spotted Chanel, wearing a red silk gown, ropes of pearls, and glittering jewels. Maggie recognized a two-headed platinum eagle and rare shield-cut diamonds as Chanel's own designs, inspired by those she had received from another lover, this one a Romanov duke.

Chanel greeted the German ambassador, then found her way to Maggie. "Miss Kelly," she said, eyeing her, "you turn up in the most interesting places." Maggie opened her mouth to speak but nothing came out. "Wearing another ill-fitting dress, I see." The couturiere sniffed. "Turn for me."

Maggie closed her mouth and did as she was bid. "It's a Schiaparelli," Chanel muttered with disgust. "*L'Italienne*," she whispered under her breath in a tone that made it sound like a curse. Maggie remembered there had been no love lost between the two designers. *Yes, but unlike you, Elsa Schiaparelli left Paris for New York when war broke out,* Maggie thought. *She, at least, didn't stay in Nazi-occupied Paris, taking a Nazi lover. She isn't trying to negotiate a separate peace with the Allies.*

"You're living history tonight—on the arm of the most famous bullfighter in the world—and you can't even move in that dress." Chanel scoffed. "Not only are you seven pounds too heavy, and the fit unconscionable, but it's a monstrosity. And with feathers, no less! Feathers! You look like a crow working as a prostitute."

"I had the same thought before I left. About the crow, not the prostitute, though," Maggie admitted. "It's borrowed."

"Beauty's a weapon, you know," Chanel said, darkened brows knit in thought. She appraised Maggie's gown once again, then took her arm. "Come with me."

In the ladies' lounge, Chanel unceremoniously ripped all the feathers from the dress's neck and sleeves. Then she knelt and tore every plume from the hem. She removed the beaded and feathered belt as well. Maggie was aware of the eyes of women, touching up their lipstick and fixing their hair, upon them, as well as how close the designer was to finding her gun.

"There," Chanel said with satisfaction, gazing at the simple but elegant sleeveless and scoop-necked black dress that remained. "I don't know what you're up to tonight, Miss Kelly, but you'll look the part now, at any rate."

She didn't discover the gun, Maggie thought, struggling to breathe normally. *Thank God.*

She spun to gaze at her reflection. The couturiere was right. The dress was significantly better—elegant, modern, fresh. As if that were in any way important at the moment.

Chanel frowned. "It needs something more." She pulled a carnation from an enormous bouquet in an urn and placed it in Maggie's hair, plucking out the feathers. Then she took off one of her own necklaces, strands of pearls with diamonds, and placed it around the spy's neck.

"Oh, I couldn't possibly, Mademoiselle—" Maggie said.

"You'll repay me by never wearing that Italian's dresses, ever again." She stepped back with a glare. "Have I made myself clear?"

The necklace was heavy and warm on Maggie's neck. "Yes, Mademoiselle."

"Have you ever heard of a glamour?" the couturiere said. She was in her element, making sure every thread was in place and looked perfect. "Not glamour—I mean *a* glamour. Beauty, you see, casts a spell. Glamour distracts the eye. It sparkles and dazzles and prevents us from seeing what's really there. Even the word itself means enchantment and magic. Just ask Dr. Goebbels. It's not by chance that his newspapers alternate lines about war with pictures of actresses. It's high time you learned to use it."

"I understand."

They made their way back to the gala. Chanel leaned in to whisper in her ear, "All best wishes to you and your *bébé*." Then the couturiere spied one of her friends. "Countess Gloria von Fürstenberg. They say the American ambassador discovered her in a Mexico City casino when she was sixteen. She's allegedly half Spanish, half Mexican. Tried to make a go of it as an actress in Hollywood but wised up and married well. At least *she's* wearing one of my dresses."

As Chanel wafted away to speak with the Countess, Maggie turned to see Heisenberg enter, dressed in black tie. He was laughing and joking with the Spanish bear of a man from the university. They made the rounds together, accepting glasses of champagne, stopping for a conversation with the German ambassador. Maggie watched him mingle and make small talk, then finally summoned the nerve to put herself directly in his path.

"Good evening, Herr Professor," she said in German with a smile. "We meet again."

He placed his empty coupe on a waiter's tray. "Miss Kelly, what brings you here?"

"I'm the guest of Juanito Belmonte," she said, gesturing to the bullfighter, still surrounded by a swarm of admirers.

"He's a star. Especially after the fight. And you lucky girl—you received the ear!"

Maggie felt nauseated at the memory but pressed on. "*You're* the star tonight, Herr Professor." Another waiter passed with a silver tray of filled coupes. Maggie took two and handed one to Heisenberg.

He gave a self-deprecating chuckle as he accepted it. "Hardly." He raised his glass. "*Prost!*"

She raised hers as well. "*Prost!*" They both took a sip. The cut glass sparkled in the candlelight, and she felt the bubbles tilt at the back of her throat, sharp as stars.

"Even though I'm Irish," Maggie said, "I grew up in the United States." She was relieved to say something truthful at last. "I know you've spent some time in America as well. New York City, am I right? Columbia University?"

"So many brilliant scientists left Germany for America. Germany's loss is the Allies' gain." She watched a shadow cross his face.

This is it, she thought. "Tell me," she said, putting her glass down on a side table and leaning in, "do you think they're working on nuclear fission? The German scientists who fled to the U.S.?" She lowered her voice, hoping to appeal to his competitive nature.

He looked at her sharply, then laughed. "Einstein's brilliant, but ultimately a poet. He found an *Alice in Wonderland* universe. The faster you move, the heavier you become, you see? And, even stranger, time slows down! Of course, none of this's noticeable unless you're moving close to the speed of light."

"But most Nazi scientists consider Einstein's theory of relativity an 'evil fantasy,' created by Jewish scientists to 'trick noble Aryans,' don't they?" Maggie asked. "They embarked upon a campaign to rid Germany of 'Jewish physics' and replace it with 'German physics'?"

Heisenberg finished his glass of champagne in silence. Maggie raised her brows at a waiter, who hurried over with his tray. *Maybe he'll say more if he's drunk.*

"They must be working on a fission weapon," she offered as Heisenberg helped himself to another. "Don't you think?"

He looked at her. "You're not drinking yours!"

She took a sip. "Of course I am!"

He sighed. "Even if they're working on a bomb, which I doubt, they can't be very far along."

Interesting . . . "Why do you think that?"

"They're not . . . real Germans."

"You mean they're Jewish?"

"They left." He shrugged. "And they simply cannot be first-rate scientists outside of Germany."

The arrogance! Maggie thought. But she said only "You yourself were accused of 'Jewish science.'" Despite being Christian, Heisenberg had been attacked in the press as a "White Jew" who should be made to "disappear" after he'd submitted a paper on the neutron-proton model of the nucleus.

The accusation hung in the air, and he stared. "You seem to know a lot about me, Miss Kelly."

"You're a public figure, a Nobel Prize winner, Herr Professor," she countered. "You elected to stay in Germany, even after they accused you."

"I'm a German," he said stiffly. "Not a Nazi."

"You've said." Maggie smiled sweetly. "You're head of the Kaiser Wilhelm Institute."

"I'm only interested in my own research."

This is it! "Which is . . . Hitler's new 'wonder weapon'?" She watched his face closely.

"We're not talking theoretical physics," Heisenberg said. "We're talking practical applications—applications that, yes, could change the war. A superweapon. Or, what did you call it? A 'wonder' weapon." Maggie could sense the Gestapo undercover security team circling.

Heisenberg noticed the attention as well. "Surely you'd rather be spending time with a glamorous bullfighter than an old man like me," he said, an edge to his tone.

A gong was struck, and the echo reverberated through the room, causing conversation to cease. "Time for dinner," the physicist said, relieved.

Juanito came up behind Maggie and offered an arm. "Ready?" he asked.

"Yes." She put down her half-full coupe and took it. "I'm starving." *And we're just getting started.*

. . .

In the dining hall, the walls were swathed in tapestries and the table covered in white damask. Maggie peered at the assembled guests as waiters in tails scurried in and out. She had hoped to be seated near Heisenberg, but no such luck. When she sat, the gun weighed heavily on her leg.

Still, even over the low hum of conversation and clinks of silver against bone china, as they ate the first course of mushroom soup, she could hear the physicist perfectly as he spoke. The physicist sat between Chanel and a famous Andalusian actress, a ravishing brunette, her dress's neck and cuffs trimmed in mink. "I just don't understand how you could have stayed in Germany," the actress was saying to Heisenberg.

He grimaced slightly and put down his spoon, then pressed his napkin to his lips, as if forcing back words he'd rather not say aloud. He reached for his glass of sherry.

"No politics!" Dr. Martinez instructed from across the table, coming to his friend's defense. Even in his dinner jacket, he still reminded Maggie of a teddy bear. "No war!"

As the waiters cleared away the soup bowls and brought in the next course, Maggie felt queasy. *Is it morning sickness? Nerves? I don't even know anymore. . . .*

"I must say that Germany's been good for France in the long run," Chanel declared as the waiter served her oysters. Another followed, pouring glasses of Albariño. To Maggie, it sounded rehearsed, but she'd probably been given talking points. Dincklage looked on approvingly, as if she were his star pupil.

"It would be wonderful if Germany and Britain could come to some kind of . . . peace agreement," Chanel continued. "So much better to keep the Russians out of Europe, yes? You know Stalin has plans for controlling the countries bordering Russia. This would keep them out. Keep Europe European."

Maggie began to feel a red ache behind her left eye. *Harbinger of a migraine,* she thought and took a sip of water. General Franco and some of the others raised their glasses, and Dincklage looked proud.

"But the war's all but lost for Germany now, no?" said the actress next to Heisenberg. The German ambassador seemed enraged, Maggie noted, but Heisenberg merely appeared sad. Or was it numb? He picked up his glass of white wine.

The actress turned back to Heisenberg, her mother-of-pearl hair comb catching the light. "Why *did* you stay, Professor?" she asked, putting down her spoon with a clink. "You remained in Germany during the war, when you had every opportunity to leave. You *chose* to stay. Why?"

The man to her right put a warning hand on her arm. "*Querida* . . ." he cautioned gently. Maggie felt the migraine slowly bloom behind her left eye. *But maybe this actress can be helpful?*

She shook her companion off. "After all, so many of your colleagues left Germany. Either they were Jews and they had to, or they were moral Germans who didn't want to be on the wrong side of the war." The actress took a long drink of wine and called the waiter over for a refill.

"I stayed in Germany—with my wife and children, and our older parents," he told her. "Germany's my home and I've responsibilities there, both to my family and to the Fatherland." He flashed a sideways glance to the ambassador. "I'm a scientist—not a politician. And, above all, I'm German."

"And we're all famished! Let's enjoy this lovely meal," the ambassador said as the plates were cleared and waiters set down tiny bowls of sharp lemon sorbet to cleanse the palate between courses. "Mademoiselle, I'd love to learn more about the Germans in France," he said to Chanel.

"Yes, of course," she replied, warming to her subject. Whatever she said would be passed back up the intelligence chain to

Walter Schellenberg, Maggie knew. "Perhaps to no one's surprise, France is far more disciplined under the Germans. More
efficient. Better regulated. Something the British and Americans should think about, if Stalin tries anything."

Heisenberg's face remained a mask as the gun's steel burned
against Maggie's leg. She forced herself to breathe.

"*I* want to hear about the bulls," Franco told the table, finishing his sorbet in a single huge spoonful. "Bulls are always
more interesting than politics." Juanito, seated across from the
general, immediately began telling him of a new breeding program guaranteed to produce even larger and more aggressive
bulls. The dictator looked pleased.

Through a haze of pain, Maggie noted Heisenberg seemed
relieved. As the waiters cleared the sorbet bowls, she saw that
the physicist's wineglass had been refilled. *Good,* she thought.
*Might make him more talkative. Although the window for
talk's quickly closing . . . and it'll soon be time to act.*

Chapter Twenty-eight

After dinner, the guests moved to yet another grand and gilded room, where the men were served Spanish brandy and the women small glasses of sweet orange juice from Valencia. Maggie put hers down untouched when she noticed Heisenberg leaving the room. *This is it,* she thought. She found a waiter and asked for a bottle of brandy and two glasses, then followed.

Outside, in the cold, Maggie sucked in her breath and checked her surroundings. No one had followed, as far as she could tell. Still wary, she headed through the courtyard.

She finally caught up with the physicist on one of the palace's balconies. It was cold and quiet; they seemed to be completely alone. The stars dazzled in the night sky as the wind picked up. She could hear faint music from the party.

"Nightcap, Professor?" Maggie's head was pounding as she set the bottle and glasses on the balcony's ledge, and she could barely see through the pain.

Heisenberg looked up; in the dim light he appeared gaunt and shadowed, like an El Greco painting. "Are you following me, Miss Kelly?"

As she poured them both glasses, she realized this was the perfect place for a kill; she could even push his body over the railing to the gardens below. "I'm in the company of one of the world's greatest minds. Of course I want to speak with you." She handed him the snifter; her hand was steady, but her knees trembled.

He accepted the glass, then gazed out over the gardens swathed in darkness. "Even if I'm a Nazi?" he said with bitterness.

"Are you?" she asked, then raised her glass for him to clink. She felt sick with pain and fear, but she gritted her teeth into a smile.

"I'm German," he said, swirling the brown liquid in his glass before taking a sip. "I work for Germany. I can't help it if a gang of criminals and half-wits have taken power in my country and given us a war nobody wanted."

That's the alcohol, Maggie thought. She took a small sip of her own but couldn't taste anything. The wind blew and goose pimples rose on her arms. "You didn't have to become involved with the Nazis. Nobody forced you to advise them on deadly weapons." She surreptitiously tipped her drink onto the stones.

"My dear, you've no idea what Germany is really like." He took a large gulp. "You didn't have to work with them. To stand by while they rode roughshod over every law and civil right. While they arrested and murdered thousands of our own citizens."

"You could have left the country." She refilled both their glasses.

Heisenberg moved closer. "You think I should have run away?"

He was so close she could smell the alcohol on his breath. But she still couldn't read the expression in his eyes. "Don't you feel any responsibility?"

"I couldn't abandon Germany to these . . . people. My responsibility kept me in Germany." Maggie thought she heard him starting to slur his words a fraction. "I've no use for Hitler, but I do love Germany," he said, raising his glass and then taking another generous sip. "That's my ancestry, you understand, my blood." He pulled a silver case from his dinner jacket's breast pocket and opened it. "Cigarette?"

"No, thank you."

He plucked one from the case, lit it, and exhaled a stream of smoke. "They're terrible for you," he admitted. "Still, with a brandy, after a large meal . . ."

Maggie knew she had to tread carefully. She shivered in the cold, coming to stand closer to him. In silence, glasses in hand, they looked out over the moonlit bluff of Casa de Campo in the direction of the Manzanares River. "You know, on a clear day, you can see the mountain pass leading from Madrid to Old Castile," he said, with a touch of melancholy.

"It's easy to see why Madrid's Berber rulers picked this spot for a fortress," Maggie said. "Easy to protect. Although I'm surprised it's still standing after the Civil War."

"The Falange never touched the Royal Palace." Heisenberg took a swallow. "It's a symbol for the Monarchists."

Another silence. Maggie put her glass down and knelt slightly, as if to adjust her satin slipper. But instead, her hand reached beneath her skirt. Her fingers eased the tiny gun from its holster. She concealed it in her hand.

Terror coursing through her veins, she moved the gun's hammer back to full-cock position as she stood. She had two shots. There was room for only one mistake. Not even that.

She was aware Heisenberg was now speaking about his wife, his children. About their beautiful garden in Germany. He toasted them in the night air.

Now that she faced him, could she really shoot him? He was unarmed, unprepared. . . . A husband and a father. Just like Connor. Her fingers felt paralyzed. *He doesn't know it,* Maggie thought, *but his own life's balanced between two quantum states. In one outcome, he'll be dead with two bullets in him. In the other, he'll live to see another day.* She felt adrenaline flood through her and was aware of a high-pitched ring filling her ears. The migraine pain grew almost unbearable.

"We're looking out over a battlefield, you know," Heisenberg was saying as he put down his empty glass. "It's the royal garden, yes—but unexploded shells are buried there."

"I'm still trying to determine your position," Maggie said, cutting to the chase.

"As am I, with you." He rested the burning cigarette on the stone ledge.

"A last question." *This is it,* she thought. "And it's not of science but morality. *Would* you build the bomb?"

"Can I?" He laughed mirthlessly. "Of course."

Maggie tightened her grip on the gun beneath her palm and slid her finger into the trigger. "No—the question is—would you? Will you? Or have you already?"

He shook his head, unwilling to answer. *Say something!* she wanted to scream. But instead she tried a different tactic. "How would it feel if the Americans got there first? Created the world's first fission bomb?"

"They won't," he said sharply. She could feel the heat of his anger and disdain. "They can't. The Germans have the edge. Germany always has the upper hand."

Ah, there it is, Maggie thought. *Finally. He's competitive. That could be his Achilles' heel.* "Are you sure, though? Germany turned on its own Jewish scientists—Einstein and the rest. Without them . . ."

"They left Germany, true. But Hahn, von Weizsäcker, Houtermans, Harteck, and I—we all stayed."

"You don't know what Einstein and the others are working on. With the British and the Americans."

Heisenberg's eyes flashed, and Maggie could see his driven nature rise again. He scoffed and picked up his cigarette. "A weapon's too far away," he said after inhaling. "Too expensive." He blew out smoke. "I do think a bomb's possible, but it needs too much time and money to succeed for this war. No one's going to be able to fund it. If the Germans can't, certainly the Americans and Brits can't. They're years behind us."

Are you sure? Maggie thought. "Too expensive?" she pressed, "for Albert Speer? Undoubtedly he's putting tons of money into his weapons development program." She could feel the gun, heavy in her hand behind her back. She tried again. "You're the head of Kaiser Wilhelm. Surely you're provided with everything you need."

His eyes flashed with rage. "Peenemünde," he said finally, with a sneer.

Maggie heard his voice rise in pitch, noted his rapid blinks, saw as he bit his lip. He made it sound like profanity. *Sore spot. Good.* "Peenemünde?"

"That's the weapons program that's won all the money, all the resources," he said bitterly. "The rockets. That's Speer's darling now."

"What happened?"

"The Allies took out the heavy water factory in Norway last year—can't be rebuilt. Since then, the German Army can't spare a man or an ounce of material. Speer's ordered work on a reduced scale. He wants us to focus on atomic power for industry."

He took another large gulp of brandy. "You couldn't understand—you're just a girl," he said, but it sounded as if he were talking to himself. "The Nazis are concentrating on weapons that can be produced quickly. The rocket program in Peenemünde received the money they should have given to us, to me, to my fission program. We have no resources, no support, no funding, no manpower. Nothing but ideas on chalkboards."

He tossed the cigarette over the rail. Maggie watched the red light arc, then fall into darkness. "We make do with scraps," he said bitterly. "Treated like peons."

In that moment, Maggie knew his position at last. *They don't have the bomb,* she realized, heart in her throat. *They don't.* She flipped the safety back on the gun, which she still held behind her back. The avatar of uncertainty was certainly a lucky man, at least tonight.

She was silent in the starlight. Despite the throbbing of her migraine, the significance of what the physicist had said echoed in her mind. The Germans didn't have a bomb. Instead, they were putting everything into their rocket program. The United States—the Allies—were inching ever closer. The Allies would produce a fission bomb first. It would decide the war. She felt a wave of relief. *But will they use it? And how many people— civilians—will still die?*

Heisenberg barked out a bitter laugh. "Do you think Speer would let me come to Madrid if I were supervising a fission bomb project?" He snorted. "I'm here for the propaganda, trotted out like a show pony." Then he looked up at her sharply, anger flashing in his eyes. "Who *are* you?"

"A fellow scientist—taught to question, hypothesize, and observe," she told him. It was over. Germany wasn't even close to creating the fission bomb. And she would *not* have to shoot him.

Maggie should have felt relief, but instead, she felt a sharp pain in her abdomen. She turned away, pretending to peer out at the gardens, and let the gun fall off the side of the balcony. She felt wetness between her legs, dripping down to the stones, and sharp, sickening cramps shot through her gut. She bent over, clutching herself. *What—?*

A *bang* echoed across the courtyard. Something whizzed by her with a peculiar buzzing sound. *A bullet,* she realized, head spinning. *Aimed at me.* Her cramps had saved her. She looked in the direction of the shot and saw a man, wearing all black, holding a glinting gun. *He must have scaled the wall,* she thought dimly. Alarm bells jangled in her head. *Ángel?*

He approached. "I've been a faithful servant of Russia since my early twenties—and if I'm ordered to dispose of British agents, that's what I do. No matter how much I might personally like you. And I do like you, Maggie, very much."

Heisenberg's eyes widened.

"You wouldn't shoot me, Ángel," Maggie told him with false bravado. "You'll be caught. Kim will discover you're a double agent."

"No." He smiled, as though to a small child. "I've let everyone know I'm in Lisbon tonight. I'm on this morning's flight manifesto and any number of my colleagues there will report seeing me at the gaming tables."

Ángel moved the pistol's muzzle a fraction, pointing it directly at her heart.

"Señor," Heisenberg began, "surely you and I, as gentlemen, can settle this—"

Ángel pointed the gun at the physicist for a moment. "Shut up. And don't even think about moving."

"You killed Connor, didn't you?" Maggie said, realizing. "Not *you,* of course—since we were dancing at the time—but someone you're working with," she said. "You had him killed so you could work this mission with me." Her voice shook with rage and sorrow. "Who stabbed him?"

"Just another comrade," he told her. "One death, or even two, means nothing in this war. It's all about who'll ultimately control Europe—Russia or Germany or the Allies. We're fighting for control of the very globe now. We're already knee-deep in the next war and most people haven't even realized it." Maggie swallowed. "You're shocked, aren't you?"

"Who was it?" she demanded, even as she felt Heisenberg readying himself to run.

Ángel also caught the movement. He took a shot and grazed the physicist's thigh. Heisenberg shouted German profanities and doubled over in pain.

"Madrid's full of characters willing to make some pocket money. Loyalty is cheap."

"What about the Marquesa?" she asked, taking Heisenberg's jacket off him and using it to apply pressure to his wound. *It's just a nick,* she thought. *Superficial.* "Doña Rosa? You killed her too? What did she know?" Heisenberg's low moans continued, and he dropped to his knees.

An expression of contempt flashed across Ángel's face. "Of course I killed her. Dropped a little potassium cyanide into her glass when the old dear wasn't looking. She was one of my subagents, one who didn't trust me—she'd overheard me talking to my NKVD handler. I couldn't have her warning you."

"But you brought me to the party to meet her!" Maggie protested, keeping an eye on Heisenberg, still on his knees, head bent low to the cobblestones. *Keep him talking. The longer he's talking, the longer he's not shooting.*

"She was communicating, with the cards," he said. "That she was on to me. She wanted to tell you in private. I'd been made." He shook his head. "And even then I might have let you go—but you wouldn't give me the damn letter. Stalin himself forbids that letter go to Winston Churchill. My orders are to make sure it's destroyed." He sighed. "And I'm sorry, but that includes you now, too."

Another shot rang out, this one from the shadows of the courtyard. Echoes bounced off the stone walls as Ángel staggered, dropping the gun, hand to his chest. She could only watch in horror as he fell to his knees. He crawled forward a few paces before crumpling to the cobblestones.

Maggie caught the faint whiff of gunpowder on the wind. *He tried to shoot me—and then someone shot him* was all she could take in before her legs gave way beneath her. She lost consciousness in her own growing pool of blood.

Chapter Twenty-nine

A gray dawn had come and gone, and morning passed as sheets of white clouds blew across the sky. As *Madrileños* left work to go home for lunch and siesta, Maggie slept on.

However, she was safe. Hospital Municipal de Cirugía, in the Latina quarter, was the oldest in Madrid and considered the best. Overhead, the dim electric lights sputtered, barely cutting through the day's gloom, and the curtains were drawn. Maggie lay semiconscious on a white enamel-framed bed in a private room.

When she'd arrived, the nurses had taken off her finery and put her in a cotton gown. A doctor had examined her, and the nurses had given her thick menstrual pads and pain medication.

Maggie, abdomen cramping viciously, had been only dimly aware of what was happening. As she flickered in and out of consciousness, she heard kind voices speaking Spanish. She didn't understand the words, but she did comprehend the tone. She was having a miscarriage. Bean was no more.

She must have been given a sedative, because she found it impossible to keep her eyes open. Everything she did to try to keep her mind alert failed, and finally she slipped into a dreamless sleep.

. . .

When Maggie woke finally, she realized that Chanel, immacu-
lately dressed, was sitting on the straight-backed chair by her
bed, smoking a Gitane. "Ah, there you are," she said in English, noting Maggie's open eyes. She'd brought a bouquet of
red carnations. "We were wondering how long you'd sleep."

Maggie blinked at the surreal scene. Chanel ground out her
cigarette in an empty ceramic bedpan. "How do you feel?"

Maggie moved a bit. Everything hurt, probably from the
fall. The room reeked of antiseptic. She looked down at her
inner elbow. A needle in her vein was hooked to a bag of intra-
venous solution.

The events of the previous evening were coming back to her.
Her hands went to the thick cotton padding between her legs.
"I'm sorry," Chanel said. "You've lost the child."

Maggie swallowed, willing herself not to cry.

"You're part of a club now," Chanel told her, not unkindly.
"A club no one wants to be in." Maggie understood what the
designer was sharing with her.

*But I want—wanted—a baby. I wanted to tell John. I
wanted us to watch my belly grow. My feet swell. To pick
names . . .* The grief she felt was overwhelming, primitive, and
she pressed her face into the pillow and exhaled a guttural
scream. *How can you have so much love for someone you
never knew?*

Bean. Maggie raised her head. *Little Bean. Mine and
John's . . .*

"You're young," Chanel told her dispassionately. "You can
have more children if you want. Take comfort in that." She
added, "Also take comfort in the fact I registered you under a
false name. You're safe for the moment. Although not for
long."

A doctor in a white coat knocked at the open door and then

entered. He was short, diminutive even, but with a great mane of curly black hair and cheeks already sprouting dark stubble. "It was early, *Señora*," he told Maggie in accented English. "I'm sorry, but you lost the pregnancy. We examined you and kept you overnight for observation. But you're free to leave today. You should know you'll bleed for one to two weeks, like a heavy period. We'll give you sanitary napkins to take with you."

By rote, Maggie replied, "Thank you, Doctor."

"It's not uncommon." He put his hand on her arm. "Happens in one out of ten pregnancies—and those are just the ones we know of. Again, you'll bleed, but any clotting, dizziness, or fainting all warrant a trip back to the hospital."

Maggie forced herself up into a sitting position. Chanel. The letter. The mission. *Bean, I'm so, so sorry. I promise I'll cry for you later.* "I'm fine" was all she said.

He nodded. "Let the nurses know if you need anything." He turned before he left. "I'll light a candle in the hospital chapel for you."

"Thank you." When he left, Maggie slumped back against the pillows.

Chanel said only "I brought you some clothes. And I took the necklace back. It wasn't really your style."

Maggie watched the ceiling fan spin. *Work*, she thought. She needed to focus on work. "Professor Heisenberg?" she asked.

"On his way back to Germany. But he was the one who got help for you—when you fainted. His leg just needed to be bandaged."

Maggie thought of the physicist, returning safely to his family. He didn't need to die. And yet, a life had been taken. Bean's. She knew there was no connection, no correlation between the lives, one hadn't been exchanged for the other. And yet it felt as if somehow a price had been paid.

Bits and pieces of the evening were returning to Maggie in bright, confusing images. She remembered Ángel, with a gun. He'd shot at her and missed. "Ángel?"

"Dead." Chanel shook her head, a hand going to the curve of her neck. "Gestapo guards shot him before he shot you. I don't know what sort of company you keep, Miss Kelly, but you may want to rethink your traveling companions." She quirked a penciled eyebrow. "Let's not forget you still need to deliver my message to the Prime Minister, yes?"

Ángel wanted to kill me . . . Maggie thought, using reason and logic to distract herself. *He was always interested in Chanel's letter to Churchill. But he knew I'd deliver it safely to the P.M.*

"The letter means nothing," she said slowly. "I've worked closely with Mr. Churchill. He'd never, ever consent to a separate peace. I'd stake my life on it. I *will* deliver it, because I promised." She breathed through the pain of an intense cramp. "But it won't make a whit of difference."

Chanel was looking out the window; the light from the wooden slats cast striped shadows across her made-up face. "I know what you must think," she said, lighting another cigarette. "I'm a 'horizontal collaborator.' Well . . ."

She inhaled, and the tip of her cigarette glowed orange. "Bullshit!" she rasped, as though Maggie had challenged her. "I'm a pragmatist." She exhaled smoke. "A *survivor*. Even with France subjugated to Germany, a truce is the only way Europe will survive the Communists."

Maggie told her the truth. "You're betraying France."

Chanel drew herself up. "I'm *saving* France!"

"Do you take any responsibility for the horrors of the Nazis in the Occupation?"

"As I've said, the discipline—"

"Bollocks," Maggie spat. "What about the Jews?"

Chanel's face shuttered. "Don't talk to me about 'the Jews.'

You've no idea what they did to me and my company. To my country."

"I know you sold your company, at a significant profit, to the Wertheimers," Maggie said. "And you regretted the sale."

"No—"

"Yes!" Despite the pain, she pulled herself up on the bed. "Since the Nazis were stealing French businesses owned by Jews, you thought you could use the new Aryan laws to get out of your contract—take your company back from the Wertheimers."

"Nonsense!" Chanel stated, although her voice rose in pitch.

"You stayed. You lived with, worked with, slept with Nazis. You're not just a collaborator. You're a perpetrator."

Chanel blinked, as though she'd been struck. "You've no idea who I am and what I've been through."

"I know exactly what you've done. What you're trying to do."

A cloud passed over Chanel's face. "I'm a survivor," she repeated. Then, "I wasn't aware of everything."

"You watched as the enemy took over your country, your city. You knew exactly what was happening and you watched. You stayed and watched. You lived at the Ritz, for God's sake!"

Chanel's eyes narrowed. "I fought for everything I received! And I still didn't know what exactly was happening—none of us did!"

"When we have privilege and status, when we're given gifts, we tend not to see beyond the benefits."

"Spatz is a handsome man. And I've lost so many other loves, you've no idea . . ."

"You were—you *are*—part of the inner circle. It's easy to overlook the bad things that are happening, especially when you're on the receiving end of all the good." Maggie let the words sink in. "Why didn't you ask more questions?"

"Life is cruel." Chanel's voice turned self-pitying. "And I'm a monster, apparently."

"You're not a monster," Maggie countered. "You're a human being. Any of us—all of us—have the capacity to be cruel, to have blind spots, to live in denial. We're all trying to survive. We all must be on guard against our own capacity for willful ignorance. But you must see—you weren't led astray. You participated."

Maggie stared at her. *Maybe I can salvage something from this after all.* "Come to Britain with me, Mademoiselle," she urged. "Leave all this behind you. Start a new life in the U.K."

Chanel was taken aback. "It's not so easy."

"None of it's easy."

"I'm a . . . monster," Chanel repeated, protesting, insisting. "A monster."

"No," Maggie told her, "but you must take responsibility. Apologize. Change. Make restitution."

Chanel shook her head, and Maggie could see then how broken the older woman was. Whatever had happened in her life—the rejection, the poverty, the powerlessness—it had damaged her. She could see Chanel splitting off, closing the door to her own humanity, lost in a hall of mirrors. *Can she ever reconnect with that part of herself?* Maggie didn't know.

Maggie glanced at the pitcher of red carnations, then she remembered: Ángel had been compromised.

Red. Not red for Spain. Red for the Soviet Union. Red for Communism. He'd been working undercover for the Russians. Kim Philby had been running a double agent. But did he know? Could Kim be part of the Soviet fifth column?

Chanel was still speaking. "I've had to start all over so many times in life, you wouldn't believe! But strength is built by failure, not success. I'll make it through this. I'll survive. Again. And again, and again, if I must."

Maggie looked over at the couturiere. "I've no doubt."

"Still," Chanel continued, as if speaking to herself. "Guilt is perhaps the most painful companion of death. I anticipate meeting up with guilt sooner rather than later."

There was a knock at the door, and Tom Burns let himself in. " 'The maddest thing a man can do in this life is to let himself die,' " he said.

Maggie realized she was glad to see him. "Who said that?"

"Don Quixote. Or, rather, Sancho Panza to the Don."

"Are you my Sancho Panza, Mr. Burns?"

He smiled modestly. "I like to lend a helping hand where I can."

Chanel drew her glossy sable coat around her. "You have a friend at the British Embassy, Miss Kelly," she said, taking a last inhale of her cigarette before crushing it out. "Mr. Burns was right with you, every step of the way last night. And now I must go." Maggie watched her stand and gather her things. "But I do look forward to hearing from Winston when you deliver the letter."

You'll be waiting until hell freezes, Maggie thought.

As Chanel settled her fur on her shoulders, she added, "I don't know why I didn't see it sooner," she mused. "But you do resemble Peter."

What? Maggie frowned. "Peter? Peter who?"

"Peter Frain, of course. I can see it in your face, your expression right now, in fact. You're his daughter. You must be."

Maggie gasped and stared. "What?" *What's she talking about? Edmund Hope was my father. . . .*

"Clara Hess was your mother." She peered closely at Maggie. "Ah, but you knew that, didn't you? Well, of course you ended up a spy. It's practically the family business!"

Maggie's mouth was open, but no words came out. *I've been made,* she realized. *My cover's blown. And . . . because of my mother?* She was cold with shock.

"When I was in Britain with Bendor, I had an atelier in London," Chanel continued. "Clara was one of my best customers and closest friends. We were inseparable for a time. I designed all the gowns she wore for her performances and her tours. She was a delight to fit. I knew you looked familiar—and not just your face. It's your figure as well."

Maggie wasn't admitting anything. "Clara Hess married Edmund Hope," she said, voice shaky.

"Oh, that one." Chanel waved a hand dismissively. "I could never understand what she was doing with him." She smiled wistfully. "She and I had an affair, you know. It was delightful. But I was with Bendor. And eventually she was with Peter—and then Edmund."

Wait, what? "You? And Clara?"

"Just a dalliance." Coco twitched bony shoulders. "But no, it was Peter she loved. Peter who was everything to her."

Maggie felt as if the world were turning into a Salvador Dalí painting, time moving in strange, unnatural ways. "But—my father—Edmund—had red hair." She'd known her father for a little bit before he'd died. And they did indeed both have red hair.

"Peter's mother was a redhead," Chanel purred. "Magnificent woman. I remember meeting her at the opera. It's not all that uncommon in Britain, after all." She sniffed. "All that inbreeding."

"This is—" Maggie waved her hands. "All too much."

"I suppose it *is* a lot," Chanel said with something approaching sympathy in her voice.

And then she was gone.

Chapter Thirty

"How are you?" Burns asked gently once Chanel was gone. His suit was rumpled, and tie askew. His coat was draped over his shoulders; face shadowed with stubble and eyes bloodshot. By the look of it, he hadn't slept all night.

Maggie lay back in the bed, watching the ceiling fan again. "How do you think?" Anger rose in her, hot and strong. Ángel had betrayed her. Connor was dead. The Marquesa was dead. Kim Philby was possibly a double agent, working for the Soviets.

And she'd lost her and John's baby.

"How did you know to come to the palace?" she asked finally.

"I'm not a novice, Maggie. I've been working in Madrid a long time. And I've been following you since you arrived. You eluded me any number of times, but I was able to give you the slip as well." He pulled the blankets over her and tucked her in, as if she were a small child. "Forgive me. It wasn't that I didn't trust you; I didn't trust anyone around you."

Maggie rubbed her eyes as a wave of fatigue threatened to drown her. "There are double agents in British intelligence," she said finally. "Working for Russia."

"We've suspected many for quite a while. They're slippery,

though. Excellent at their jobs. Some, we believe, have been in place since the early thirties, just waiting. They have the perfect cover."

"Connor?" she asked, heart sinking.

"Connor Sullivan did gamble, and incurred quite a debt," he told her. "However, we think it was more likely, given the timing, that he was killed because he was your handpicked partner."

Maggie closed her eyes, overcome with guilt. "It's my fault."

Burns shook his head. "You recognized an agent you could trust and asked to work with him. *You* didn't kill him."

"He was married, you know. With a small child." Instinctively, her hands went to her abdomen.

"We know," Burns said. "And it's horrible, terrible, that Connor was murdered. But it's not your fault. You can't blame yourself."

"Ángel?" Maggie thought back.

"Yes. Ángel was working in concert with an NKVD handler and other Russian agents in Lisbon. But we hadn't been able to prove anything yet. Portugal's a neutral nation, and if it looks like the death was for a gambling debt, it's not in their police's best interest to investigate further and become involved with spies."

"What about London?"

"While you were sleeping, I contacted London through our channels at the embassy. They know the Lisbon and Madrid cells are blown and Ángel was a double agent." He glanced down. "Your hands are shaking." They were. She gripped the blanket tightly to keep them still.

"And you? You're a spook, too?"

"I'm the press attaché for the British Embassy," he said, with a courtly bow.

That's as much as I'm going to learn, at least for the moment, Maggie thought. "Of course. And—we had a meeting with British intelligence agents in a cellar in Lisbon. . . . Were *they* even real?"

"They were real," Burns told her. "Those are ours. Ángel had them all fooled as well. His Disney background made him the perfect fit for Portugal and Spain. Except it was a cover for his work for Russia. He'd formed Marxist sympathies at Columbia University and was recruited there by the NKVD. He managed to infiltrate British intelligence—possibly with the help of other double agents. His facility with languages was an asset."

"Surely the Soviets didn't take the idea of Britain's making a separate peace seriously? Churchill would *never*."

"But they did," Burns said, "especially with rumors of the P.M.'s illness after the Tehran Conference. Many Russians were terrified of the idea of Coco Chanel bringing a legitimate peace offering not only to Churchill—but to his successor, who could have been not only Conservative but pro-fascist."

Maggie thought. "Then I suppose it's up to whoever marches fastest and invades first." She blinked. "That's the next war, isn't it? The Russians against the Allies."

"Indeed." *And with one or both sides having a fission bomb.*

"And Kim?" she asked. "Kim Philby? What happens to him?"

Burns sighed. "We have our suspicions, but nothing concrete. Not real evidence. It's possible, of course, he wasn't involved."

Maggie thought of Kim, his charm, his perfect manners, his old-boy accent. Who'd ever suspect him? But he *had* dabbled in communism at Cambridge—she remembered reading that about him. "Does Kim know what's happened—with Ángel?"

"Since Ángel's dead, Philby has no way to contact you. I could provide you access at the embassy, of course—"

"No!" Maggie said. She pushed the covers off and sat up

with difficulty. Her hands were no longer shaking. "I need to pick up the letter and leave Spain. It's best if Kim—or anyone—doesn't know." She felt cramps rack her body and steeled herself. "We need to go. I need to finish this." She began to climb out of bed.

"You might want to dress first," Burns said, leaving to give her privacy.

At the Palace Hotel, Maggie walked slowly to the front desk on Burns's arm; she was still in significant pain. She pulled out her key to the safe from her purse. "*Buenos dias, señor*—I'm checking out," she told the man on duty. "I have something in the safe I need to collect."

At the counter a few feet away from Maggie, a young woman with thick black hair and a fur-trimmed wool coat was checking in with her young son. She reached down and ran her hand absently through his silky hair as she spoke with the concierge. The gesture, so ordinary and yet so loving, sent a shaft of longing and loss through Maggie. She could almost feel the soft hair under her own hand, then felt her abdomen twist again.

"Of course, *señorita*." The man flicked his eyes to an associate. "Security will accompany you."

"I'm fine on my own."

"It's hotel policy, miss."

In the hotel's subterranean vault, there were stacks of long wooden drawers, each marked with a bronze plate with a number and a lock. Maggie matched up the number of the key with the correct drawer and opened it. There, nestled on red velvet, was the envelope Coco Chanel had entrusted to her.

"*Such fuss over nothing,*" *Aunt Edith would say.* "*Tempest in a teapot."* Except Connor lost his life over this *"nothing."* As well as Doña Rosa. And who knows how many others?

Maggie had just picked the letter up when she felt a blade pressed to the side of her throat. *"Por favor, señorita,"* a voice growled. A man's large hand reached for the missive.

Let go, part of her thought, as her abdomen tightened like a vise. But she'd promised to deliver it. She'd promised John she'd return. And she needed to pay Peter Frain a visit.

No. She handed the letter over. When the man accepted it, she felt the pressure from the blade lessen. She took the opportunity to grab the knife, hard, and twisted it away from him.

With what strength she had left, she rammed the thick blade into her attacker's open hand. It pierced his palm, the blade protruding on the opposite side. He let out a guttural cry and dropped the letter to grab his wrist as blood began to gush. Maggie snatched up the envelope he'd dropped and ran to the stairwell. But she wasn't fast enough.

A man grabbed her arm and said something in Spanish. "Burns!" she called desperately, hearing the elevator doors open.

"No" came a low, Spanish-accented voice. "Juanito Belmonte, at your service."

Her attacker turned and gaped, his jaw dropping. Maggie had a split second to be amused that even a goon could be distracted by the famous bullfighter before she kicked him hard in the kneecap. He yelped and she pulled away, stumbling toward the stairs.

As the man growled and lurched after her, Juanito said coolly to Maggie, *"Querida,* would you mind giving me a little room?"

"Despite what you may think, I'm not some damsel in distress," she snapped. "I'm trained for this."

"Still. Allow me." Juanito sized up the man wearing the Palace's doorman uniform. He was a head taller than Maggie, with dark hair, a beaky nose, and unwavering eyes. The man had removed the knife from his palm, making a fist to stop the flow of blood. He turned to point the bloody dagger at Juanito and lunged.

Juanito removed his cape with a flourish, just as he had in the ring, then twirled it, throwing it in the attacker's face. The man used the dagger to slice at it, to no avail. While he was temporarily blinded by the heavy black fabric, staggering backward, Maggie slipped back in and kicked him again in the same kneecap. He howled in pain.

As Juanito whipped his cape away, the attacker attempted another slice. The cape wrapped around his arm. "When I arrived at the hospital, you were gone," the bullfighter told Maggie, easily pulling the man around with his cape. "I had to make sure you were all right."

With the dagger still trapped in his hand, the man lurched at Juanito. Maggie slammed the heel of her palm into his nose. The man screamed.

"So I came to the hotel, and your friend, Señor Burns, recognized me. Told me to come down to find you. It's a good thing I did!"

"I'm perfectly fine," Maggie retorted.

The attacker growled in rage, thrusting the knife toward Juanito, who sidestepped it with grace, throwing his cape over the man's head with a cry of *"¡Olé!"* Blinded and disoriented, the man hit the opposite wall and crumpled to the floor.

"I could have handled this," Maggie told him. "Alone." But her abdomen was cramping, and she felt faint. She took a moment to put a hand to the wall for balance and to catch her breath.

"Of course," Juanito said. "I am here only as your 'man of swords.' Your Sancho Panza." The matador silently offered his arm, which Maggie accepted. Slowly, they made their way back to the lobby.

. . .

They met up with Burns under the rotunda. He appraised Maggie's rumpled clothes and Juanito's glowing smirk and uttered a string of profanities.

"Not in front of a lady!" Juanito insisted.

Burns ignored him. "We've got to get you out of here," he said. "I can put you on a flight back to London."

"From Madrid?"

"No—they'll be searching for you at the airport. You'll leave from Gibraltar. I have a train ticket for you. From there, you'll go to the airport."

"Do you need a ride to the station?" Juanito offered. He gestured to the front door. There was his shiny, cream-colored car. "I'll take you anywhere you need to go."

Maggie knew someone might still be watching them. "Pull the car around to the back, Juanito, please," she told him. "We'll jump in. You're coming, too, Mr. Burns."

Juanito bowed his head, then looked up. "Who *are* you?" he asked, eyes wide with curiosity and not a small amount of awe.

She shrugged. "Just a woman."

"I highly doubt that—but I will respect your privacy."

As the bullfighter left to get his car, Burns and Maggie could hear him muttering to himself, "Bulls! Bulls I understand. . . . Women—never!"

Chapter Thirty-one

Juanito's car shuddered in the wind as they drove along the Paseo del Prado to Puerta de Atocha, Madrid's art nouveau train station. A huge drop in temperature heralded a storm, and the sky turned a bilious shade of green. On the way, Maggie and Burns both watched for tails, but there weren't many cars out on the streets. A few people were en route to the Prado, dashing with scarves covering their faces, to protect them from the windstorm's dust.

"We're clean," Burns assured Maggie.

Juanito pulled up in front of the station, a huge wrought-iron structure located at the convergence of several of Madrid's major streets. "They say all roads lead to Rome," he tried to joke, "but really, they all lead to Atocha."

"Thank you, Juanito," Maggie said as she and Burns exited the car into the bitter wind. "I'll think of you every time I see violets. And I'll read all about you in the papers."

His dark eyes were melancholy. "Will I ever read about you?"

Maggie's mouth twitched in a smile, and she kissed his cheek. "Not if I do my job well."

"*Despedida, querida. Vaya con Dios.*"

Farewell, she understood. *Go with God.* "*Gracias,*" she told him sincerely.

Burns offered her his arm, and they passed through the doors of the train station. The huge lobby had a soaring ceiling and the air was perfumed with cooking oil and fried dough. Children wandered, begging for coins, while soldiers in khaki sat on the floor, playing cards for cigarettes. A young mother nursed her baby under an embroidered wool shawl, while her husband ignored their toddler, who was exploring the doors leading to the tracks. Nazis, out of uniform but identified by swastika pins, waited patiently, smoking fat cigars.

In a quiet corner, Burns pulled something from his breast pocket. It was a roll, wound taut inside a transparent envelope. It was shiny, even in the dimness of the spluttering gaslights. "Microfilm."

Maggie nodded. "Of course."

"I don't like to *send* people into danger," Burns told her, "but you're in rather deep already, and we need to deliver this to London."

"Should I even ask what 'this' is?"

As he handed her the roll, he whispered, "Contact information for those in Spain willing and able to help our agents. Took us years to put together." It was surprisingly light in her palm.

"You'll take the train to the airport in Gibraltar. From there, you'll take a plane that'll take you to the RAF base at Northolt. You'll go to St. Mary's Church directly and wait in the last pew in the back. A man will meet you—he'll be wearing a sky-blue scarf. Sit close to him, pretend to pray, and then pass him the film. No talking, no nothing. Just pass the film."

"Just there—in a church pew." Maggie had made a few drops before. "This is your great plan?"

"No, that's my dicey as fuck plan—excuse my language—but I do think simple's best."

Maggie smiled crookedly in agreement. The wind was even stronger now, and rain was slapping the glass of the ceiling.

Burns handed her a ticket. "This will take you to Gibral-tar," he said. "Remember, you're in British territory there. A car will be waiting at the train station to take you to the air-port. If you're picked up on the way, you must destroy the microfilm."

Maggie slipped the roll into her brassiere. "Understood."

Burns glanced up at the flipping letters and numbers on the board. "Your train's arrived," he told her.

She looked at the number on the board, then matched it with the one on her ticket. "You're not coming with me?"

"Alas, no," he said with a sad smile. "But you'll be fine," he told her, patting her shoulder awkwardly. "Just fine."

Maggie was still cramping and bleeding, but he didn't know that. "Thank you," she told him. "For everything."

"As they say in Spain," he said, shrugging, *"de nada."*

Maggie boarded the train. Her heart raced as the conductor checked her name on his clipboard. Her identification matched, and she made her way down the narrow corridor to sleeper number 2, still checking if she were being tailed.

Inside her cabin, she locked the door, then looked around. The space was small and shabby, with dark furniture, velvet flocked wallpaper, and brass fittings. But it was private. The train's whistle blew, and the cars creaked into motion.

Maggie sat on the worn sofa, feeling waves of pain shoot across her abdomen. She gazed through the curtains as the city flashed by—Madrid, then the city's outskirts, then countryside. Rain began to fall in earnest, streaming like tears down the window glass. She put her hand to the roll of microfilm; it was still there, reassuring and solid. She opened her purse and checked for the lipstick case. It was there, too, along with Coco Chanel's letter. Her purse felt impossibly light without the gun.

There was a knock on the door. *"¿Quién es?"* she called.

She heard a man's flat, emotionless voice reply, *"La policía."*

Her stomach clenched, but she rose and cracked open the door with her sunniest smile. "The police! To what do I owe the honor?" Her heart was hammering loudly, and she felt certain he could hear it.

"Your passport, *señorita,*" the officer demanded. He was bulky and florid, with a large black handlebar mustache with waxed tips.

"Of course." She reached into her purse, took out the passport, and handed it to him. He squinted at it.

"And your travel permit?"

What? "Travel permit?" Maggie barely got the words out. *What fresh hell is this? Burns didn't mention a bloody travel permit.*

"New regulation," the officer told her, his breath smelling strongly of cigarillo smoke and fried onions. "Foreigners need a travel permit to leave Madrid now."

"Oh, dear," she said, trying to appear small and helpless. "Or . . . what?"

He handed her back her passport. "Or else I must arrest you."

No, Maggie thought. *No, no, no, no* . . . But at least it seemed just a paperwork mix-up; the policeman didn't seem German. Or Russian. *But then again, who knows?*

"When we arrive in Gibraltar," he told her, "I will take you to the police station."

Maggie smiled and reached for her purse. "You know," she said, "I'm leaving Spain and have no use for this—" She pulled out a wad of bills. "Care to take it off my hands?"

"*¡Señorita!* Are you trying to bribe an officer of the law?"

"No, no!" she replied, stuffing the money back in her bag. "I just don't know what to do with it. . . ."

"It is yours," he told her. "We reach Gibraltar in about twelve hours. Do not attempt to escape."

Maggie locked and chained the door again, then retreated to the small lavatory, with its marble sink and Venetian cutglass mirror. She sat on the toilet, changing out the thick pads the hospital had given her for the train's plush monogrammed hand towels, holding back tears. *No time for crying, Hope,* she told herself. *You can cry all you want when you've delivered the letter and the microfilm and you're back in London.* Then, *If you get back to London.*

The night passed with Maggie curled up in a blanket, looking out into the darkness, feeling the wind buffet the train. Finally, though, the swaying motion helped her sleep, at least for a little while.

When she woke, she blinked for a moment, disoriented, until the memories flooded her, and she put her hand to the film. Still there. She remembered the impending arrest and tried to take deep breaths to quell the wave of terror that threatened to engulf her.

She sat staring out the window as the train rumbled along, barely able to focus on the countryside as it passed. The pale gray light of dawn showed a track curving through rocky fields studded with palm trees.

The skies were clear; they'd outrun the storm. There were no more requests to inspect her papers, and as the train entered Algeciras, Maggie barricaded herself in the lavatory. The Spanish police officer rapped at the door. "Come now, miss," he said. "It's time. Don't make this harder than it needs to be."

She cracked open the small window as far as she could and shouted, "No! I won't go with you. I'm in British territory now. You have no jurisdiction over me here!"

The rapping continued, growing louder. On the train platform, a man in a British police officer's dark blue uniform and helmet overheard and approached. "What's the trouble, miss?"

"They're trying to arrest me!"

There was the sound of kicking and profanity. "Did you do anything?"

"No! And I'm an Irishwoman with an Irish passport!"

The train's security must have brought in tools; they made a cacophony. "I came from Madrid on the express," Maggie told him, straining her voice over the sounds of the *policía* breaking into the lavatory. "I've a passport, but no exit permit. And they want to arrest me! Ambassador Samuel Hoare at the British Embassy in Madrid can vouch for me. I can clear this up with a phone call."

The Spanish officer finally broke down the door. "Miss! You are a prisoner of Spain!"

"No, no, *mi amigo*," the British officer called through the window. "This is Gibraltar—British territory. You've no authority here."

Relief flooded Maggie as the Spaniard mouthed a profanity, shook his fist, then turned on his heel and left, banging the door in frustration. "Thank you," she called, a hand on the microfilm.

The officer saluted, then told her, "My mother's Irish." He winked and walked on.

At that, Maggie felt at least some of the tension she was holding suddenly ease. She exited the train and the station. Outside was a black Packard with diplomatic license plates. The driver looked up. "Miss Kelly?"

"Yes?"

"Mr. Burns told me to expect you." He opened the car door for her. "It's not far to the airport."

Chapter Thirty-two

The wind was still strong as the car pulled up on the tarmac. A man with a sunburned face, wearing a woolen cap, opened the door for Maggie. "Miss Kelly?"

"Yes."

"This way." He walked her through the gusts to the ladder leading up to the plane door.

"Thank you," she said. Before she embarked, she checked for the microfilm. It was still there. And the letter. *Thank heavens.*

She found her worn upholstered seat. A few other passengers were already aboard, some smoking. *Probably diplomats,* Maggie thought, *or other agents.* She looked closely at all of them. Most appeared tired, ready to get some sleep on the plane. In the row in front of her were two men in dark suits and wool overcoats. One was tall and lanky with a curly lock of brown hair falling over his brow. Next to him was a shorter figure with a shock of bristly blond hair, sunburned cheeks, and vigilant blue eyes. "I wonder if this is what it was like for Leslie Howard," the tall one said in a surprisingly high-pitched voice. "On his last trip."

"That was out of Lisbon," his friend replied.

"Still," the tall man said, "Howard was returning from a tour of Spain, following *Gone with the Wind,* as part of a campaign to win Spanish support. Burns himself set that trip up."

Burns? Maggie swallowed. *Tom Burns?*

He continued. "But this is 'the Rock.' Gibraltar. It's ours."

"Krauts are attacking everything flying over the Atlantic—doesn't matter where it's coming from," the smaller, blond-haired man said. "Oh, and don't forget about Poland's General Sikorski."

Maggie remembered that the general had been killed, but not the details. "Was that Lisbon?"

"No, here in Gibraltar. Last June. General's plane crashed after taking off from this very airport," he said. "Killed him and several others on board."

"Does anyone know what happened?"

The man shrugged. "Lots of speculation, plenty of conspiracy theories. Some believe it was an assassination."

"Who?"

"British, Russian, or even a Polish operation . . . Sikorski was the best-known leader of the Polish exiles. His death was a brutal blow to the Polish cause." The man took a monogrammed silver flask from his jacket pocket and offered it to his seatmate. "Calm your nerves? It's good Spanish brandy—better than that pretentious French swill, if you ask me."

The other man declined. He opened his briefcase and pulled out a cobalt-blue thermos. "Doctor says I need to travel with water," he said, shrugging. "Kidney stones."

"Sorry, mate."

Just as the pilot was ready to shut the doors, another man entered. He was young, no more than twenty-five. He wore a dark, voluminous coat, like the ones favored by men in Madrid. However, Maggie thought his face looked English, with pale eyes and pasty skin. She watched as he took his seat at the back of the plane, then pulled his homburg hat's brim low on his forehead as if to settle into a nap.

The pilot announced takeoff and they all fastened their seatbelts. The plane's engine roared to life and, slowly, the aircraft began to taxi down the runway. It gathered speed and then lifted off the ground, surging into the air.

Maggie gazed out the window at the yellow sun, the waves shimmering, and pressed a hand against the microfilm yet again to reassure herself. Then she checked one more time, too, for Chanel's letter in her bag. *Both accounted for. Check and check.* She felt the cords of her neck relax incrementally. Even her cramps were slightly less painful.

For a moment, lulled by the hum of the engine and the low conversation of the other passengers, she allowed herself to close her eyes.

She opened them again when she smelled smoke. She sat up and glanced around. In the rear of the plane, the pasty man had taken off his oversize coat. Maggie saw he had a parachute strapped to his back. "Hey!" she shouted, standing. "What the hell?"

He was wearing flight goggles that obscured his eyes and a black leather helmet. He was struggling with the emergency exit door, which seemed to be stuck. As he struggled to open the door, a few of the other men stirred themselves from their fog of cigarettes and brandy.

Maggie stood, climbed up on her seat, and looked back. Her stomach lurched as she saw a ring of plasticine and a long red cotton wick: an SOE bomb. The wick was lit. But the string was long, longer than they'd been taught to use in training, and burning slowly. *The only time you'd use that,* Maggie thought, *was if you had to leave the scene—and didn't know how fast you'd make it. . . .*

"No!" she shouted, shrugging out of her own coat. She realized he'd set up a bomb on the plane and was about to parachute out, leaving them all to die in the explosion. "A bomb! He's set a bomb! Stop him!"

The tall man in front of her roused himself, realizing what was happening. "You buggering bugger!" he yelled. He leapt from his seat and ran down the narrow aisle to tackle the bomber. Maggie threw her coat on the sparking wick, then jumped over a seat back to put the fire out with her hands before it could reach the plasticine.

The man tackled the bomber against the exit door, but he was hit hard in the throat, then knocked out.

Meanwhile, more of the men had risen. The British man with the flask and the parachutist grappled, each landing blows so loud that Maggie could hear them above the keening of the engine.

Someone must have alerted the captain and the plane dipped to a lower altitude. It hit turbulence and Maggie fell. Crawling up the aisle as the plane bumped and bounced, she finally reached the bomb. Her coat hadn't smothered the wick, as she'd hoped, but was itself going up in bright orange flames, acrid black smoke filling the cabin.

The bomber punched the man's shoulder, who howled in pain. The bomber grabbed him by the back of the neck, swung him around, then pushed him hard. Maggie heard his body hit the back wall with a sickening thud.

The parachutist reached for the red latch of the emergency exit. The door popped open; cold wind filled the plane. He was about to jump, but the shorter man spun him around and landed another punch. They all watched in silent horror as the parachutist fell out of the plane, unconscious.

Maggie, using the parachutist's own heavy coat, finally managed to put out the fire. Her hands were singed and covered in soot. She wiped sweat from her face, leaving a trail of ash.

The short man closed and latched the plane door, and they all looked at one another. "What an arse," he deadpanned, helping the tall man up.

Maggie lifted the coats to make sure the wick was truly extinguished. "Does anyone have any water?" she called.

"Here!" The shorter man threw his blue thermos over several rows of seats. Maggie caught it with one hand, opened it, and poured water over everything. Another puff of black smoke rose. When she was satisfied the fire was completely out, she raised her head. "Absolute arse" was all she could say.

After sharing the flask of brandy and making small talk, the passengers and pilot finally landed safely at RAF Station Northolt, a key airport in the Battle of Britain. The roofs of the hangars were covered with forest camouflage, with house rooftops and gardens, while a gray-blue stream was painted over the runway. When the plane finally touched down, the passengers cheered.

Peter Frain, head of MI-5, met Maggie at the airport's waiting area. When he caught sight of her, he frowned in concern. "You look terrible," he said in his most irritatingly British tones as he walked to her. He took a cambric handkerchief from his pocket. "I think you have a little something on your face."

Maggie gazed at him, speechless as she accepted the fabric. She took in his familiar countenance. Did she look anything like him? He like her? They stood awkwardly at arm's length as she wiped ash from her face. He opened his mouth to continue, but Maggie held up a hand. "Not now, Peter," was all she said. "We need to talk—someone tried to plant a bomb on the plane, to start—but before that, I need to go to St. Mary's."

The plain white wooden church of St. Mary's with its heaven-pointing bell tower was ancient, sections of it having been built around 1290. Its bells rang out across the town's rooftops, echoing in the frosty air. Inside, the sanctuary was shadowy, with flickering lights. The worn wooden pews smelled of beeswax polish. A parishioner knelt near a leaded-glass window, his head bowed and hands folded, while a woman with white hair in a low bun placed vases of fresh-cut evergreen boughs and forced snowdrops on the altar.

The last pew was empty. Maggie shrugged out of her coat, slid in and prepared to wait. As an organist began to practice the sweet, solemn notes of William Henry Monk's "Eventide," Maggie fished the microfilm from her brassiere, then took a hymnal from the rack in front of her. She placed the tiny canister of film between the angled pages. As she did, she doubled over in pain, as yet another shuddering cramp passed through her.

A man entered the church, a hand-knit, sky-blue scarf around his neck. He was wrapped in a bulky coat, and he'd left his hat on, pushed low over his face. He sat on the other end of Maggie's pew, not meeting her eyes.

Maggie saw the blue scarf and slid the hymnal with the precious film down the polished wooden seat. The man took the hymnal, held it in his hands, then removed the film and slipped it into his inside breast pocket. The transaction was complete. He made the sign of the cross, then rose and left.

Maggie remained until the organist finished, the music's final, reverberating notes low and haunting. When she rose at last, she saw that she'd left a smear of blood on the pew.

Chapter Thirty-three

Frain drove slowly through the blackout from Northolt to London. Maggie stared, unblinking, at the darkness outside the window, pierced by cold stars and a dazzling moon.

She gazed at Frain's profile, trying to see if he looked like her. Or, rather, if she looked like him. She felt a deep sadness: *He may or may not be my father. He may or may not have lost a grandchild.*

She felt sorrow at the ephemeral nature of life, how people slip through your fingers, even when you try so very hard to hold on to them. *Everything changes, everything ends,* she thought. *And yet, every beginning comes from an ending.*

And then there was the great, aching sadness of knowing the world was forever and irrevocably altered by the theory of the bomb. Even if the Allies got it first, and Maggie truly hoped they did, there was no way to understand the new world they were all hurtling toward. What was it the beginning of?

Still, she had to stop imagining the worst. Too much was at stake to let conjecture get in the way. She had to control her sadness. And her fear. *Get ahold of yourself, Hope. Just hang in there, a little while longer.*

.   .   .

Her next stop was Number 10 Downing Street.

It feels almost surreal to be back, Maggie thought as she entered through the back door and the kitchen. Mrs. Tinsley, one of Winston Churchill's typists for decades, rushed to greet her. "Miss Hope, how are you?" Maggie had worked with Mrs. Tinsley, then sharp, critical, and disapproving, when she'd first been employed as Mr. Churchill's typist during the Blitz. But in the following years, the women had become friends.

When Maggie struggled to reply, Mrs. Tinsley said merely, "Never mind, it's good to have you here safe and sound. We'll bring you tea."

Tea, Maggie thought with gratitude, almost tearing up. *Always tea.*

Mrs. Tinsley looked Maggie over, then said, "First, why don't we girls go to the lavatory?" She turned to Frain. "We'll be back in the shake of a lamb's tail, sir." Frain huffed in response.

Maggie removed her heavy coat and cleaned herself up in a stall as well as she could, and when she was washing her hands, Mrs. Tinsley removed her navy-blue cardigan. "Here," she said gently, handing it to Maggie. "Tie it around your waist."

Maggie realized what she meant. "Thank you," she said numbly while doing as Mrs. Tinsley bade.

The older woman reached above the mirror and pulled out a comb. "I keep this here for emergencies."

Maggie splashed water on her face, rinsed out her mouth, then did the best she could with her hair.

"Are you ready for His Nibs?" Mrs. Tinsley asked, putting Maggie's coat over her arm. It was what she and Miss Stewart, another typist, called Mr. Churchill when he was being difficult.

Maggie almost laughed out loud, remembering how even

the thought of being in Mr. Churchill's presence to take dictation used to terrify her. How far she'd come. "Ready as ever."

Mrs. Tinsley escorted Maggie and Frain up the grand cantilevered staircase, past black-and-white engravings of all Britain's past prime ministers in chronological order, back to Sir Robert Walpole.

She left them at the door to the Prime Minister's study. "I'll send up that tea," she told Maggie. For a moment, it seemed as though the older woman might actually embrace her, but then Mrs. Tinsley straightened, passed over the coat, turned on her heel, and walked briskly away. *She's English, after all,* Maggie thought with affection. She knocked on the door.

"Come in" rumbled the familiar voice.

She opened the door and there he was—Prime Minister Winston Churchill. He was seated at his desk, with John and David in front. They all stood when she and Frain entered. A fire burned cheerfully behind brass andirons. "Miss Hope!" the P.M. called cheerfully. But Maggie could see the toll his illness had taken on him. He was thinner, with a gray tinge to his face that was new. His hand shook slightly as he gestured to the study's sofa. "Please, have a seat, Miss Hope. 'We need Hope in this office!'" he exclaimed, quoting himself when he'd first hired her. Then, "Frain."

Frain replied only "Prime Minister."

"Tea! We need tea!" the P.M. bellowed.

It had been only days, but John looked different, at once strange and familiar. The light from the desk lamp and sconces emphasized his fine features. Yet Maggie couldn't meet his eyes as she sat. She had lost their baby, and he didn't even know. *No time for this now,* she thought and focused only on the present.

"Mrs. Tinsley is fetching some, I believe," John told him.

"Good, good!" the P.M. rumbled. He gazed at Maggie with

cloudy blue eyes. "Well, Miss Hope, this is your new vocation? My personal mail courier?"

"I do what's required, sir."

"You were in Spain, Miss Hope."

It wasn't a question. "Yes, sir. I met with Mademoiselle Chanel and Ambassador Hoare at the British Embassy in Madrid."

"Coco . . ." he said, as if to himself, "such a vibrant girl. I remember her with Bendor. Such spark. Such wit, such elegance!" Then, "A shame what's happened to her."

"What *did* happen?"

"Who can say? Nazism is the disease of our time. The curse of a generation—the 'lost generation,' yes . . . And by Nazis, I don't mean just Germans. There are many German Nazis, yes, but also English and American Nazis. And, as Coco shows us, French, as well."

He shook his head, chins wagging. "Coco's brilliant," he said. "Strong, smart." He sighed. "But she always fell in with the wrong people. The wrong men. It seems she's continued that trend."

"What creates a Nazi, then?" Maggie asked him.

"I can only guess what created Coco. First, she was educated by anti-Semitic Catholic nuns—oh yes, I've heard her stories about convent life. And then she ran with a fast crowd who had beauty, money, and vigor, yes, but no real education or intellect. Because of all the money, the power, the lack of intellectual discipline, Coco remained childish. She focused on aesthetics, appearances—but she neglected the soul."

He looked to Maggie. "What do *you* think, Miss Hope? You've known a few Nazis yourself."

"I think we all have the capacity," she said slowly. "I don't in any way believe the world divides into the so-called good ones and the Nazis. In real life, there are no white and black hats, like cowboys in the American movies. I think fascism's always a danger—for all of us. And the solution of a strong leader's most seductive in a crisis. And we've had many, many crises in a short period of time. Endless propaganda and reinforcement of fascist ideas. As well as a certain moral nihilism."

She had something on her mind, something she'd held back for a while. This seemed as good a time as any to say it. "And even the so-called 'good' countries can do terrible things, Prime Minister. President Roosevelt's Executive Order 9066, which sent Japanese in the U.S. and Americans of Japanese descent to camps. *Concentration* camps, in America. The U.S. military's horrific treatment of Negro soldiers."

"Well, the Yanks—"

"But it's not just the Yanks, sir. There's the Great Famine in India. As well as the issue of India's self-governance. The British colonies must have self-rule—or they'll simply take it.

"And we women need better treatment, stronger roles. The working class, as well. We've all shown what we can do in this war. We've all fought, and we've all paid the price. It's high time for us to have a place at the table."

There, she thought. *I've finally said it.*

The P.M. narrowed his eyes. "You're tired, Miss Hope. I'll put this . . . outburst . . . down to exhaustion." There was a long silence, unapologetic on both sides. "How did you find Mademoiselle?"

"She seemed well," Maggie said. "At least as well as can be expected in wartime."

The P.M. chuckled ruefully. "Yes, all of us are a bit worse for wear, myself included."

"I'm sorry you were ill in Tehran, sir."

"That's all behind us now, Miss Hope." He looked to John and David. "Good to have Hope back in the office, yes?"

They both smiled and John said, "Indeed."

"I have something for you, sir." Maggie opened her purse and took out Coco Chanel's letter, containing Walter Schellenberg's peace offer. It was creased and wrinkled. She handed it to him.

David rose and brought the P.M. a silver letter opener, its handle tipped with a lion's head. Churchill opened the letter, pulled out all the pages, then read in silence, broken by the occasional throat clearing and loud *harrumph*.

Mrs. Tinsley arrived with a tea tray, complete with a plate of Dundee cake slices. She poured and served.

"None for me," Churchill growled, letter in hand, still reading. "Gimme scotch."

John went to the sideboard and poured the P.M. a tumbler of scotch, then added a fair amount of water.

The P.M. glanced up suddenly, his eyes tired and shadowed. "Perhaps you'd prefer scotch as well, Miss Hope?" he said, taking his glass from John.

"No, thank you, sir," Maggie said, accepting a cup of tea from Mrs. Tinsley. "Tea is perfect." It was hot and strong, and she sipped it with gratitude, sharing a smile with the older secretary.

Mrs. Tinsley left, and the P.M. reread the letter. "Oh, Coco," he said finally, shaking his head and sighing. He tossed it into the fire, where it burned brightly before crumbling into ash and releasing a puff of black smoke. Maggie felt justified, relieved. And angry. She'd sacrificed so much for this letter. So much. Even knowing how it would be received in the end.

"I feel it's my duty to tell you, Prime Minister," Maggie said, setting down her teacup, "that Mademoiselle indicated she had some sort of . . . intelligence on you."

"Ha!" Churchill waved a blue-veined hand. "Not as much as I have on her!"

Frain said quietly, "We didn't hear about any other big news . . . coming from Madrid this past week."

"No," Maggie said. "Our 'German friend'—well, he doesn't have the bomb. *They* don't have the bomb."

Churchill exalted, raising his tumbler. "Thank God."

Frain sipped his tea. "How did you determine that?" he asked.

"I grew up with an academic," Maggie said, thinking of Aunt Edith and all the Chemistry Department funding battles she had and the bitterness that etched itself on her face. "I could recognize the professor's disappointment and frustration. The German rocket program in Peenemünde's receiving all the money and resources that could have gone to the fission bomb project, and Heisenberg let some of his resentment slip. So be aware of that."

The P.M., John, and David all exchanged a look. "We're on it," David said smoothly.

Churchill nodded. "What else?"

Maggie took another sip of tea to steady herself. "My first partner, Connor Sullivan, was killed in Lisbon. Connor was replaced with another agent, Ángel Ramos, who murdered Doña Rosa, who was working with the Allies. I've Tom Burns, the press attaché for the British Embassy, to thank for my life."

She set down her cup. "I believe my mission was compromised. I believe Ángel Ramos was a double agent, working for NKVD. His plan was to kill me to stop you from receiving Mademoiselle Chanel's letter and Schellenberg's peace proposal. Doña Rosa was about to tip me off when he had her killed."

The P.M. raised his eyebrows. "Frain?"

"We're looking into it."

"Who oversaw the mission?" the P.M. asked Maggie.

"Kim Philby." She sat up. "Sir, I think—"

"Oh, he's not a double agent," the Prime Minister said with a chuckle, as if he'd heard the insinuation before. He took a sip of his whiskey. "Philby's one of us, you know."

"And what does that mean, Mr. Churchill?" Maggie asked, an edge in her voice.

The P.M. barked at David, "Gimme a cigar!" The younger man obliged, taking one from the ebony box on the desk, then lighting it for Churchill, slipping a cut-glass ashtray in front of him.

The P.M. took a long inhale, then leaned back in his chair. "Philby's been working for us since 'forty," he said. "He went to Westminster, then Trinity. His father's Jack Philby, for God's sake." He jabbed the air with his cigar for emphasis. "A long line of Philbys have belonged to the Athenaeum Club!"

Well, then, Maggie thought, exchanging a glance with Frain. *As if coming from a particular family, attending certain schools, and being a member of exclusive clubs implied decency and honor.* She knew all too well, starting with the real Paige Kelly, that looks could be deceiving. Still, now wasn't the time.

"We can fully debrief tomorrow, on all aspects of your mission," Frain said. "Maggie, you must be exhausted."

I am, Maggie thought, *but I would never admit to it.* She looked up and met John's eyes. "It's good to be home."

Chapter Thirty-four

Maggie finally returned home, staggered up to her room, crawled into bed, and stayed there.

Days passed as she battled a deep and devastating grief. She thought of her friend Sarah, of how she'd lost her baby in Paris, also on a mission. How had she coped? How did *any* woman cope? Chuck brought up meals on trays that were barely touched. John brought bouquets of flowers—snowdrops and daffodils. David brought a bottle of Plymouth gin, left untouched. Griff, with Chuck's help, made soft warm carrot cookies. Frain called and left messages with Chuck.

These gestures, wordlessly offered, were gratefully accepted. Yet Maggie didn't leave her room. K barely left her side. He sat at her feet, keeping watch while she slept, or curling against her hip and purring loudly when she sat up.

Finally, Chuck knocked at Maggie's bedroom door. The house's clocks were all chiming noon. "Hullo!" she said cheerfully. "Shall I change the sheets?"

"It's fine," Maggie croaked, her voice rusty. She was sitting up in bed, wrapped in her tartan robe with K nestled in her lap, staring out the window as the treetops swayed in the gentle wind. She petted his soft fur absently. "I'm fine."

"No," Chuck told her through the door, "today's Saturday. It's Fresh Sheets and Towels Day!"

Maggie exhaled.

"I know no one cares about Fresh Sheets and Towels Day except me." Chuck slowly opened the door a crack. "But laundry's on my weekly schedule. I'm a nurse—or at least used to be a nurse. Hygiene's important!" She opened the door wider and, when met with no resistance, entered.

Maggie groaned and stood. K jumped down with his odd "*Meh!*" and left. She started taking the sheets off the bed.

Chuck assisted. "How are you?"

"I'm fine."

"No offense, but you don't seem fine." Chuck noticed dried bloodstains on the sheets. "Jesus H. Roosevelt Christ, Maggie," she said. "This is not fine."

"You're a nurse." Maggie fell into a wing chair. "You know what's happening."

Chuck blinked, realization dawning on her face.

"The job I did is . . . over," Maggie said. "We did it." She thought of Connor and his family. "Well, not really . . . but it's over." She took a ragged breath. "And now—I don't know who I am anymore." Chuck sat on the bare mattress covered in blue-and-white-striped ticking.

"I lost someone I barely knew existed," Maggie said softly. "I knew them for only a few days, and, even then, I never had time to really sort out what it all meant."

"Oh, sweetheart," Chuck said, her eyes wide. "I'm so sorry."

"I can't hold the baby. I can't bury the baby. It's just . . . gone." She sniffled and wiped at her nose with her hand. "And it's probably because of me—let's face it, it *was* because of me. Because I was traveling, because I was under so much stress, the things I did—almost did . . ."

Chuck passed her a clean handkerchief, which Maggie accepted. "You can't blame yourself," she said, putting a hand to Maggie's knee. "It's not your fault."

"Except it really is."

"It's *not*. It's this bloody war." Chuck sighed. "Have you told John?"

"Not yet. I know I need to. I just can't yet."

Chuck offered, "I had a miscarriage once. After Griff, while Nigel was away. It was . . . so lonely."

Maggie raised her head. "You didn't tell me!"

"I was living at the other flat, the old flat."

"Still," Maggie said. She put her hand on Chuck's. They were both members of the club no one wanted to be in. "I'm sorry."

They sat together, in silence, until the telephone rang. Chuck rose. "It's probably that Mr. Frain. Calls all the bloody time— even during Griff's naps. Mr. Philby, too." She made a face. Maggie could hear the toddler start crying from his room. "Do you mind answering that, while I tend to him? Or let it ring, I don't mind," Chuck said as she left, calling, "Yes, darling! Mummy's coming!"

Maggie, stiff from lying in bed, padded to the hall telephone. "Hello?" she said into the cold black Bakelite receiver.

"Frain."

"Yes."

"I've been trying to reach you."

"Yes."

"We need to debrief."

Maggie was silent.

"I can come to you, if that's better. Your friend says you've been unwell."

"This afternoon," Maggie said finally. "Three o'clock."

"I'll be there."

Chuck had taken Griff to Regent's Park; Maggie and Frain sat stiffly in the library. She didn't offer him tea and he didn't ask.

Next to Maggie, K kept watch, staring down the head of MI-5 without blinking, body tense and prepared for attack.

"Let's debrief, shall we?" He handed her a fountain pen and paper. "Here you go."

Maggie, who'd managed to take a bath and dress in fresh clothes, was still not used to speaking. Her voice rasped as she replied, "Let's," and began to write a report of her "overseas activities."

The report took the better part of an hour. When she was finished, she signed it, then passed the paper and pen back to Frain, exhausted.

"Ángel worked directly under Kim Philby . . ." she said slowly. "I think Kim's at the heart of this. He *must* be. He could have been the one to order Connor killed and insert Ángel. Who killed Doña Rosa. He's the one who warned me against Burns, who ultimately helped save me and the mission."

"Burns has always been . . . complicated," Frain said.

"Burns was undermined by Kim. He could be working secretly to destabilize General Franco and prepare for a Russian takeover in Spain."

"No—"

"Yes! If he were working for Russia, Kim would see pro-Franco Burns as an enemy, and he tried hard to have him sacked, or at least undercut. Even with me, he tried to identify Burns as a security risk—a Brit compromised by his Catholicism."

"I can see how you'd come to that conclusion. There are coincidences, yes," Frain admitted.

"There are never coincidences in this game," Maggie told him. "You of all people should know. And what about the plane?"

"That must have been a tail on Burns, who then followed

you." She was silent. "Maggie, I know you were let down by SOE in Paris. . . ."

"More than just SOE in Paris," she snapped, not wanting to revisit painful memories. "And it just shows how it can happen again. How British agents in the field can be betrayed." *I was betrayed, but Connor and Doña Rosa are dead.*

Frain shook his head. "Philby's an Englishman, through and through. A patriot. I know him. I know his wife. I know his family." He raised his hands. "He's no Communist, Maggie. Believe me: I of all people would know."

"We're going to have to agree to disagree, then." She raised an eyebrow. "And what about you?"

He looked surprised. "What about me?"

"I hear you're an old friend of Coco Chanel's. At least, that's what she said in Madrid."

A strange expression flickered on his face. "She mentioned me?"

"Yes," Maggie said, sensing his apprehension. "Apparently she reached out to you, an old friend, when she wanted to pass a message through British intelligence. That's how she requested me. As you well know."

"You know I can't say. . . ."

Maggie looked at Frain as if she were examining him through a microscope. "She thinks you're my father."

He was perfectly still. "She does, does she?"

Maggie pressed on. "Yes. You and Clara Hess—allegedly you had an affair. While she was married to—to Edmund Hope."

"It is . . ." Frain said delicately, "possible. But I'm not sure the dates line up. And you have Edmund's red hair."

"Chanel said your mother had red hair." He was silent. "Did she?"

"She did," he admitted finally.

Oh my God, so perhaps it is true. "Is Clara still alive?" Maggie thought she was, thought she'd seen her in London, in Clerkenwell—thought her mother had saved her life—but she wasn't sure.

"Your mother, that is, Clara—" Frain, usually so polished, so formal, stumbled. "You know I can't say," he finally repeated.

"Can't or won't?"

"Maggie . . ."

"Let me understand this—you might be my father. My mother, a notorious Nazi intelligence agent, might still be alive and living in London under an assumed name. But you can't tell me anything."

Frain gazed out the window at the twins playing tag, avoiding Maggie's eyes. "Edmund, Clara, Coco, and I were all friends in London, decades ago. It was a different time," he said slowly. "I was a different person. We were considered the 'Bright Young Things' back then, if you can believe that. It was well before Hitler came to power."

Maggie cut to the chase. "I was born March first, nineteen fifteen," she said. "Do those dates match? You would have been with Clara sometime in June of nineteen fourteen."

"I— It was a long time ago."

Maggie fixed him with her gaze. "Perhaps you can review your old diaries."

"Perhaps."

"And in terms of my mother—that is, Clara Hess—I thought she was dead. That she'd been executed in Berlin."

"It's all covered under the Official Secrets Act," Frain told her.

"Which I've signed, Peter. My clearance level is high, almost as high as yours. And my, shall we say, 'sabbatical' in Scotland certainly proves without a doubt my ability to keep secrets."

"Understood." Frain had the grace to look uncomfortable.

"But since I do believe she and I met up recently, and under extraordinary circumstances, I deserve to know."

He glanced out the window at the swaying bare branches of plane trees. "Your mother didn't die in Germany," he admitted finally. "She was captured with several other high-ranking Nazis and taken to a particular prisoner of war camp in Britain."

Maggie laughed harshly. "Oh, I bet she loved that."

"It was a special camp. A country house, with books and music and excellent food. Daily papers brought in. Access to the wireless."

"How . . . posh. And when so many others in Britain were suffering."

"We had microphones hidden everywhere," he told her. "Our agents listened to the prisoners around the clock. So any scrap of intelligence they let slip could be used."

"And did she let anything slip?"

"No. But we do think she set fire to the house."

Maggie quirked an eyebrow. She looked to K, who returned the gaze. They both turned back to Frain.

"We thought all the prisoners died in the fire. But Clara used it as a diversion. To escape."

"So she's in London now?"

He sighed. "She is."

"She's created a new identity?"

"She has."

Maggie sat back. "So she's out there"—she gestured at the window—"somewhere."

"Yes."

"And you're in contact with her."

"It's good to keep your enemies close."

Maggie made an irritated face. "*Is* she the enemy? Are you using her? Or is she using you?"

"It's . . . complicated." Frain ran his hands through his graying hair, an unusual gesture of frustration. "She contacts me through coded messages. She's still in touch with some of her friends in Paris and Berlin, again through code. She says she wants to work for us as a double agent."

"And you believe her?"

"With her network . . ." He spread his hands. "Well, she would be invaluable."

"She could also double-cross you. Easily."

"Yes."

"Do you trust her?"

"I trust very few people, Maggie."

She snorted. "I understand the feeling." Then she repeated, "Do you trust *her*?"

"I'm a professional."

K stared balefully as Maggie asked, "Are you sure, Peter?"

"I wasn't going to bring this up today, but since we're on the subject—I'd like you to work with her."

"Me?" Maggie scoffed. "You must be joking."

"She knows valuable people in Berlin. There's also the question of your sister."

Maggie frowned. Peter wasn't joking. "What question about Elise? She's safe in the convent in France, isn't she?"

"For now," he said. "But the nuns in Elise's convent are hiding Jewish children and then helping them escape to England."

"And that's a bad thing?" she asked drily.

"It's dangerous for everyone involved. And Clara wants to get Elise out before the invasion."

Maggie was speechless. Peter, her mother—and now Elise. "You mean she wants to put together a rescue mission?"

"I've given you much to think about, I know." Frain gathered his belongings and rose. Maggie stood as well. "I'll let you rest," he said. "Thank you for the report."

She led him to the front door, then he turned. "I hope you feel better soon."

"Thank you," she said, feeling more confused than ever. "Me, too."

"I'll be in touch."

Chapter Thirty-five

A warm spell gripped London, giving everyone a heady promise of spring. Icy puddles melted, and a yellow sun shone from a dazzling blue sky. While a windstorm had battered the city the previous night, sending dead leaves to the gutters and branches to the pavement, this morning was still. Goldfinches sang in the trees as Maggie walked through Regent's Park to Queen Mary's Gardens.

She met John at the entrance. He was whistling Rina Ketty's "*J'attendrai.*"

The perfect song for January nineteen forty-four, Maggie thought. Waiting was what she felt she was doing, what everyone felt, as they stared down the new year. There was a sense of time suspended as Europe's leaders, like giants in the sky, plotted their next moves, ones that would affect the globe.

The invasion of France by the Allies was imminent, everyone knew. There were massive numbers of soldiers in London now—from America, Canada, Australia, New Zealand. . . . Maggie had even given directions to a young Tasmanian soldier on Baker Street recently.

And now, a select few knew that somewhere in the United States, the Manhattan Project was creating and perfecting the world's first fission bomb. A bomb that could destroy all of humanity. A small, single, airdropped mechanism that could change the wages of war from imperialism to annihilation. The story of life on earth had a possible end.

Maggie knew history would be forever separated into the before—the now—and the after. It was difficult to trust the now when it was unclear what the after would bring. While she mourned Bean, she also knew bringing children into the current war-torn world would be difficult, if not impossible. But also she knew it wouldn't last forever. Life did go on.

John looked different—or perhaps it was just she who was different now. He didn't speak when he saw her, just enfolded her in his arms. Maggie felt his heart beating fast, just like her own. Without words, she pressed against him, inhaling his warm, familiar smell of soap and wool.

They strolled through the gardens, named for the wife of King George V, which had opened to the public in 1932 and now boasted London's largest collection of roses. They meandered among walls of shrubbery that bestowed a sense of peace and privacy.

In the clear sky above, several Spitfires flew over, leaving trails of vapor; Maggie felt an ominous dread. "Something's coming," she said. "There're so many soldiers in London. I could hardly find a space on the Tube."

"Something's coming, yes," John said, as Maggie took his hand. "But not today."

They walked close to each other and finally stopped at a wooden bench and sat. A gardener worked nearby, clipping the brown, dead roses from the bushes, tossing them into a growing heap, making room for new blooms. Even in winter, new buds were pushing up through the stems. "*The force that through the green fuse drives the flower,*" she thought.

Maggie could smell the grass, the earth, the loamy scent of the dead flowers, and the sharp, fresh scent of the warm air. She took a deep breath. It was time.

"I was pregnant . . ." she blurted. " 'With child,' as they say. And . . . and I lost it."

John froze for a moment. Then he grasped her gloved hand. "I'm so sorry."

"I—think it was because of what I was doing. Where I was. My job." While she couldn't give specifics, she knew he'd understand what she meant.

John put a comforting arm around her. "You can't blame yourself."

"I know. And yet, here I am." They watched as the gardener moved on. Finally, she stirred and gazed at him. "How can you come back from this place?" Maggie asked. "From what might have been?"

"I don't know that you do," he told her. "But I do think you go on." In the far distance, church bells pealed. For a moment it was just the two of them, without past or future, just the present.

"I jotted down a quote from Cervantes that made me think of you," he said.

"What's that?"

He took a scrap of paper from his pocket and read, " *'The phoenix hope, can wing her way through the desert skies, and still defying fortune's spite; revive from ashes and rise.' "*

"Thank you." Maggie smiled and kissed his cheek. "I'll hang on to this," she said, taking the paper and slipping it into her coat pocket. "In other words, 'Keep Buggering On,' as we used to say in the office."

"We still say KBO. And I'll always bet on Hope rising like a phoenix," John told her. "By the way, my mother's in town. Would you like to meet her?" He chuckled. "I'll understand if you say no."

"Your *mother?*"

"After all, I've met Aunt Edith—and K—so I think it's only fair you get to meet my family. I thought we'd start with just my mother. For now."

Maggie had heard about John's parents and seen photographs, of course, but she'd never met them. "Yes," she said. "Yes, I'd like that very much." *And you may be able to meet my real mother and father soon, too,* she thought. *But not too soon. Let's see what happens first.*

"I'll arrange tea at Claridge's."

"Sounds delightful." They sat in silence, watching a pair of cardinals. "And about that question you asked—"

"Yes?"

She put a hand on his. "Why don't you ask me again—when the war's over."

They kissed, a promise. "It's getting cold," he said, drawing her in tighter. "Would you like to go somewhere inside? Tea? A film?"

"A film's an excellent idea. I'd love to escape reality for a bit." Maggie stood. "Do you know what's playing?"

John rose as well. "I walked past the Classic on Baker Street on my way here," he told her as they began to stroll back through the park, the wind still for the moment. "They've got *For Whom the Bell Tolls*. Any interest?" It was the film version of Hemingway's novel. "It's in Technicolor . . ." he added.

Will there be a bullfighter character based on Juanito Belmonte's father? "Maybe *not* something set during the Spanish Civil War," Maggie told him.

"*Song of Bernadette?*"

She thought of Elise. "Too many nuns."

"What about *Casablanca?*"

"Oh, I heard that's good!"

"I read an interview with Ingrid Bergman," John said, their feet crunching on the gravel path as they exited the park. "She said she played the whole movie without knowing how it would end." He chuckled. "Rather like life."

Maggie smiled and linked her arm through his. "Rather."

Acknowledgments

The first person I want to thank is—you. Thank you for reading.

It's been a joy to research and write the Maggie Hope books. And the reception has been both unexpected and overwhelming. So many of you have told me you see yourself in Maggie and her friends, how you've been inspired by them—and I can't express how happy that makes me.

You've also told me how the books have kept you company through medical journeys, anniversaries of loved ones' deaths, and other challenging times. It's been my privilege to provide even a few moments of distraction. And it's been an honor to meet and become friends with many of you over the years.

I want to thank my husband, Noel MacNeal, for his support. It's Noel who always tells me I can do things (even when I don't believe it) and always believes in me.

Likewise, our son, Matt, has been a stalwart supporter, and I thank him for his love and generosity. (And patience. So much patience!)

Shout-out to Londoner James Byrne, who gave me a copy of *Time Out London* back in 1999—and pointed out the Cabinet War Rooms, saying, "Despite what you Yanks might think, World War II didn't start with Pearl Harbor." My subsequent visit to the War Rooms was the inspiration for Maggie Hope and the series.

All my gratitude to Idria Barone Knecht, *mia amica cara,* for reading many, many, many versions of all the manuscripts, and for keeping track of pretty much everything (even things I've forgotten).

My love to Victoria Skurnick, a warm and supportive agent and friend—and all the wonderful people at Levine Greenberg Rostan Literary Agency, as well. I'm thankful for an agent (and agency) who sees me as a person, not just a set of numbers.

I have immense gratitude for fellow scribes Kim Fay and Mariah Fredericks, for sensitive edits through the years, and especially of this book.

Thanks to editor Jenny Chen. Applause for Mae Martinez, a terrific editorial assistant. Gratitude to marketing goddess Allison Schuster and assistant marketing goddess Emma Thomasch. Standing ovations to publicity stars Sarah Breivogel and Katie Horn.

Big thanks to the copy editors—I'm in absolute awe of your talents. To everyone in production, rights, art, and sales—and their assistants, of course—my endless gratitude. Thank you also to artist Mick Wiggins for the gorgeous covers. And I have such respect for the booksellers and independent bookstore owners—thank you.

Many people were kind enough to give me space and silence to write this book. I want to thank Mrs. Maurice (Molly) Thompson for letting me stay in Charleston, and Mary Linton Peters and Steve Peters for writing retreats in Cambridge.

Thanks also to Michael Pieck and Alexa and Kaia (and Callie) Pieck for generously sharing their Tribeca and East Hampton homes, along with Heather Beckman. (And "wicked smart" Michael for reading the physics scenes!)

A special thank you to Laura Wollstadt Patterson.

Hugs to Dr. Meredith Norris for providing medical expertise.

High fives to historian Ronald Granieri, Ph.D. I wouldn't want to write about the twentieth century without you, my friend—it wouldn't be half as much fun. A special thank-you to physicist Victoria Centarino, as well.

Nosegays of pink roses to Claire Ayoub, Elizabeth Hara, Kimmerie Jones, Dru Ann Love, Michael Jay McClure, Goran Sparrman, and Janet Somerville for your support, expertise, and friendship.

Bouquets of yellow roses to fellow historical novelists Tasha Alexander, Lauren Belfer, Melanie Benjamin, Nancy Bilyeau, L. A. Chandlar, Kim Fay, Mariah Fredericks, Andrew Grant, Naomi Hirahara, Anna Lee Huber, Piper Huguley, Brenda Janowitz, Pam Jenoff, Lynda Cohen Loigman, Sujata Massey, Elizabeth Kerri Mahon, Rachel McMillan, Karen Odden, and Kate Quinn for the friendship and camaraderie.

KBO, as Maggie and her friends say—Keep Buggering On.

Historical Notes

Truth really is stranger than fiction—and I'm delighted to share some of the facts behind the inspiration of this novel.

Let's talk first about Coco Chanel. Back when I was writing *The Paris Spy,* I was fascinated by the nonfiction book *Sleeping with the Enemy* by Hal Vaughan, which details Chanel's affair with Nazi spy Hans Günther "Spatz" von Dincklage. There wasn't room in *The Paris Spy* to go too far into Chanel's story with the Nazis, but I never forgot—and I'm so glad I was able to go back to it.

Was Chanel a spy for the Nazis? Yes. Did she have a lover who was a well-known and high-ranking Nazi? Yes. Was she a collaborator? Yes. Was she a Nazi? I can't answer that.

However, according to all the research I did, Chanel was virulently anti-Semitic—even for Paris in those days—and willing to use the Nazis' Aryanization laws in France to wrestle her perfume company back from the Wertheimers, who were Jewish.

But as the fashion model and spy Toto said to Laura Aitken, in Alan Frame's *Toto & Coco: Spies, Seduction and the Fight for Survival:* "It might seem strange that Coco had lovers who were Nazis and such rabid anti-Semites at the same time as being friends with Winston Churchill and [his son] Randolph. But that's how it was before the war. Everyone hoped some arrangement could be made to stop Hitler from going further. Of course that never happened, and it was then that we all had to make up our minds about which side we were on. I knew quite a few German officers, and, with few exceptions, they were smart, very civilized and charming. They weren't all monsters but, sadly, it only took a few monsters to start a war and bring about such unimaginable horrors. I should know. When all that became clear, that's when Coco should have turned her back on the Nazis. But no, she was too concerned with her own wealth to worry about what was right and wrong."

The facts are that Coco Chanel really was Agent F-7124, code-named Agent Westminster, and she took two trips to Madrid for the Nazis during the war, both under the pretext of opening a new shop. I've used more of the second trip as inspiration, but the first was in service of freeing her nephew from a concentration camp and is worth reading about in detail in Vaughan's book.

The mission from Heinrich Himmler and intelligence chief Walter Schellenberg is factual. They wanted Chanel to use her social connections with Winston Churchill and other high-ranking British to send a message regarding the offer of a separate peace with Germany sans Hitler. *Himmler's Secret War: Covert Peace Negotiations* by Martin Allen goes into detail for those who want to know more.

And how did Chanel avoid arrest and retribution after the war?

Although she escaped all charges, the matter of her collaboration did resurface briefly in May 1946, when Judge Roger Serre of Paris brought a suit against Chanel for espionage. In court, when confronted with the facts of Operation Modelhut as well as her attempt to use her Nazi connections to take Parfums Chanel away from the Wertheimers, Chanel simply denied everything. When pressed, she offered only lies; for example, she said she didn't know anyone in the German military. The court knew she was lying, and the transcript reads: "The answers Mlle Chanel gave to this court were deceptive." But she was never arrested or charged.

In *Sleeping with the Enemy,* Vaughan speculates that Churchill intervened to shield Chanel from prosecution. "One theory has it that Chanel knew Churchill had violated his own Trading with the Enemy Act (enacted in 1939, which made it a criminal offense to conduct business with the enemy during wartime) by secretly paying the Germans to protect the Duke of Windsor's property in Paris. The duke's apartment in the Sixteenth Arrondissement of Paris was never touched when the Windsors were exiled in the Bahamas, where the duke was governor.

"A Windsor biographer claimed 'had Chanel been made to stand trial for collaboration with the enemy in wartime she might have exposed as Nazi collaborators the Windsors and a number of other highly placed in society. The royal family would not easily tolerate an exposé of a family member.'

"The royal family was so touchy about the duke's collaboration that Anthony Blunt, the royal historian, was sent to Europe in the final days of the war. Blunt, who was later exposed as a Russian spy, traveled secretly to the German town of Schloss Friedrichshof in 1945 to retrieve sensitive letters between the Duke of Windsor, Adolf Hitler, and other prominent figures. (The duke's correspondence with Hitler and the Nazis remains secret.)"

And while General Walter Schellenberg could have told all about Operation Modelhut—he never did. Schellenberg was sentenced to six years in prison at the Nuremberg Trials for war crimes. He was released after two years on the grounds of ill health. During his time in prison, however, he had written his memoir, *The Labyrinth* (still in print today). But there isn't one mention of Chanel.

Apparently she paid him off, giving him and his wife a house in Switzerland and then a villa in Italy. She also paid his medical bills for treatment of terminal liver cancer. Before he died, Chanel made sure she had his word that her name would not appear in *The Labyrinth*.

Historian Katrin Paehler, author of the excellent *The Third Reich's Intelligence Services,* states: "Schellenberg subsequently contacted Coco Chanel who eventually called on Schellenberg—in a black Mercedes nonetheless—and handed him 30,000 francs. Indeed, it appears that Chanel had already given Schellenberg a substantial sum in June 1951, after learning that he intended to publish his memoir. Chanel had collaborated with both the Abwehr and SD—including yet another ill-fated attempt to contact the Western Allies, in this case the British in 1943—and might have hoped to keep her name out of Schellenberg's book.

"Schellenberg's widow Irene, who eventually handled the book's publication, stated, 'Madame Chanel offered us financial assistance in our difficult situation, and it was thanks for her that we were able to spend a few more months together.'" Schellenberg died in Turin at age forty-two on March 31, 1952.

The looking-glass opposite of Coco Chanel on the Allied side is Aline Griffith, also known as the Countess of Romanones. Griffith was an American, working for the OSS (the United States's new intelligence section and the precursor to the CIA) during World War II, and she told her stories in a series of books, including *The Spy Wore Red: My Adventures as an Undercover Agent in World War II*. As she herself says in the introduction: "In the course of lecturing over the past eight years, I've discovered that people enjoy (and need) authentic, firsthand information about espionage, a topic on which reliable information is (understandably) difficult to come by. What I have attempted in this book is to inform and to entertain."

From this book, I learned how a secret agent from an Allied

nation would operate in neutral countries, such as Portugal and Spain. I also learned about her fellow agent, Edmundo Lassalle, who was from Mexico and the United States and worked for the Walt Disney Company. Although I based certain aspects of my character Don Miguel Ángel Ramos on him, Lassalle was not a Communist and not a double agent.

Like Griffith, Maggie meets a legendary bullfighter, the very real Juanito Belmonte, who courts her, as he wooed Griffith in real life. (And Griffith went on to marry him!) And Griffith knew Tom Burns and Ambassador Samuel Hoare. My Doña Rosa was inspired by her Doña Mimosa. And Maggie is given the task of smuggling microfilm out of Madrid, just as Griffith was.

The Spy Wore Red is so fantastical, I checked up on Griffith's research by reading Larry Loftis's excellent *The Princess Spy: The True Story of World War II Spy Aline Griffith, Countess of Romanones*. And yes, according to Loftis, almost everything is factual—except she changed her code name from Butch to Tiger (which is understandable).

And while we're talking about real heroes of the war, a shout-out to the owner of the Embassy café, Margarita Kearney Taylor. An Irishwoman from France, she brought the concept of British high tea to Madrid, as Maggie enjoyed with Burns. But Taylor was also a leader of a covert wartime operation that helped Allied servicemen and Jewish refugees escape Nazi-occupied Europe. They would be smuggled secretly to her tearoom in Madrid, then sent on to ports in Gibraltar and Portugal, and, ultimately, to freedom in Britain and the United States. Maggie and Tom Burns had their tea with Jewish refugees hiding in the rooms above the tearoom. I couldn't fit this detail in, but Taylor certainly deserves her own book.

Where to start with spy and would-be assassin Moe Berg? You may already know him from the 2018 film *The Catcher*

Was a Spy, starring Paul Rudd, or some of the excellent biographies, such as Thomas McDonough's *Moe Berg: The Secret Files,* which I relied on.

Like Griffith, Berg was an American working with OSS. A former professional baseball player for the Red Sox, Berg was ordered to assassinate German physicist Werner Heisenberg, believed to be finished with, or close to finishing, Germany's first atomic bomb.

I'm fascinated with Berg's story for many reasons, but not least of all because he used his intelligence to intuit that Germany did *not* have the bomb, and so Heisenberg did *not* need to be assassinated. A life saved instead of taken.

How did it happen? In late 1943, Heisenberg was scheduled to speak at the Swiss Federal Institute of Technology in Zurich. Berg attended the lecture and listened for clues as to whether or not the Germans were close to building an atomic bomb. Like Maggie, he carried a gun and a suicide pill. If the scientist indicated that the Germans were on the brink of nuclear warfare, he was to kill Heisenberg. The suicide pill was in case he was caught and might reveal the secrets of the Manhattan Project.

After the lecture in Switzerland, the Gestapo sent a message to Heisenberg's superiors, stating that he had made defeatist statements in Switzerland. Those pessimistic statements, perhaps made to or in front of Berg, probably saved his life. As McDonough writes, "The avatar of uncertainty was certainly a lucky man."

What I love about this historically grounded assassination attempt is that Maggie started out as thwarting one in *Mr. Churchill's Secretary* and goes on to become a would-be assassin herself. When she began, she was excellent at math and codes, and not so comfortable with her fellow human beings. Now, she's relying as much on her emotional intelligence as her intellect.

Kim Philby (eventually revealed to be a Soviet spy and one

of the infamous "Cambridge Five") really did train SOE agents, and oversaw British espionage on the Iberian peninsula. His own memoir, written in Russia after he escaped Britain—*My Silent War: The Autobiography of a Spy*—was an excellent resource.

In my imagination, Maggie Hope, along with John, David, Sarah, Chuck, Griffin, Freddie, and Mr. K (of course), all make it to V.E. Day and beyond. I've always had the final image of the series in mind—Buckingham Palace during the victory celebrations, with the prime minister and royal family out on the balcony, waving to the crowd. And, out of sight and behind them, Maggie, John, David, Sarah, Peter Frain, and so many of the people who worked behind the scenes to help the Allies win.

So many real people *did* toil anonymously, many giving their health, their sanity, their very lives to save democracy and the free world. Most were never awarded medals. In many cases, they never even spoke of what they did during the war, and never got the recognition they so richly deserve.

Hats off.

Sources

BOOKS

Allen, Martin. *Himmler's Secret War: Covert Peace Negotiations of Heinrich Himmler.* Da Capo Press.

Berkeley, Roy. *A Spy's London.* Pen & Sword.

Burns, Jimmy. *Papa Spy: Love, Faith, and Betrayal in Wartime Spain.* Walker & Company.

Cassidy, David C. *Beyond Uncertainty: Heisenberg, Quantum Physics, and the Bomb.* Bellevue Literary Press.

Chaney, Lisa. *Coco Chanel: An Intimate Life.* Viking.

Dawidoff, Nicholas. *The Catcher Was a Spy: The Mysterious Life of Moe Berg.* Vintage Books.

De Courcy, Anne. *Chanel's Riviera: Glamour, Decadence, and Survival in Peace and War, 1930–1944.* St. Martin's Press.

Dorries, Reinhard R. *Hitler's Intelligence Chief Walter Schellenberg.* Enigma Books.

Field, Leslie. *Bendor: The Golden Duke of Westminster.* Weidenfeld and Nicolson.

Frame, Alan. *Toto and Coco: Spies, Seduction, and the Fight for Survival.* Kelvin House.

Garelick, Rhonda K. *Mademoiselle: Coco Chanel and the Pulse of History.* Random House.

Hemming, Henry. *M: Maxwell Knight, MI5's Greatest Spymaster.* Arrow Books.

Jeffery, Keith. *The Secret History of MI-6 1909–1949.* Penguin Press.

Jenkins, Roy. *Churchill: A Biography*. Farrar, Straus, and Giroux.

Lochery, Neill. *Lisbon: War in the Shadows of the City of Light, 1939–45*. Public Affairs.

Macintyre, Ben. *A Spy Among Friends: Kim Philby and the Great Betrayal*. Crown.

McDonough, Thomas R. *Moe Berg: The Secret Files*. Self-published.

Paehler, Katrin. *The Third Reich's Intelligence*. Cambridge University Press.

Philby, Kim. *My Silent War: The Autobiography of a Spy*. Modern Library.

Pike, David. *Franco and the Axis Stigma*. Palgrave Macmillan.

Ridley, George. *Bend'Or: Duke of Westminster*. Robin Clark.

Romanones, Aline, Countess of. *The Spy Wore Red*. Random House.

Schellenberg, Walter. *The Labyrinth: Memoirs of Walter Schellenberg, Hitler's Chief of Intelligence*. Da Capo Press.

Smith, Nancy. *Churchill on the Riviera: Winston Churchill, Wendy Reves, and the Villa La Pausa Built by Coco Chanel*. The Educational Publisher/Biblio Publishing.

Vaughan, Hal. *Sleeping with the Enemy: Coco Chanel's Secret War*. Vintage Books.

ARTICLES

Messenger, David A. " 'Against the Grain': Special Operations Executive in Spain, 1941–45." *Intelligence and National Security*, vol. 20, no. 1, 2005.

Vale, J. A., and J. W. Scadding. "In Carthage Ruins: The Illness of Sir Winston Churchill at Carthage, December 1943." *Journal of the Royal College of Physicians of Edinburgh*, vol. 47, no. 3, 2017.

DOCUMENTARIES

Churchill and the Fascist Plot, directed by Peter Nicholson.

Coco Chanel & Arletty: An Auvergne Destiny, directed by Adrian Sibley.

The Decent One, directed by Vanessa Lapa.

Inside Fascist Spain: The March of Time (1943 documentary), Twentieth Century-Fox.

ABOUT THE AUTHOR

Susan Elia MacNeal is the *New York Times* bestselling author of the Maggie Hope mystery series. She won the Barry Award and has been nominated for the Edgar, Macavity, Agatha, Left Coast Crime, Dilys, ITW Thriller, and other awards. She lives in Brooklyn, New York, with her husband and son.

susaneliamacneal.com
Facebook.com/MrChurchillsSecretary
X: @susanmacneal
Instagram: @susaneliamacneal
Threads: @susaneliamacneal